the
THIRD

the THIRD

ABEL KEOGH

Bonneville Books
SPRINGVILLE, UTAH

This is a work of fiction. The characters, names, incidents, places, and dialogue are products of the author's imagination and are not to be construed as real.

ISBN 13: 978-1-59955-494-5

Published by Bonneville Books, an imprint of Cedar Fort, Inc., 2373 W. 700 S., Springville, UT 84663
Distributed by Cedar Fort, Inc., www.cedarfort.com

LIBRARY OF CONGRESS CATALOGING-IN-PUBLICATION DATA

Keogh, Abel, 1975-
  The third / Abel Keogh.
    p. cm.
  Summary: In the year 2065, the government passes a law that no one may
have more than two children unless they purchase a credit from someone
else. Ransom Lawe learns that his wife is pregnant with their third child, but
he cannot afford to purchase a credit. His love for his wife and unborn child
comes up against the risk that the Census Bureau will discover his family's
secret.
  ISBN 978-1-59955-494-5
  1. Science fiction, American. 2. Population policy--Fiction. 3. Birth
control--Fiction. 4. Families--Fiction. I. Title.

  PS3611.E69T48 2010
  813'.6--dc22

2010043974

Cover design by Angela D. Olsen
Cover design © 2011 by Lyle Mortimer
Edited and typeset by Megan E. Welton

Printed in the United States of America

10 9 8 7 6 5 4 3 2 1

Printed on acid-free paper

To Marathon Girl

Also by Abel Keogh

Room for Two

T he tram's doors hissed open, flooding the platform with the heat and stench of a hundred human bodies packed tightly together.

Standing on the platform, Ransom Lawe put a hand over his nose and mouth as the air washed over him. He took a step back, waiting for the passengers to exit. Only a gray-haired man wearing a patched, navy blue suit pushed his way toward the exit and off the tram. He held a worn leather briefcase above his head. Once the man's feet touched the platform, the waiting crowd shoved its way up the stairs and onto the tram.

Ransom took a deep breath and surged forward with the others. Once on board, he used his mass to push toward the missing window opposite the door. Most of the tram's windows were rusted shut from years of neglect, and though closed windows were nice in the winter, at this time of year they turned the trams into cauldrons of heat. The second car on the tram Ransom caught to the Recycling Center each morning had a back window that had been broken for years, allowing the hot, dusty air to flow through the cabin, providing some relief.

Ransom reached the window just as a bell gave out a sharp ring, and the door snapped shut. Setting his metal lunch bucket on the floor, he grabbed a handrail, and the tram surged forward.

A hot breeze began drying the sweat from his face, and he took a deep breath of the dusty air, happy to have a momentary reprieve from the stench-filled car. Glancing around at the other passengers, he was bored to discover that most looked familiar. There was the man with the pockmarked face who wore the same bow tie every day and always got off on the 23rd Street stop. The woman with short hair and coffee-colored skin who always had her nose in a worn paperback. And the three employees wearing blue power company uniforms who stood in a tight circle at the back of the car, talking. They were people he saw every day on his commute to work, but he knew none of their names—strangers brought together by the thirty-minute ride into the heart of the city where it seemed almost everyone worked. No one made eye contact. Instead, they stared out the dirty windows or looked down at the floor in silence.

The lucky ones sat on blue plastic benches that lined the inside of the tram. Ransom looked down at the two women who sat in front of him. They wore identical work uniforms—black slacks and white blouses with the words *Census Bureau* embroidered across their left pockets in black lettering. Ransom recognized the narrow-faced older woman, her blouse yellowed around the collar from sweat and age, but he hadn't seen the other woman before. She seemed like a duplicate of her companion, only without the crow's feet and the permanently etched worry lines across her forehead. The younger woman's blouse was clean and pressed. Ransom figured she must be the older woman's daughter, a recent Census Bureau hire. There was no other way to account for the snow-white blouse.

The tram arrived at the next stop, where the platform was packed. As the doors opened, a dozen people headed toward the exit and off the tram. Then the new passengers pushed forward. It was obvious there wasn't going to be enough room for everyone.

For the better part of a minute, people tried to force their way onto the tram. Ransom could feel the crowd press against him. He held tight to the handrail, determined not to lose his spot by the window.

The bell rang. The doors tried unsuccessfully to close. Over the crowd, Ransom could see three people holding the car's rear doors open as they fought for room. The bell rang a second time, and the tram began moving forward. Two of those trying to board let go as the tram picked up speed. The third man held on to the railing, probably hoping to make it to the next stop. But a hand from the woman directly in front of him shot out and caught him on the shoulder. The push caught him off guard, and he tumbled onto the platform as the doors banged shut.

Ransom peered out the back window as the tram sped down the tracks. The man who had been pushed off leaned up on his elbows, stuck his thumb between his middle and index fingers, and shook his hand at the departing tram. Two dozen disappointed passengers still remained on the platform behind him. Half of them watched the tram speed away while the rest looked in the opposite direction, most likely hoping to catch sight of the next one.

A baby's loud, piercing cry surprised Ransom. Looking toward the front of the car, he tried to catch a glimpse. At six feet five inches, he was taller than most of the passengers, but he still couldn't manage to see the baby or mother. He did, however, notice that several riders near the front seemed to be looking toward the left corner of the tram. The woman and her child must have boarded early enough to land a seat.

The tram pulled up to the next platform and stopped. Between each wail, Ransom could just make out the frantic hushes of the mother trying to quiet the child. It didn't help. The baby's cry grew louder and more acute. Ransom felt bad for the mother. With the heat and smell of the car, he couldn't blame the baby, though he did wonder what the woman was thinking, bringing a child onto a packed morning tram.

"I wish it was illegal to bring kids on these things," a female voice said.

Ransom looked down at the bench in front of him, thinking that one of the two women was talking to him.

"Why'd she even bring it?" the younger woman asked, looking at the older one. "Doesn't her building have a care center?"

"From the way it's crying, it sounds like it wants attention. Maybe it's a third and she doesn't have enough time to care for it properly," the older woman guessed, her voice full of contempt.

Ransom felt a flash of anger at the woman's comment but didn't say anything. Instead, he bit his lower lip and stared out the window. He preferred not to hear more of their conversation, but they were sitting too close, and he couldn't just move to another part of the tram.

The doors swung shut again, and the train lurched forward. The baby continued to howl. Ransom did his best to put the women and the baby out of his mind. He leaned forward into the dry air.

The tram came to a sudden stop. The tightly packed passengers stumbled in one mass toward the front of the car. Ransom gripped the handrail tightly to avoid being thrown. As he looked around, he noticed that everyone seemed to be okay. He leaned his head out the window to see what was going on, his knees bumping those of the older woman as he did so.

"Hey, watch it!" she barked.

Ransom ignored her. Fifty yards ahead was the 16th Street station. A crowd of people stood on the platform, staring at the stopped tram. He turned and looked down the tracks. A tram heading the opposite direction was stopped about twenty yards down the line. That could mean only one thing: a power failure.

He pulled his head back inside and checked the time. It was quarter to eight. He still had fifteen minutes to get to work. If he started walking now, he might make it on time.

The infant's cry, which had come to an abrupt end when the tram stopped, started up again.

"Open the doors!" a man shouted somewhere near the front of the car. His voice was loud and momentarily drowned out the baby's wails.

"Be patient. The power will be back on in a minute," suggested a female voice from somewhere in the middle of the tram.

"Shut up!" the man retorted. "Some of us have places to go."

Two men who were pressed up against the middle doors turned and tried to pry them open.

Things were quiet for a beat. Then the baby let out another scream. Ransom looked at the men struggling with the doors, hoping they'd open them soon. A bit of fresh air and more space was what everyone needed.

"I don't care if it's sick," the man blustered. "I have a right to ride to work without your little parasite screaming in my ear."

There was another pause, then something that sounded like the mother trying to hush her child. The baby continued to cry.

"If you won't shut it up, then I will!"

There was the sound of scuffling, followed by the cry of, "Give me back my baby!"

Ransom looked to the front. A large, muscular arm held the infant high in the air by one of her legs. The baby looked about two months old. She had dark eyes, olive skin, and a large mat of brown hair that hung in loose strands toward the ground. She wore pink shorts. The bottom of her white T-shirt hung down to her neck, exposing her soft belly. He couldn't see the face of the person holding her, but the man's cruelty was obvious.

The baby quieted for a moment, seemingly surprised to find herself upside down. Then her face turned crimson, and another cry burst forth.

A more delicate arm reached up and tried to grab the child, but it was quickly swatted away.

The man with the deep voice chuckled. "A breeder like you needs to be taught some parenting skills, like how to rock it to sleep."

The man swung the little girl back and forth by her leg. Ransom cringed as the baby's head just missed the car's front wall.

"Give her back, right now!" the mother demanded.

"I'm just putting it to sleep," the man said. "As soon as it shuts up, you can have it."

"If you don't give her back now, I'll kill you!" the woman yelled.

Ransom felt a bead of sweat run down his back. He glanced over at the men who had been trying to open the door. They'd stopped working and were staring toward the front of the car. Just about everyone was trying to get a glimpse of the commotion, but no one made a move to step in.

Helping out was simply asking for trouble, of course. Better to mind your own business and go on with your life. Ransom looked down at the lunch bucket between his feet.

"Don't threaten me, breeder," the man snarled, "or I'll bash its head!"

The man swung the baby far enough that her head lightly struck the wall. It was so quiet on the tram that the small thud echoed through the car. The baby's face puckered up, and she let out a piercing cry.

The woman screamed. Once again, she reached for the child.

The man raised his free hand and brought it down on the woman. There was the sickening sound of flesh meeting flesh. "Try that again, and I'll spill its brains all over the floor!" The man's voice rumbled through the car like thunder.

Ransom found himself pushing through the crowd. He ignored the cries and cursing from the other passengers as he shoved them to the side. A moment later he stood across from the man, the baby, and the woman.

For the first time, he got a good look at the mother. She was probably five and a half feet tall, with an olive complexion like her daughter. Her black hair was pulled back into a ponytail, and she wore a tiny gold cross around her neck. Her right eye was swollen and puffy, and blood ran from her nose onto a navy blue T-shirt. Her fists were clenched, and her eyes filled with anger.

The man holding the baby had small, deep-set green eyes. His shaved head glistened with sweat, and the muscles in his arms and neck pulled at the sleeves and collar of his black shirt. He looked to be Ransom's size, even though Ransom had a good five inches of height on him. He wore black boots and black pants. Around his waist was a belt containing handcuffs, mace, and a nightstick. A silver shield with the Census Bureau logo imprinted on it was pinned to his front pocket.

Ransom paused. Census Bureau Sentinels only had jurisdiction when it came to population crimes. Their main job was to round up women who were concealing an illegal pregnancy or children for whom their parents didn't have a replacement credit. As a result, they had earned the nickname *snatchers*. They had the reputation of having little respect for the law when it suited their purposes, so their jurisdiction usually didn't stop them. They were commonly known for their strength, fierceness, and cruelty. They inspired enough fear that even the police rarely bothered to investigate complaints against them. When it came to sentinels, the unspoken rule was to leave them alone and hope they'd do you the same courtesy.

The baby's continued screams drew Ransom's attention back to the child. Her face was bright red. Two steady streams of tears ran from her eyes and down her forehead to the floor.

She was just out of reach.

Another two feet forward and to his right, Ransom could at least make a grab for the child. He took a half step toward her when the deep voice of the snatcher reverberated through the car.

"Move any closer, and I'll drop the baby on its head."

Ransom stopped and faced the sentinel, who stared at Ransom through his tiny green eyes. "Back up," the man barked. "This matter doesn't concern you."

"Give the baby back." Ransom did his best to keep his voice flat and steady.

The sentinel's eyes betrayed a faint element of surprise. He likely wasn't used to someone talking back to him. "If you know what's good for you, you'll mind your own business," he said, looking back at the baby as though the conversation was over.

"Give the baby back to her mother," Ransom demanded, his voice rising.

Now Ransom had the sentinel's full attention. His eyes went from Ransom's face to the Recycling Center logo on Ransom's breast pocket.

"Are you kidding me? You're just a recycler. Why don't you go pick up some trash?"

Ransom ignored the taunt. "I'm not going to ask you again."

He took a step toward the sentinel so there was about six feet between them. Out of the corner of his eye, Ransom saw the mother move closer. The sentinel saw it too. His eyes darted from the mother to Ransom, then back to the mother. He seemed to realize that he couldn't stop both Ransom and the baby's mother from grabbing the child.

Without warning, the sentinel pushed the mother, dropped the baby, and lunged at Ransom. The woman's head made a dull thud as it smacked against the window. Ransom ducked under the sentinel's arm and managed to catch the infant just before her head hit the floor.

The mother sat up and rubbed the back of her head. She looked at Ransom, then rose to her feet and grabbed the baby from his arms. She retreated to the corner of the tram, where she held the child close to her breast.

The baby stopped crying.

Ransom stood and turned to face the sentinel, who had fallen into the crowd and lay atop three passengers. Everyone else was backing up, trying to get out of the way.

The sentinel rose to his hands and knees and shook his head. He grabbed a handrail and pulled himself to his feet, turning to face Ransom. Then he caught Ransom unprepared, his swing connecting with the side of Ransom's jaw, despite his failed attempt at ducking.

Ransom's mouth filled with the coppery taste of blood. His legs gave out from under him, and he found himself facedown on the tram's floor. Then there was a sharp kick to his side. The air rushed out of his lungs, and he curled up, fighting for breath.

Two strong hands grabbed him by the shoulders and flipped him on his back. The sentinel looked down at him with a smirk on his face. A bead of sweat fell from his forehead and landed squarely on Ransom's chest.

"I told you to mind your own business," the sentinel growled. "Maybe next time you'll listen."

He raised his leg, positioning his boot over Ransom's face.

Ransom instinctively raised his arms and waited for the blow.

It never came.

Through the spaces between his fingers, Ransom caught a flash of silver, then the sentinel swatting his neck as if bitten by a mosquito. Ransom lowered his hands and saw the sentinel staring at a small object between his fingers. It was about an inch long, half of its length in the form of a thin needle. The sentinel glanced in the direction of the woman and opened his mouth to say something, then suddenly grabbed the pole next to him for support. His body swayed from side to side before he fell to his knees. Eyes rolling to the back of his head, he fell to the floor, face-first, next to Ransom.

It was absolutely quiet on the tram.

Ransom pulled himself to his knees. He could feel his breath coming back to him. He spat blood out on the floor. His jaw hurt, and a few of his back teeth felt loose.

He looked over at the woman, confused by what had just happened.

Suddenly, the sounds of the men trying to open the doors started up again. Moments later, there was a hiss as the middle doors were forced open. A blast of fresh air rushed through the car.

The passengers made for the exit as fast as they could.

The woman picked a yellow sling from the floor and put it over her shoulder. A drop of blood fell from her nose to the fabric. She placed the baby in the sling and stepped over the body of the sentinel, heading for the exit.

"Wait," Ransom called.

The woman turned and looked at him. "Thank you for saving my baby," she said. "One day I'll repay you."

"What did you do to him?" Ransom asked, looking at the motionless body.

"Thanks for reminding me."

She knelt next to the sentinel and pried open his hand, retrieving the silver object. She slid it into her pocket, then pulled herself to her feet and checked the baby, brushed the dust from her pants, and headed toward the door.

"Who are you?" Ransom tried again.

"He'll wake up soon. You should get going."

"Wait," he called, but the woman had hurried down the steps of the tram.

Ransom pulled himself to a standing position. His jaw and side throbbed with pain. He staggered to the tram's open doors and spotted the woman thirty yards down the street. She was walking fast, weaving her way in and out of the throngs of people. Ransom hurried down the stairs and started after her. He was still winded and stiff from the fight. Within twenty yards, he had to put his hands on his knees while he caught his breath.

When he looked up again, she was gone.

Then he heard a high-pitched police whistle. Three cops were running down the street toward the tram. The middle one had a silver whistle between his lips that he blew as he ran.

Quickly, Ransom got in the back of a nearby line for a grocery store. Once the police ran past, he hurried down the street as fast as he could walk, anxious to put as much space between him and the tram as possible. It wasn't easy. He was still dazed and hurting, and the sidewalks were crowded with people going to work, groups of kids in their yellow-and-green uniforms hurrying to school, and people standing in line waiting for stores to open. To make faster progress, he stepped off the sidewalk and walked in the gutter. But even that path had obstacles. Donkey carts were parked in front of stores, their drivers unloading burlap bags filled with produce and supplies. There were piles of manure—some fresh, others days old—that had been swept to the gutter but not yet collected. Ransom ended up back on the sidewalk.

As his distance from the tram increased, Ransom's adrenaline ebbed and was replaced by fear. He wondered if the sentinel would be able to give the police a good enough description to ID him. The man had seen his uniform and knew where he worked. If police showed up at the Recycling Center, it wouldn't be too hard to figure out who he was. It was a rarity for people to be much taller than six feet. As far as Ransom knew, he was the tallest employee at the center.

He chastised himself for intervening in something that wasn't his business. The last thing he and his family needed was for him to miss work and spend a few weeks in jail. Money was tight enough as it was. What had he been thinking?

A pack of stray dogs ran out into the street. The lead dog, a German shepherd with spots of fur missing from his body, looked at Ransom with sad brown eyes. Ransom reached down to the gutter and pretended to pick up a rock. Immediately, the pack of dogs turned and ran across the street.

Ransom checked his watch. It was eight o'clock. He was late for work.

Ignoring the pain in his side, Ransom picked up the pace and hurried the remaining blocks to the Recycling Center.

two

The Recycling Center was a four-story, windowless concrete building that took up an entire city block. Etched in the side of the building was the universal recycling symbol of three bent arrows chasing each other in a Möbius loop. There was only one public entrance to the facility—a plain-looking, smoked-glass door bearing the hours of operation in inch-high, gold-colored paint. Next to the door was a plaque the size of a dinner plate that read:

**This building is made from 100% recycled material
New Earth Initiative Project #4562**

Ransom entered the doors at fifteen past eight. Off to the right was a small public waiting room. Eight metal folding chairs lined the perimeter of the room, but they were unoccupied. Past the room was a small window where a red-headed receptionist was too busy looking at her fingernails to notice Ransom as he walked by. Beyond the receptionist was another door that was propped open. A bored-looking security guard sat on a chair next to the door with his arms folded across his chest.

Ransom flashed his work ID card at the man.

The guard didn't look at it but just smiled and nodded. "Power's still out," he said. "You want a candle?"

Ransom shook his head. "I'll be fine." He could get to the cargo bay even if the hallway was pitch-black. Straight back, then take the first right. The door was at the end of that hall. But it wouldn't be dark—at least not during normal office hours. As he hurried down the hall, orange candlelight radiated from the open doors of offices on either side. The soft glow reminded Ransom of walking down an unlit road at twilight.

Ransom glanced in some of the office windows and open doors as he passed. Most people were bent over their desks, reading or filling out paperwork. A few had phones pressed to their ears. A middle-aged man with a large white candle on his desk and a pencil over his ear waved at Ransom when he walked by.

Ransom was in too much of a hurry to wave back.

He turned right and stopped at the door at the end of the hall. A bright white light emanated from the crack at the bottom. Ransom opened the door and stepped into a large cargo bay. Sunshine streamed through dozens of skylights in the ceiling. Five recycling trucks, painted forest green, were parked by the far wall. The trucks were twenty feet long and had a twelve-by-twenty-foot cargo hold on the back.

Two other trucks were backed up to a wall on the right. Their cargo holds were filled with wooden beams, chunks of concrete, and scrap metal. Next to the trucks stood half a dozen men. A few leaned against a large conveyor belt that took material from the trucks into the recycling machinery in the center of the building. With no power, there was no point in unloading the trucks.

Suddenly there was a click, followed by a humming sound. The reverberation of clanking machinery emanated from the heart of the building as the power came back on. Four of the men ran to either side of the conveyer belt as it rattled to life, and the other two jumped into the back of the trucks and started unloading the material.

Ransom headed to the row of gray lockers. He grabbed the work order taped to his door, read it, then shoved it in the front pocket of his jumpsuit. He pulled a small key from another pocket and opened the door, grabbing his canteen and toolbox.

Standing at a large, stainless steel sink next to the lockers, Ransom let the cold water run through his fingers. This was the only sink Ransom knew of that didn't have a water meter attached. The meters automatically shut off the water after five seconds and were mandatory for all homes, businesses, and government offices.

No one knew exactly why this sink didn't have one, but rumors circulated that the meter was packed away in a supervisor's office or had been "accidentally" put on the conveyor belt and sent with a load of material to be recycled. Whatever the reason, Ransom wasn't about to complain.

There was a rumbling sound as one of the cargo doors opened. In the mirror's reflection, he saw the driver honk and wave. Ransom gave the driver, Dempsey, a half wave in return. He turned and looked at the clock over the door. Why was Dempsey driving the truck outside this early? He shook his head. He'd ask later.

As he looked in the mirror, he saw that his face was flushed from the quick walk in warm morning air; beads of sweat ran from his close-cropped hair past green eyes and down his cheek. Dried blood covered the corners of his mouth. He touched the spot and smarted where the sentinel's fist had connected with his mouth.

Ransom stuck his head under the faucet, closing his eyes. The water washed the sweat from his face and reduced the throbbing in his jaw, but it did nothing to calm his fears.

After a minute, he pulled his head from the tap. Water rained from his brown hair to his face and splattered on the concrete floor. He looked around for something he could use to dry off. All he could see was a grubby, blue rag on a hook by the side of the sink. He used his sleeve instead.

"Hey, quit wasting water," a voice hollered.

Ransom turned and saw a young man staring at him incredulously. What was his name? Jared? Joseph? Jesse? Jesse, that was it. He had been hired two weeks earlier and was assigned to one of the recycling crews that worked Green Zone 4. In that short period of time, Jesse had garnered a reputation as an overexcited know-it-all. Ransom was glad Jesse wasn't part of his crew.

"There's only so much water to go around." Jesse stepped past Ransom and turned off the faucet. "I can't believe they haven't installed a water meter on this sink."

Ransom took a hard look at the teenager. He turned the tap back on and held his canteen under the water. In a few moments, water was overflowing from the top. Ransom kept the canteen under the tap, letting the water cascade down the sides.

Jesse angrily reached for the tap.

"Don't do it," Ransom said. "Not today. I'm not in the mood."

Most days, Jesse's attitude would have only inspired Ransom to harass the younger coworker. He might have poured his canteen onto the floor and joked about the lost life of a fish or something, just to get a reaction. But today was different. He was still uptight about the morning's incident. Anger, fear, and adrenaline pumped through his body, needing an outlet.

Jesse paused, his eyes studying every inch of Ransom's face. He moved to shut off the tap anyway.

Ransom dropped his canteen and grabbed Jesse's right arm, twisted it behind his back, then squeezed the tendons between Jesse's thumb and pointer finger as hard as he could.

Jesse's back arched in pain. He tried to wriggle free from Ransom's grasp. Ransom squeezed harder.

"You're wasting water," Jesse said through clenched teeth.

"And you're wasting my time," Ransom said. "Now get back to work and mind your own business, or I'll keep this water running all day."

He let go of Jesse and pushed him away. Jesse glared at Ransom, then headed for the closest green truck, rubbing his hand.

The men near the conveyor belt had stopped to watch the commotion.

"What are you looking at?" Ransom yelled.

The men shook their heads and muttered amongst themselves before returning to their backbreaking labor.

Ransom picked up his canteen from the floor and filled it again. He screwed on the lid and shut off the tap.

Dempsey was leaning against the front of their truck when Ransom put his toolbox in the truck's side panel. He had a half-smile on his wrinkled face that told Ransom he had seen the commotion near the sink. "Congratulations. You beat up the new guy. You want to tell me what that was about?"

Ransom ignored the question.

"Looks like you ran a marathon," Dempsey noted.

"Tram lost power, so I had to walk in," Ransom said, looking in the side panel to make sure they had all their tools and equipment.

"Everything okay? You usually don't snap like that."

Without a word, Ransom climbed into the passenger side and slammed the door. He needed to calm down before he talked with anyone.

He heard Dempsey close the side panel of the truck before he climbed in the cab and got behind the wheel.

"Where we going today?"

Ransom pulled the work order from his pocket and handed it to Dempsey. As Dempsey read it, Ransom looked at him. Dempsey was finally aging. His burly build seemed slightly diminished, and the hair seemed more gray than black now, contrasting well with his chocolate-colored skin. He also had more heavy wrinkles under his brown eyes and across his forehead, which he blamed on the stress of being a father.

Dempsey handed the work order back to Ransom.

"A new assignment—a home to tear down. That will be a nice change from hauling trash."

Dempsey pushed a button next to the steering wheel, and the dashboard lit up as the electric motor came to life. But then he tapped at the power dial under the glass, as though he thought the reading was wrong.

Ransom looked over at the dashboard. The orange power dial hovered just above the halfway mark.

"We're only half full? How much driving did you do this morning?" Ransom asked.

"Not much," Dempsey said. "I was just taking it for a test drive. Had to replace one of the batteries this morning. Wanted to make sure she was running good."

"Must have been a long test drive."

Dempsey just smiled. "Truck didn't fully charge," he guessed. "Probably had a power outage or something during the night."

"Do we have enough to get us there and back?"

"Yeah, we should be fine. But if it doesn't fully charge tonight, we might have a problem going anywhere tomorrow."

Dempsey put the truck in drive and honked the horn so the

others in the cargo bay would know they were in motion. The truck moved toward the large bay doors on the north wall. The two men by the doors stood and pulled the chain as the truck approached, and the bay doors slowly opened.

Dempsey nodded to the men as he drove past. He guided the truck around the back of the building to the street. He then looked both ways before honking his horn and pulling the truck onto Edward Abbey Boulevard—or "the 'Vard," as everyone called it.

Ransom looked at the work order. "Says here the owner died three days ago."

"Think there'll be anything left of it?"

"Only if they posted a guard."

"A guard doesn't mean anything. You know that." Dempsey laughed. "They're human too. Doesn't take much for someone to look the other way—especially if he has mouths to feed at home."

Ransom didn't reply. He looked out at the city as they drove past. Dempsey was right. Odds were they'd show up to the house and find that anything of value had been stripped.

As they drove through the streets, Ransom finally felt the anger and tension slowly ebbing from his body. Suddenly Dempsey slammed on the breaks to avoid hitting a teenager who walked into the road. Ransom's hands were braced to stop himself from hitting the dashboard, and Dempsey laid on the horn and cursed. The teen stood in the middle of the road and looked at the truck for a beat before walking to the other side.

"Stupid kids don't know to look both ways when they cross the street anymore," Dempsey groused.

"Considering almost no one drives anymore, that shouldn't be a surprise. Not all of us are old enough to remember streets filled with cars."

"Doesn't help that you can't hear these electric engines," Dempsey went on. "That's one thing I miss—the purr of a powerful motor. I don't care what they put in the air. You could hear a good one coming a mile away."

"I'll take your word for it." Ransom smiled.

Dempsey put his foot on the throttle and continued down the 'Vard, honking his horn more frequently.

"You aren't that young, are you?" Dempsey asked as he took a left on 12th Street, heading west. "I thought you were old enough to remember when just about everyone owned a car."

Dempsey honked the truck's horn, and Ransom watched as a lady reading the news board jumped in the air. He could remember car-filled streets, but the memories were few and hazy. The clearest was of him sitting in the backseat of his family's minivan, looking out the window as his mom pulled into a parking lot filled with cars. Perhaps he remembered it so well because the summer sun had reflected off their windshields and reminded him of a sky filled with stars.

"I was five, maybe six, when the carbon taxes went into effect," Ransom said. "I remember my dad coming home from work and telling my mom that they couldn't afford to drive anymore. Sometime after that, I think the car was sold or given to a recycling center."

"You're making me feel old," Dempsey said. "Old, but useful. What are you going to do when people my age die? You won't have anyone to drive you outside the town."

"By the time you die, there won't be any houses left in the Green Zone to recycle."

"Yeah, right. There's probably what, only two hundred or so homes left? In five to ten years, all their owners will be dead, and we'll be out of a job."

"I wouldn't worry about not having a job. There's always something that needs to be recycled. At the very least, there's always trash that needs to be picked up."

Dempsey laughed. "That would be ironic."

"What?"

"Turning us back into full-time garbage men," Dempsey said. "That's where I started, you know. Back when you were a kid, we were called garbage men. Good, steady job, but not the kind most people dreamed of having. Then they passed a bunch of green laws and started calling us recyclers. Change our title, and suddenly we have more respect in the community. Funny thing is, it doesn't matter what you call us; in reality, we're still a bunch of garbage men."

Ransom raised his eyebrows.

"Think about it, Ransom. We simply take what other people don't want and put it somewhere else. We just take all of it to a recycling center instead of putting it in a big hole in the ground."

"There's one difference. A lot of people want what's left behind. That's why most of the houses we visit are stripped."

Dempsey's eyes twinkled. "Yeah, but since there's nothing of value once we get there, we're basically picking up trash."

Ransom let out a laugh, and out came the last of his anger and tension. He smiled the rest of the way to the security checkpoint.

* * *

There was one other recycling truck in line when they reached the security checkpoint. Dempsey put the truck in park and turned off the electric engine. They watched the two guards do a security sweep of the first truck.

The first guard walked around the truck with a mirror attached to a long pole to look under the bottom. The second guard waited while the back of the truck's container opened on its hydraulic hinges. Once it was open, he looked into the back, then banged twice on the side. A moment later, the hydraulic hinges started to close.

When the two were satisfied, a third guard came out of the shack and approached the driver.

"Looks like we're going to be here awhile," Dempsey said.

Ransom looked up just as the driver handed the guard his paperwork. The guard was a short, pudgy-faced man with a goatee and close-cropped black hair and notorious for taking a long time to examine paperwork. He took the clipboard and licked his lips. It looked like he was examining every word with the thoroughness of a secondary school English teacher. All he was missing, Ransom thought, was a fat red pencil.

It was getting hot in the truck. Ransom opened his door and hopped out. "Looks like we've got at least a ten-minute wait," he said. "I'm going to stretch my legs."

He walked to the back of the truck on Dempsey's side where there was some shade. He leaned against the truck, his eyes tracing the razor wire atop the fifteen-foot-high fence that encircled the city. He followed the wire until it reached a guard tower about a half mile away. Ransom could just make out a guard slowly pacing in the tower.

Ransom turned his attention to the line of twenty or so people waiting to leave the city. Based on the size of their backpacks, Ransom figured most of them were heading to the farming community of Cheney, a couple hours' walk to the west. Two people near the front of the line, a man and a woman, carried large backpacks on their shoulders with sleeping bags attached to the top. Ransom wondered where their journey was taking them. Yakima, perhaps. Seattle. Maybe even Portland. Wherever they were going, they looked anxious to start. Ransom couldn't blame them. It was getting hotter by the minute, and the longer they waited, the more time they'd have to spend walking in the heat of the day.

The braying of a donkey brought Ransom out of his thoughts. A guard lifted the stop pole and waved the man driving a donkey cart through the checkpoint. The driver wore a wide-brimmed hat and a long-sleeve shirt. The back of the cart held burlap bags filled with ears of corn. Ransom felt his mouth water at the sight of the green husks sticking out the top of the bag. The driver gave the reins a shake, and the donkey picked up speed. Ransom made a mental note to stop by the store near his apartment on the way home. He might as well see if some of the corn had made its way to their shelves.

He thought about getting some food from his lunch pail when he realized he'd left it on the tram. Cursing under his breath for forgetting it, he knew there was no point stopping by the transportation department to see if anyone had turned it in. No doubt some enterprising person had already eaten the food and sold the bucket at the Station or planned on using it himself. Steel buckets like that were expensive to replace—if one could even find a replacement. He'd have to come up with another solution after he got home. He simply couldn't carry an armful of food onto the tram every day. In the meantime, his carelessness meant he was going hungry for lunch. He leaned against the truck and closed his eyes. It was going to be a long day.

The truck lurched forward. Ransom looked up and saw the guard waving Dempsey to the checkpoint. The other recycling truck was already making its way down the road, leaving a trail of dust in its wake.

Ransom circled to the passenger side and climbed back into the cab. He handed the work order to Dempsey, who handed it to the guard. Then they sat in the cab for five hot minutes while the same short, pudgy guard examined it. Several times, Ransom was tempted to tell the guard to hurry, but he kept his mouth shut. Any comments simply meant the guard would take more time signing the paperwork. Ransom had waited in line for an hour once because the guard had overheard him make a snide remark to Dempsey about the delay.

"Open the back of your truck," the guard ordered.

"Why? We're empty," Dempsey said.

"Just open it, sir," the guard replied.

Dempsey pushed a button on the dashboard, and the whine of hydraulic hinges filled the air.

A few moments later, someone pounded on the side of the truck, and Dempsey pushed the button to close the doors.

The guard signed the paperwork and handed it to Dempsey.

"Sorry for the delay," he said. "A family has gone missing. We believe they're trying to leave the city."

He handed Dempsey a piece of paper from his clipboard. Dempsey glanced at it, then passed it to Ransom. It was a grainy copy of a photograph of a pretty woman with big eyes and dark hair.

"If you see this woman while you're out in the Green Zone, let us know. Her name is Amber. She might be traveling with a man and three children."

Dempsey nodded. "Will do."

The guard waved them through the checkpoint. Dempsey drove down the dirt road at the truck's top speed—thirty-five miles an hour.

Ten minutes later, Dempsey parked the truck on the brown, matted grass of a red brick bungalow. Ransom figured it had been built during the post–World War II housing boom that had filled up much of the land west of town. There was a detached garage on the rear of the property and a rusting swing set in the backyard.

"I don't see glass in the windows," Dempsey said as they got out of the truck. "I told you this place would be stripped."

Ransom walked up to the house. There was a large, empty square where the front window had been. He walked up the concrete stairs to the tiny porch. The front door had three small, rectangular windows that went down at an angle. The glass was missing and so was the doorknob. He pushed the door open, listened a moment, then headed inside. Dempsey followed close behind.

They stood in the middle of what had been a living room. The carpet had been torn up and removed. Small pieces of padding were still stuck to the floor. The outlets were ripped from the wall. There were holes in the walls where the wiring had been pulled out. One gash went all the way to the ceiling, where a light fixture had once hung.

Ransom headed down a short hall to the kitchen. As expected, the kitchen sink had been removed, along with all the piping, cabinets, and countertops. The only thing that looked untouched was the linoleum-covered floor.

"We've got a bedroom and bathroom in similar shape," Dempsey said, coming into the kitchen. "Double or nothing, the furnace and everything worth taking in the basement is gone too."

They stood in silence for several moments. Then Ransom said, "Get the tools out of the truck. I'll inspect the rest of the place."

"Look on the bright side," Dempsey said, smiling. "Whoever did this saved us a lot of work."

The basement, it turned out, was just as bad. There were holes in the ceiling where the copper piping had been ripped out. In what had been a utility room, there were only dark squares where a washer and dryer had once stood. The salvageable remains were next to zero. If they were lucky, the wooden frame would be in good enough condition to be reused. But with the house being over a hundred years old, Ransom didn't have high expectations.

He stopped in what had once been a bedroom. The walls were

painted pink with big brown polka dots. The color combination was not to his liking. Still, he stood in the middle of the room and wondered who had lived in the house over the last hundred years. He wondered whether the home had seemed small and cramped or large and spacious to its occupants. He felt a twinge of jealously. This home was easily twice as large as his apartment. It probably boasted eighteen hundred square feet. Granted, he had recycled homes twice this size, but still, he'd love to be able to give his boys their own rooms and paint the walls their favorite colors.

Ransom headed up the stairs and out the back door to examine the rest of the property. His first stop was the detached garage. He opened two large, white, wooden doors and stepped inside. It was instantly twenty degrees hotter and smelled like dust. The garage was empty except for a pile of shriveled leaves and dust in one corner and faded oil stains on the cement. The drywall was still relatively intact, but it was yellowed from water stains in a few areas near the floor. To his surprise, there were power outlets on the far wall along two wooden shelves. Ransom found it odd that someone would take the effort to strip out the house but leave the garage untouched. True, there wasn't much to take, but the few power outlets and wiring in the walls held some value.

He headed to the backyard. Next to the swing set was a large cherry tree. The green leaves were wilting. Despite its large size, Ransom figured it wasn't going to last long—at least not without regular care. Not that it mattered anyway—once the house was gone, someone would come and take the tree down too. Cherry trees weren't native to this part of the Green Zone, so it would have to go.

Ransom kicked at some dried cherry pits on the dead grass, then moved to the swing set. The metal frame was pockmarked with rust. The swing seats were cracked and bleached white from years of exposure to the sun. Ransom wondered why no one had bothered to remove the frame. It was heavy, and the metal alone would easily bring a month's worth of wages if one could find the right buyer. He got down on his knees and pulled back the brown, foot-high grass that surrounded the base of the poles. The swing set was anchored in cement. It appeared that someone had tried to chisel it away but had given up.

Ransom stood up and looked around the yard. It was about a quarter acre in size. He found his mind drifting back to his two boys and wondered how they'd enjoy having this much space to run around. The play area next to their apartment building was crowded with kids, and there was always a fight for the swings or other playground equipment. But if they lived in this house, his two boys would have their own place to play. He stood for a minute and imagined them running around the yard, chasing each other and playing on the swings. The thought of his boys made him smile.

"Hey, where do you want to start?"

Dempsey's voice brought Ransom out of his reverie. He turned and saw Dempsey standing at the back door with his toolbox in his hand.

"The garage," Ransom said. "For some reason, they didn't touch it. We should get everything out of there now. They'll come back and take it tonight if we don't."

Ransom watched Dempsey head into the garage. A moment later, he could hear the sounds of the drywall being pried back from the walls. He was glad they had found something of value. His family needed the extra income that the outlets and wiring would bring.

three

Teya grimaced as Lia inserted a needle into her arm. She watched as the small vial filled with blood. Then the needle was removed, and a patch of cotton was taped to her arm to stop the bleeding.

Teya pulled down the sleeve of her blouse and watched Lia cap the vial and affix a label with Teya's name and ID number to it. Her eyes moved from the vial to Lia, then back to the vial. She fought the urge to take the small glass tube out of Lia's hands and wash its contents down the drain, but such an action would be futile. All it would do was raise suspicion, and she'd eventually be forced to give another sample.

Lia turned and set the vial of blood in a tray containing thirty other samples. She brushed her auburn hair out of her eyes and picked up a clipboard from the counter. "All right," she said. "You're the last one. Let's get started."

Teya randomly selected a vial from the tray. She read out the patient's name and ID number and inserted the vial into the top slot of the Incubus. She shut the lid and pushed a button. Exactly twenty seconds later, a buzzing sound came from the Incubus, and the red bulb next to the slot lit up. While Lia wrote down the results, Teya dumped the blood down the drain and placed the vial in a bucket in the sink.

One down, thirty to go, she thought as she placed another sample in the machine.

While it was processing, Teya stared at her sample in the tray and thought of ways she could get Lia out of the lab for a minute. Sixty seconds was all she needed to swap the label on her vial with the label on another. She had done it for her last two tests. She could do it again.

The Incubus buzzed, and the red light lit up. Lia yawned and recorded the results. Teya removed the vial and glanced at Lia to see if she was looking. She wasn't. Teya let the vial slip from her fingers. Glass and blood spilled across the cement floor. Lia jumped backward to avoid the mess.

"Oh, how clumsy of me," Teya said, standing up. "Let me get something to clean it up."

"I'll get it," Lia said, setting the clipboard on the counter. "I need to stretch my legs anyway."

Once Lia walked out the door, Teya quickly moved to the tray with the vials. She picked up two vials, one with her name on it. Noting the name on the other sample—*Eloise Johnston*—Teya carefully peeled back the label. She had to work slowly or the label would tear. While she worked, she counted to sixty in her head— the time she figured it would take Lia to return.

Ten . . . eleven . . . twelve . . . thirteen . . .

Once the label was off, she placed it upside down on the counter and pulled back the label from her own vial.

Thirty-three . . . thirty-four . . . thirty-five . . .

Carefully, she switched the labels.

Fifty-five . . . fifty-six . . . fifty-seven . . .

Done.

She let out a sigh and dropped both vials back in the tray.

"Teya?"

She jumped at the sound of her name, spinning around to see the director of the Paul Ehrlich Clinic standing in the doorway. Dr. Geoffrey Redgrave was a short man with a protruding belly and a receding hairline. He wore a ragged white lab coat that was several sizes too big, giving him the appearance of wearing flowing white robes.

Teya's heart was racing. The way Dr. Redgrave held the doorknob made her think he'd been standing there for a while. She stood speechless under his gaze, trying to think up a natural excuse for what she had done.

"I didn't mean to startle you," Dr. Redgrave said as he pushed his glasses up the bridge of his nose. "I just wanted to tell you I'm leaving a little early, so I'll need you to drop off the day's test results with the Census Bureau."

Teya inwardly groaned. She usually looked forward to unexpected clinic-related trips to the Census Bureau. They were an excuse to get out of the small, cramped lab and outside for a couple of hours. Plus, she could stop by her sister's office for a while and chat. But today, the Census Bureau was the last place she wanted to go.

Talking her way out of the assignment wasn't an option, however. Due to confidentiality laws, the report had to be delivered by the head of the clinic or the head lab technician. And if Dr. Redgrave couldn't do it, the task fell to her.

Teya took a calming breath before answering. "Not a problem. I'd be happy to."

"Thanks," Dr. Redgrave said.

He looked over Teya's shoulder at the vials. Teya followed his gaze, her heart skipping a beat.

"We've got quite a few samples today," Dr. Redgrave said.

"Yes, well, it's almost the end of the month," she answered. "Most women wait until the last possible day before getting their blood drawn."

"That's right. July's almost over," Dr. Redgrave said, shaking his head. "That means we'll be plenty busy the rest of the week. Well, thanks in advance for running that errand." He turned to leave, then stopped and glanced around the room. "Where's Lia? There should be two of you in the room when you're testing."

"I'm right here, Dr. Redgrave," Lia said as she scooted around him with a rag, broom, and dustpan in her hands. She knelt down and began picking up pieces of glass with her fingers and tossing them in the garbage can.

Dr. Redgrave looked at the mess on the floor as if seeing it for the first time. "You did test that before it broke, right?" he asked.

Teya nodded. "Yep. Another negative."

Dr. Redgrave massaged his forehead with his fingers. "Good. Getting women back in here to have their blood drawn again is a headache." He turned without another word, leaving the door to the laboratory ajar.

While Lia soaked up the blood with a rag, Teya looked out in the hall. It was empty. Quietly closing the door, she leaned against it and fought back tears of relief.

She'd be more careful next time—if there was a next time. Her pregnancy was a week or so away from entering the second trimester. She couldn't hide it forever, especially where she worked. Twice a year, everyone at the clinic received training on how to tell if a woman was concealing a pregnancy. She had been careful not to wear larger or baggy clothes, even though her clothes felt tighter around her waist. And she felt sure Dr. Redgrave or someone at the clinic would have noticed her breasts enlarging. But no one had said anything.

Teya returned to her stool, fighting the temptation to put her hand on her stomach by reminding herself that such an action was the number one sign that a woman was pregnant. She noticed that the needle Lia had used to draw her blood was still on the counter. She tossed it in the sink with the bucketful of others that needed to be cleaned.

She let her body relax as Lia swept up the last of the glass, dumped it in the garbage can, rinsed the blood from the rag, and washed her hands thoroughly. She was glad she had enough seniority that she didn't have to clean up the mess. Washing the blood-stained vials and used needles was bad enough. She always worried about getting poked and contracting some horrid disease. Sometimes she wished they used the throwaway supplies some of the older doctors wistfully talked about when the topic arose. It would be more convenient and sanitary, they would say, to throw away used medical supplies instead of washing and reusing them. Even if the doctors were right, using disposables was impossible since there were no landfills or incinerators in which to put the waste. And even if there were, the clinic didn't have enough money to buy large amounts of medical supplies—let alone pay the carbon taxes that would be required to ship them from Texas or wherever they were made. Unless the laws were changed or someone came up with a better solution, they were stuck with the status quo.

When Lia was done, she picked up the clipboard. "Ready?" she asked.

Teya gave her a weak smile, then looked at her sample—the one with Eloise's name on it. She couldn't bring herself to test it, at least, not right away. Instead, she picked up a vial on the other end of the tray and placed it inside the Incubus. She shut the lid and pushed the button.

While it was processing, she picked up her sample and held it between her fingers. The vial was warm from the fresh blood inside. She held it up to the lightbulb that hung by a single, frayed wire from the ceiling. Tipping the vial back and forth, she watched the red liquid move from one end to the other. She wondered how Eloise would react once she received a call asking her to return for a second test.

Teya had made that call often enough that she knew it didn't matter how many times the person on the other end was told that the Incubi weren't perfect and occasionally came back with false positives. All the patient would hear was that the clinic wanted to run another test. It was like telling someone they had cancer. It didn't matter how curable it was or if the doctor had caught it early enough to be treated. At the word *retest*, everything else became white noise.

The Incubus buzzed, bringing Teya out of her thoughts. The red light was on, another negative result. She removed the vial from the machine as Lia scribbled the information on the form. Then, taking a long, hard look at the vial that bore Eloise's name, she placed it into the Incubus and pushed the button.

After what seemed like an eternity, the Incubus buzzed. She lifted her head and saw that the green light was on.

Lia gasped. "A positive! We haven't had one of those in a week."

Teya didn't reply as Lia checked the extra boxes on the form. She couldn't open her mouth without confessing what she had just done. She quickly removed the vial and put it in the small container on the counter so it could be tested again.

I'm so sorry, Eloise. I promise to make your next visit here as short as possible, Teya thought as she loaded the next sample.

* * *

On her way out the door, Teya gave Eloise's contact information to Nevaeh. The red-headed receptionist smiled in return. Of the two girls who took turns scheduling appointments and passing out birth control, Teya thought Nevaeh was the most sensitive. She was the best at telling women they needed to return to the clinic. She had a soft voice and kept a steady, unemotional tone when she talked on the phone. It was the kind of reassuring voice women needed on the other end of the line, even if they didn't hear most of what she said.

"Only one call today?" Nevaeh asked.

"Be nice to her, okay? If she gets concerned, tell her the Incubus is having problems."

Nevaeh smiled. "I'll do my best."

"I'm out for the rest of the day," Teya said as she headed toward the door, the report in her hand and her purse over her shoulder.

Outside, the temperature was pushing one hundred degrees. Teya headed straight for the tram stop a block away. Halfway there, she saw the tram pull up. She debated whether or not to run to catch it but decided that sprinting for a tram wouldn't be good for the baby. Another train would be along in about fifteen or twenty minutes. She could wait. Since she'd left work early, she might as well enjoy the time off.

A man sprinted past her. She watched him wave to the conductor to hold the doors. The conductor smiled, then shut the doors just as the man made it to the platform. The man banged on one of the windows, startling the handful of passengers inside, but the tram picked up speed and was gone. He shook his fist before wandering over to one of the benches, where he sat down and wiped the sweat from his forehead.

Teya arrived at the platform a few minutes later. A paper carrier brushed by and hurried to the news board. Teya took her to be about sixteen. The girl wore a faded black baseball cap with the logo of the local paper on it and carried a bucket under one arm and a metal tube under the other. Teya watched the paper carrier set both items on the ground before removing the lid from the bucket and tearing down the morning's newspaper from the news board. She swung a backpack off her back and placed the discarded paper inside. Then she took a brush from her back pocket and dipped it into the bucket to spread glue in a z-like pattern over the news board. Finally, she pulled a large sheet of newsprint from the metal tube and pressed it against the board.

"It's the evening edition," the girl said to Teya as she hurried away.

Teya took a minute to skim through the paper. There was a story of the city council's debate over whether or not to reduce the meat and milk rations this winter, how the triple-digit temperatures and water usage were affecting the city's wells, and the latest updates on Sunday's New Earth Day celebration. Then a headline in the left corner of the paper caught her attention.

ALLEGED PREGNANT WOMAN SOUGHT BY CENSUS BUREAU
Woman thought to be pregnant with fourth. Family also missing.

Teya looked around the platform before continuing to read. The man who had missed the tram was still sitting on the bench, resting his chin on one of his hands. Three others stood on the far end of the platform in the sliver of shade offered by a community message board.

Satisfied that no one was paying attention to her, she bent down to read the article.

A woman believed to be pregnant with her fourth child is missing, along with her husband and three children.

According to Census Bureau reports, Amber River, 34, failed to appear for a mandatory pregnancy retest at the Rachel Carson Women's Clinic yesterday morning. After repeated attempts by the clinic to contact her, Census Bureau Sentinels were dispatched to her apartment and found it uninhabited.

River had received a first positive test two days earlier.

Census Bureau spokesperson Thomas Ramirez declined to comment, citing the ongoing investigation when asked whether or not River or her family might have fled with a terrorist organization. He did, however, mention that steps were being taken to ramp up border enforcement to make sure River and her family couldn't leave the city.

According to Census Bureau records, Matthew and Amber River are the parents of three children, Hope, Robert, and Adela, who range in age from two to six. The records show the Rivers bought a credit for their third child from Amber's sister almost three years ago. No other credits were listed in their name.

According to Mary LaFeur, a counselor who specializes in mental health assessments for women who want more than two children, women faced with an unplanned pregnancy often find themselves in an emotionally vulnerable state.

"They're often confused about what they should do. Those who want another child may not be able to obtain a credit for it," LaFeur said. "Sometimes it causes them to make irrational decisions."

Last year, 157 people were arrested for population crimes. Nearly three-fourths of them were women pregnant with children for whom they had no credits. The others were husbands or boyfriends who aided the women in concealing their pregnancies.

If anyone knows the whereabouts of Matthew or Amber River, or their children, they are encouraged to contact the Census Bureau immediately.

The article was accompanied by a black-and-white photo of Amber. She had wide, innocent eyes and a large smile. Her dark hair fell just past her shoulders. Teya knew it was the kind of face that would make most men stop and turn if they were to pass her on the street.

Teya's stomach growled, bringing her out of her thoughts. She walked to the edge of the platform and looked for a tram. The next tram appeared to be three stops down—at least another ten minutes away.

She sat on one of the empty cement benches, but the heat burned through her slacks. She moved to the partial shade offered by the news board. Inside her purse were a few salt crackers she had wrapped in a napkin for times like this. Chewing slowly, she looked around.

Across the street, a donkey cart stopped in front of the grocery store. The driver grabbed a few burlap bags from the cart and headed inside. Teya made a mental note to stop at the store on her way back in case there was some fresh food they could have with dinner. She wiped a bead of sweat from her brow and wondered if the baby inside could feel the summer heat.

Teya knew she was running out of time. She thought about the conversation she desperately needed to have with Ransom. Although he loved the two boys they already had, he wasn't going to be happy when she told him about the pregnancy because it would put their family and jobs in danger. They'd always had an open, trusting relationship, so when he learned she had kept this information from him for nearly three months, he was going to be even more upset. She thought of different ways to tell him about the pregnancy, changing what she'd say and trying to guess how he'd react. She just hoped that when she finally had the courage to tell him, instead of becoming angry, Ransom would hold her in his arms and tell her that everything would work out.

The tram pulled up to the platform. It wasn't any cooler inside. She looked around the car and took a seat near the door. Only a dozen or so people were on board. Most of them were fanning themselves with pieces of cardboard or folded-up paper. Teya looked inside her purse but didn't have anything she could use. She'd just have to deal with the heat.

Twenty minutes later, the tram stopped in front of the Census Bureau. Teya exited and stared at the five-story, black glass structure. She hesitated before entering the building.

Get in, then get out, she thought. *You'll be inside less than five minutes.*

As Teya walked through the revolving doors, she was met with a blast of cold air. She stopped just inside and closed her eyes, taking in the welcome change in temperature. The Census Bureau was the only building in the city with an air-conditioning waiver from the Sustainability Agency. During the summer, the inside of the Census Bureau was kept at a constant seventy-five degrees.

She took a long drink at a water fountain near the door and headed toward the bank of teller windows on the left wall.

Teya had always thought the main floor of the Census Bureau to be a little over-grand. The large lobby extended one hundred feet from the door. On either side were ten teller windows, and between them were rows of wooden benches where people sat waiting for their number to be called. It seemed especially silly to have so many windows when only half were regularly occupied. A third of the benches were filled with bored-looking people holding numbers in their hands.

Fortunately for Teya, she didn't have to take a number. Instead, she walked straight to the window with the word STATIS-TICS over it. She pulled the clinic's test results from her purse and slid the paper to a middle-aged clerk with black hair and a yellowed collar. The woman quickly looked over the paperwork and, when satisfied everything had been filled out correctly, handed Teya a receipt to sign.

Teya signed the paper and slid it back to the clerk. The clerk tore a yellow copy from the back of the receipt and handed it to Teya, who put it in her purse. She turned to leave and saw a sentinel standing directly behind her.

Teya froze. The sentinel was at least a foot taller than she was.

"Are you Teya Lawe?" he asked.

"Yes."

"I need you to come with me."

"I'm sorry, what is this about?"

"Everything will be explained shortly," he said. "If you would, please head to the elevator."

He motioned to a lone door along the far wall behind the security checkpoint.

Suddenly Teya felt hot. Maybe Dr. Redgrave had seen her switch the tests, realized she was pregnant, and used his excuse of leaving to get her to the Census Bureau. Maybe he called ahead and told them to arrest her.

She glanced over at the main doors and thought about running but decided against it. Running wouldn't solve anything. She took a long look at the guard, then headed for the elevators— well aware that every eye in the lobby was following her.

She passed through a metal detector, and a sentinel patted her down. Afterward, he handed her a safety pin and a yellow pass with the word GUEST printed in big, black letters. This wasn't what she had expected.

"Put this on your blouse. Make sure it's visible at all times," he said in a bored monotone.

Teya's head was buzzing. She clipped the pass to her breast pocket and followed the sentinel past the security checkpoint to the elevator. The sentinel held the elevator's door open for her. She stepped inside, and he shut the door behind them.

Teya's heart pounded in her chest all the way to the fifth floor.

four

As Teya followed the sentinel out of the elevator, her feet sank into the soft, gray carpet of a small lobby. A brown-eyed receptionist sitting behind the desk looked up as the sentinel approached. They exchanged a few words, then the receptionist looked over at Teya. She smiled in recognition and waved.

"I see your sister gave you an escort today," she said.

"My sister? What is this about?" Teya asked.

The receptionist shook her head and picked up the phone. "I have no idea, but I'll tell Mona you're here."

While the receptionist waited for an answer, Teya's mind raced, trying to figure out why her sister wanted to see her. Maybe Dr. Redgrave had called Mona directly and reported her lab results. No, that couldn't be it. As far as Teya knew, Dr. Redgrave and her sister didn't know each other. There had to be another reason.

The receptionist hung up the phone. "She'll be a few minutes. Why don't you have a seat while you wait?" She motioned to the couch against the wall, then glanced at the sentinel. "The director says you can go now."

Teya slowly paced the lobby until she heard her sister's voice coming down the hall. Around the corner came another sentinel, followed by her sister. Teya's heart skipped a beat, and she felt her legs start to lose their strength. It was a trap after all. Somehow her sister knew about her pregnancy.

"Hey, Teya!" Mona exclaimed. She stepped around the sentinel and bent a little to give her sister a hug. "I'll be with you in just a second."

Teya turned and watched Mona escort the sentinel to the elevator. The man was bald and thick with muscles. He had a bruise on his temple. He glanced at Teya as he passed, then his head swung around as he looked her up and down. Teya had received that stare many times before, but there was something extra creepy about the way this snatcher looked at her. It was as if he knew about the child growing inside her. It sent chills down her spine.

"I promise we'll find the two who attacked you," Mona was saying. "Now, if you're feeling okay, I need you to go to the Infirmary to see how we can improve our security down there. I don't want to lose another patient."

The sentinel nodded and pushed the button for the elevator.

"I appreciate your not filing a report with the police," Mona continued. "But for our own purposes, be sure to give detailed descriptions of your attackers. We need to track these people down."

The sentinel entered the elevator and nodded to Mona before closing the door.

Mona turned, smiling at Teya. "I'm so glad you came today," she said, walking across the lobby. "I called the clinic this afternoon and was told you were dropping off the pregnancy report. I hope the sentinel didn't scare you. I've been dealing with some unexpected issues all day and just wanted to make sure we had a chance to talk."

Before Teya could say anything, Mona caught her by the elbow and guided her to the office at the end of the hall.

"Is everything okay?" Teya asked, glancing over her shoulder. She couldn't shake the feeling the beady-eyed sentinel had given her.

"It is now that you're here," Mona answered. "It's been one of those days. One of our top sentinels was attacked on the tram this morning for no apparent reason. There've been other security issues as well. Sometimes I wonder why I took this job in the first place."

They stopped in front of a door where the words POPULATION DIRECTOR were written in large, gold letters. Mona opened the door and motioned for Teya to enter.

Mona's office in the southeast corner of the building was filled with diffused sunlight that streamed in through the windows and gave the room a soft, yellow glow.

Mona stretched out in the black leather seat behind the desk. She wore a white blouse underneath a business suit the same color as the chair. The suit seemed to emphasize her narrow face and added severity to her dishwater-blonde hair. Their mother's features weren't quite as soft on Mona.

Teya took one of the two chairs on the opposite side. She glanced down at the desk. Amid the papers scattered across it was an open folder with a picture of Amber River, a color version of the one Teya had seen in the newspaper. Her hair and eyes were the color of dark chocolate, and it appeared there were freckles on her face. A stack of papers an inch high lay beneath the photograph.

Mona closed the folder and moved it and a few papers to the side of her desk.

"Okay, I've got some good news," she said. "What are you guys doing for New Earth Day?"

Teya was caught off guard by the question. She still had a queasy feeling in her stomach, thinking that any moment, Mona was going to call her out on the pregnancy. Teya paused as she tried to remember what she and Ransom had planned. "I think we're taking the boys to the parade."

"Perfect!" Mona exclaimed. "I just learned this morning that we have an opening on the Census Bureau float. A family canceled at the last minute. So, I thought of a perfect family that could fill in." She gave Teya a quizzical look.

Teya gave her a half smile in return, not sure what to say.

"Come on, sis, this is a great opportunity."

"I'm sorry, Mona. What is it you want my family to do?"

"I want you to be part of the parade!"

All at once, the worry Teya had carried since Dr. Redgrave had dropped by her lab evaporated. She felt like crying with relief. "I—I don't know what to say," she said, fighting back the tears.

"Say 'yes,' " Mona said with a laugh. "Just think of how much fun your boys will have. Instead of standing on a hot, crowded sidewalk, they'll get to be part of the action. It's a day you'll all remember for the rest of your lives."

Teya thought of James and Warren riding atop the float and smiled. "Well, I guess the boys would enjoy it. I'll have to okay it with Ransom."

"You know Ransom's not going to object. He'd do anything to make the boys happy. He's a great dad. Besides, the two of you deserve to be up there more than anyone. You both do things that make the world a better place. You're people that everyone should admire."

Teya looked at the floor and pressed her foot into the carpet. The things she cared about changed when she became a mother. She'd felt slight differences between her and Mona in their approach to life as they were growing up, but their attitudes had drifted further apart over the last few years. As sisters, they looked very similar, both getting their mother's green eyes, facial features, and tall, lanky figures. If it wasn't for the dark hair Teya had gotten from their father, they could almost pass as twins. Despite their appearance, however, they were very different people. Mona had always known what she wanted to do with her life. She went straight from college to the Census Bureau, worked hard, and was appointed Population Director soon after the election and the new governor's swearing-in. That had been three years ago. There had really only been one hiccup in her well-planned life. Years ago she'd married a sentinel, but the marriage had lasted less than a month before it was annulled. Teya had never known why and had given up asking—the subject always reduced Mona to tears and stubborn silence.

Teya, on the other hand, had taken her time getting a chemistry degree. She shuffled around from one job to another, never really focusing on anything until she met Ransom. After they'd married, she finally settled down and, thanks to Mona's connections, landed her current job. Two children had followed, and now Teya found herself busier than she'd ever imagined.

And it was the arrival of her children that, at least in Teya's mind, turned the differences between the sisters from a crack to a chasm. Having children had changed the way Teya looked at the world. Instead of seeing one that was falling apart, she saw a world with problems, yes, but one that could be improved and made a better place to live. She wanted her boys to have more and better opportunities. She wanted for them to use their talents and abilities to make things not only better for themselves, but for others. Her children were assets to the world, not a burden. More than anything, Teya wished her sister had the same hope for the future as she did. She desperately wanted to confide in Mona about her pregnancy and share their deepest secrets as they had done as children. But if Mona even suspected her sister was pregnant, she would consider herself legally obligated to find the nearest snatcher and have Teya arrested.

"We're not a perfect family, Mona. You know that," Teya finally said, hoping her silence had been read as humility.

"You're better than most. My job puts me in contact with lots of families every day. Most of them are nothing but selfish. They look for ways to get more than their allotted rations or bypass our population controls."

For the second time in as many minutes, Teya felt like bursting into tears.

"Are you all right?" Mona asked.

Teya had to let out a half smile. Mona had always been good at reading her. Apparently they still had a sisterly bond after all.

"I'm just tired," Teya said. "It's the heat. I never do well in it—you know that. I guess I could really use a pick-me-up."

"Oh, that reminds me," Mona said. She opened up a desk drawer and put a bulging cloth sack on her desk. "This is for you."

"What is it?"

"Take a look."

Teya opened the bag. She gasped in surprise and pulled out an apricot. "Where did you get these?"

"Blind date from the weekend. The guy was a loser, but he happened to be one of the orchard supervisors. He brought those as a gift."

"There must be two pounds of apricots here. I can't just take them."

"Yes, you can. You have two growing boys to feed. Besides, I still have plenty at home—more than I can eat. If you don't take them, I'll just give them to some of my neighbors."

Teya took a bite from one of the apricots and savored the fruit's sweet flesh on her tongue before swallowing it. At least she wouldn't have to stop at the store on the way home and scavenge the remnants for something fresh. She took another bite and listened to Mona talk about her date.

"It started out okay, and the guy was handsome enough, but we're eating at a café on the south end of town, and in the middle of dinner he starts talking about all the money he's getting from his replacement credit. He's selling it to some family that has three kids already." Mona shook her head. "Sometimes I just want to throw in the towel when it comes to finding Mr. Right. You know the most difficult part of dating? It's definitely not finding a man who doesn't want kids—there are plenty of those. The hard part is finding one who doesn't want to sell his replacement credit. Not everything can be about money. You have to think about the greater good."

Teya couldn't let her sister's last comment go unchallenged. "People sell their replacement credits all the time. There's nothing wrong with that. Besides, think what you could do with the money. You could give it to an environmental charity or buy some trees and plant them. Heaven knows this city could use some actual green."

"Yes, but the greater gift is not enabling others to have one more mouth to feed."

Mona stopped and looked at Teya as if she just realized that her last remark could be taken the wrong way. She reached across the desk and touched Teya's arm. "Don't take my comments personally. You know I respect your decision to have two children. The law allows for that, and I like having two nephews to spoil whenever I visit."

"And they like having an aunt who enjoys spending time with them," Teya said, forcing a smile. She wished Mona wasn't so stubborn about this issue. Buying Mona's replacement credit was something Teya had been thinking about ever since she found out she was pregnant. Even if it would take the rest of her life to pay it back, she wanted to have this child. It was more than a motherly instinct that came with her previous pregnancies. She had a strong feeling that this child had a special purpose and *needed* to be born. "But the law also allows you to sell your credit if someone wants more than two children," Teya said. "Surely you can let someone who can afford the credit take care of another child."

Mona leaned forward in her chair. "You already know how I feel about this, Teya. Why do you bring it up? You know someone who's in the market for one?"

Teya pursed her lips. For a moment, she thought about telling Mona everything. Instead of being horrified at the news, Teya imagined her sister squealing in delight and giving her a hug. Then they'd sit on the soft gray carpet, and Teya would tell her how much she wanted a girl, and they'd spend hours talking about the baby and possible names. That's how it had been with the first two, and it seemed odd that Mona would loathe the news now.

Teya pushed the chair back and walked over to the window. Mona's office offered a clear view of the 'Vard and the Recycling Center on the opposite corner. To the east was an entire block of ten-story apartment buildings. She loved this view and could never figure out why her sister positioned her desk so her back was to all the activity outside.

She looked down at the people on the street below. A tram stopped. People got on and off. Children wearing their yellow-and-green school uniforms burst from the doors of a nearby building and spilled onto the street.

School was out. It was getting late. She'd have to head home soon in order to pick up her children from the sitter's.

Mona's voice cut through her thoughts. "What's on your mind, sis?"

Teya turned and leaned against the glass, surprised how cool it felt against her back. Mona was still in her chair but had turned so she was facing Teya. There was a concerned look on her face.

"Oh, I can't get this woman out of my mind. She came in for a retest last week," Teya said. "When she tested positive again, the woman became hysterical. Didn't want to give up the child for anything and begged me to sell her my credit until I told her I had already used it. I just feel bad for her, that's all."

It wasn't the full truth, but it wasn't a lie either. That scene had played out in the clinic last week. That's what occasionally happened when women were escorted back to her office and the second test confirmed an unplanned pregnancy.

Mona stood and walked over to the window. She put her arm around Teya and pulled her close. "You can't blame yourself for the irresponsible actions of others."

"You sound just like Dad."

Teya's words made them both pause for a moment.

"Yeah, you're right," Mona said. "Sometimes there's more of Dad in me than I'd like to believe."

"I think there's more of Dad in both of us than we'd like."

Mona let go of her sister. "So, can I plan on your family being part of the float?"

"Yeah, put us down. If Ransom doesn't want to do it, I'll call you." She picked up the bag of apricots from the desk. "I need to get the boys. Thanks again for the apricots. I know Ransom and the boys will love them."

"You be sure to eat them too. Your face is looking a little thin."

Teya gave her sister a weak smile. "I'll see you on the parade route."

Mona gave her sister a hug, and Teya showed herself out of the office. As she walked through the door, she glanced back over her shoulder and saw Mona open the file with Amber River's photograph.

As Teya headed out of the building, the weight in her stomach felt heavier than ever before.

five

Ransom's stomach growled as he followed the twenty or so other passengers off the tram. It had been twelve hours since he'd last eaten. Combine that with a pounding headache and exhaustion, and all he wanted was food and sleep. He hoped Teya had found time to go grocery shopping. When he'd packed his lunch that morning, their food was getting dangerously low.

From the platform, he made his way down an alley to an open plaza. Most of the crowd broke off toward one of three buildings on the far side. Ransom headed to the middle building and glanced up at the farthest fifth-floor balcony, catching sight of Teya's silhouette. She was leaning forward with her arms spread along the railing—probably trying to see if he was among the crowd. Ransom let out an audible groan. Usually when he came home this late, Teya was in bed reading or washing the boys' clothes in their largest metal tub. Whenever she stood on the balcony, it meant there was something she wanted to talk about. The growing heaviness in his stomach squashed the hunger pains. Talking wasn't something he wanted to do tonight.

Ransom suddenly winced at a burst of pain in his side and touched where the snatcher's boot had connected with his rib. The painful reminder about the morning's incident caused him to glance around the plaza, looking to see if the police were standing near the entrance to his building or waiting in the shadows. He didn't see anything out of the ordinary, but the thought made him pick up the pace. He hurried up the five flights of stairs as fast as he could, expecting at every landing for someone to step from the hallway and grab him. But no one did. The only sounds were his footsteps echoing off the cement walls and someone shutting a door somewhere several floors above. But he didn't relax until inside his apartment with the door locked.

Down the hallway and through the kitchen, he could see Teya standing on the balcony, her back to him. Ransom removed his boots and headed down the hall. Right before the kitchen, he stopped at James and Warren's bedroom door. Warren had kicked off his sheet, which now lay on the floor. He snored softly. James was lying on his side, hugging his pillow tightly. His brown hair drooped over his eyes, and the smile on his face indicated a pleasant dream. Ransom felt a pang of regret that he hadn't spent much time with them that day, but he reassured himself that tomorrow was Friday, and he could usually knock off early and be home at a decent hour. Maybe they could eat dinner together, then go to a park. The thought of finally spending some time with his boys made him smile, and he entered their room, giving them each a quick kiss before heading toward the balcony.

Ransom stopped short when he saw the bowl of apricots on the kitchen table, grabbed a handful, and popped one in his mouth. The apricot's flesh was firm but sweet. To get fruit this good, Teya must have stopped at the store just after a farmer had delivered. He smiled at Teya, wondering what else she had been able to find at the store. He stepped onto the balcony. Teya turned, smiled, and gave him a quick kiss on the lips.

"How was work?" she asked.

"Fine." He moved to the side and set the apricot pit on the railing before biting into a second serving of fruit.

Teya put her arm around him. "You didn't answer my question."

"I did. I said it was fine."

"*Fine* as in, it was just another boring day, or *fine* as in, it was so great, so full of good finds, you want to spend the next hour telling your wife all the exciting details?"

Ransom smiled. "The former. The only exciting thing that happened was that the garage we were tearing down nearly collapsed on Dempsey when he accidentally knocked over a support beam. But all it did was scare us, so I doubt I could go on for an hour."

"So, nothing useful to sell at the Station?"

Ransom felt a twinge of guilt every time she brought up the Station. He had coaxed her into his dishonest world of keeping parts from the homes he recycled in order to sell them. At first, Teya was aghast that he was engaged in illegal activity. Ransom wouldn't just lose his job if he were caught, but he could spend several years at one of the prisons in the Klamath Mountains. Whenever Ransom was late from work, Teya went into a panic, thinking he'd been caught. But Ransom explained that enforcement was spotty, and word usually got out ahead of time when the random locker and body inspections were going to take place. Only the stupid employees who tried to steal large objects like washing machines, heaters, or large amounts of piping or wiring were ever caught. As long as he took just enough stuff to hide in a lunch pail, no one was the wiser. Over time, when she realized he was likely safe, and when she saw how the little bit of extra money helped buy more food or treat the kids to an occasional surprise, she had come to accept it. Ransom justified it because even with both of them working, they could still barely afford to feed the family and keep the lights on.

He brought his mind back to Teya's question. "The house had been cleaned out before we arrived. Whoever it was didn't leave much behind. There might be a few small things I can take tomorrow."

"I hope you can find something." Teya sighed. "The electricity bill came today—over forty dollars. That doesn't leave much for food."

Ransom suddenly relaxed—the electric bill was the reason she'd been standing on the balcony. She was worried about finances. That wasn't unusual. He put his arm around her waist and pulled her close. "Even if I can't find anything at the house, I'm sure I can find something lying around the Center in the next day or two. Someone's always misplacing junk of one kind or another." His stomach growled, and Ransom looked at the kitchen. "I need to get some dinner."

"You need a shower first," Teya said, wrinkling her nose playfully. "Clean up. I'll put something together for you."

He kissed her appreciatively and headed to the bathroom. He stripped off his clothes and put them in a pile outside the door, then stood in the middle of the bathroom and angled the showerhead so it pointed to the far wall, hoping the spray on the sink and toilet would be minimal. Then he put his hand on the shower button and closed his eyes. Even though the cold water felt good after a long day of physical labor, he still had to psych himself up every night for the icy blasts. He had three ninety-second bursts of water to work with, but he'd long since timed everything so he could finish in two blasts simply because the cold water made his body ache.

He took a deep breath and pushed the button.

* * *

Teya carried the bowl with the remaining apricots to the living room and set them on the coffee table. Then she picked up Ransom's dirty clothes in the hallway and put them in the hamper.

She sat on the lumpy green couch just as the first ninety-second shower burst emanated from the bathroom. Her stomach was churning, and she felt sick. She considered waiting until the weekend to tell Ransom about her pregnancy, but after a few moments she decided against it. She had to get this off her chest before the worry and guilt ate her alive. At least Ransom had come home in a somewhat good mood. He always reacted better to bad news when his spirits were high.

A second shower burst came from the bathroom. She glanced at the bowl of apricots and realized she had promised to find him some real dinner. Hurrying to the kitchen, she found a half dozen slices of cheese, a partial loaf of bread, and a small container of carrots in the refrigerator. She grabbed two pieces of cheese, cut a thick slice of bread, then flipped through the cupboards. All they had was a glass container filled with spaghetti noodles, a couple bottles of peaches, a bottle of plum sauce, a box of salt crackers, and a half-empty carton of dried milk. She bit her lip, wishing she'd stopped at the store on her way home.

As she mixed up a glass of milk, she heard the bathroom door open and Ransom's bare feet walking down the concrete hall. She put the cheese and bread on a plate and returned to the living room, setting the food next to the apricots.

Then she waited.

A few minutes later, Ransom emerged from the bedroom, dressed in a worn sleeveless shirt and cutoffs that had once been state-mandated jeans. She'd turned them into shorts last summer when the holes in the knees got too big. He smelled clean, and his skin felt cool to the touch. Teya leaned in and put her arms around him.

While he devoured the cheese and apricots, she mentally replayed the conversation she had practiced all evening.

"Thanks for putting my clothes away," Ransom mumbled between chews.

"No problem. You seem extra tired."

"Yeah, it was a long day."

Teya ran her fingers lightly across the top of his back. After a minute, she felt the muscles in his shoulders relax and his breathing slow. *So far, so good*, she thought.

They sat like that for several minutes, baking in the dry heat of the July evening until Teya moved her fingers from his back to his stomach. When they brushed his side, Ransom jerked his body away from her.

"Are you okay?" Teya asked, startled. She lifted up Ransom's shirt and caught a glimpse of the dark purple bruise. He brushed her hand away and moved off the couch.

"Yeah, I'm fine."

"What happened to you?"

"Nothing."

"That doesn't look like nothing," Teya said, standing.

Teya saw Ransom look away. She knew what he was about to say was a lie.

"Dempsey was carrying a two-by-four and wasn't watching where he was going. He ended up poking me in the side with it."

She paused momentarily but decided not to pursue it. "You

should put something on it. I think there's some arnica ointment in the medicine cabinet."

"I'm fine," he said. There was a sharp tone to his voice that dispelled the progress Teya thought she was making with his mood.

"I'm sorry. I—I was just trying—"

"Don't worry about it," Ransom said. "I'm just tired."

Teya gave her husband a long look, then carried the apricot bowl to the kitchen. She threw the pits in the small can for biodegradable waste and rinsed out the bowl.

On her way back to the living room, she stopped in the bathroom. She leaned against the sink, trying to drum up enough courage to break the news to Ransom.

For what seemed like the millionth time that day, she debated when to tell him. Maybe tomorrow would be better. Ransom usually made it a point to come home early on Fridays. Maybe if she waited, the right moment would just arrive.

Deep inside, she knew she was lying to herself. It had been nearly three months since she'd found out, and the opportune time had yet to present itself. Her expanding waistline would reveal the truth if she didn't. Besides, the burden of this secret was crushing her spirit. She splashed cold water on her face before turning for the living room.

Ransom looked up from the couch as she walked in.

Suddenly, her courage failed her. Instead of returning to the couch next to her husband, she leaned against the wall on the opposite side of the room as a tear rolled down her face. She took a deep breath and locked eyes with him. "I'm pregnant," she said, her voice quivering.

This wasn't how she imagined it happening, but right at that moment, she didn't care. The relief of telling her husband flooded over her fears. Teya wiped her eyes and looked at Ransom, searching for a hint of how he felt or would react.

Ransom kept sitting there, his face expressionless. Then he cocked his head to one side. "You're what?"

* * *

Ransom's mind was racing. He'd braced himself for bad news

when he'd seen the worried look on Teya's face as she walked into the room. But an unplanned pregnancy was the last thing he'd expected. Teya repeated her statement before bursting into tears and sliding down the wall to the floor.

He thought back to the last few months. They had always been good about using the state-required birth control once Warren had been born. Teya regularly took her pill, and if there was ever a day she missed or was worried about becoming pregnant, they always had other birth control on hand, just to be safe. But even with all the precautions, accidental pregnancies happened. That was just the way things were.

He looked over at his wife, who lay on the floor weeping, and pushed aside the feelings of panic and fear welling up inside of him. There would be time for that later. Right now, Teya needed comforting.

He sat next to her on the cement floor and reached down and held her close. He felt the hot tears run from her cheeks to his arms.

"I'm sorry. I'm *so* sorry," she said as another wave of tears fell.

Ransom ran his fingers through her hair. He kissed the top of her head.

"Are you sure? I mean, is your period just late? That happens. We've been low on food. Remember last winter when you missed a period because we didn't have enough to eat?"

Teya shook her head. "I know I'm pregnant. I've tested myself at work I don't know how many times."

Ransom's mind flew through the different choices they had to make. There was always abortion, but he wasn't sure how Teya felt about it. He had never thought it was a decision he and Teya would have to make. Now that the decision was personal, it made him pause.

Keeping the baby would require purchasing a child credit from someone. Finding a seller and a way to pay for it would be difficult. Of course, they could always give the baby up for adoption. Adoption was the most attractive—simplistic—solution, though Ransom didn't know if he could bear seeing his child given to someone else. He'd heard stories about human trafficking and exploitation—always risks with would-be adoptive parents. Maybe it wasn't a better solution after all.

He waited until Teya stopped crying before he spoke again. "What do you want to do?" he asked.

Teya reflexively put her hand on top of his and looked him in the eye. "I'd—I'd like to find some way to keep it," she said.

"Keep it for ourselves or give it to someone else?"

"It's our baby. I want to find someone who will sell us a credit."

"What about Mona?" Ransom asked, though he already knew the answer.

"She'd never sell it. I had to run the daily report to the Census Bureau today, and I spoke with her. The subject came up in a roundabout way, and she was adamant she'd never sell hers."

"There are other people who might," Ransom said. "I'll stop by the Census Bureau tomorrow and look at the baby board. There's always someone who's willing to sell."

Though he wasn't going to say anything to Teya about it, trying to buy a credit terrified him. He had to be careful whom he asked. If someone—anyone—suspected that Teya was pregnant, that person was legally obligated to notify the Census Bureau.

"Since you're breaking the news instead of me getting a call from some bureaucrat, I'm assuming no one else knows about it?"

Teya nodded. "I've been doing the tests on the side or fudging the results on days I'm required to submit blood."

Ransom placed his hand on Teya's stomach and wondered what the baby was doing. Sleeping? Doing flips? Maybe it was just a clump of cells—a growth—and not doing anything.

They sat quietly for several minutes. Teya kept her head on Ransom's chest. He continued to run his fingers slowly through her hair as he calculated her due date.

"April," he said. "It will be nice to have a spring baby. It will balance the boys' fall birthdays out a little."

Teya lifted her head off Ransom's chest and looked directly in his eyes. "It's going to be a winter baby. January. Just like you."

"January? How can it be? For January, you'd have to be—" He stopped mid sentence and did the math in his head. "How far along are you?"

"Twelve weeks. Maybe thirteen. I don't know for certain. But I should be heading into the second trimester any day now. I'll be showing soon, and at work they're always on the lookout for women who—"

"How long have you known?" Ransom moved so he and Teya were facing each other and stared into her pale blue eyes.

"Three months. I found out at the end of May. I know I should have told you weeks ago, but—"

"*Three months?*" He stood and began pacing back and forth across the living room. A feeling of betrayal surged through him. They had always had an open and honest relationship, and suddenly he felt as though she had been keeping secrets. He looked at his wife, and, for the first time in their marriage, it felt like he was looking at a stranger. "I thought we had some time to figure this out. If you're three months along, we only have another month—at most—to find a solution!"

Teya winced at his words. "I'm sorry. I was scared. And I thought maybe the test results were wrong. That happens, you know. And there was always a chance I'd miscarry. I did before, remember?" Tears started running down her cheeks again.

"If you had told me three months ago, maybe we'd have a backup solution in case none of those things happened!"

"Ransom, sweetie, I'm so sorry. You're right. I should have told you sooner. But I'm sure we still have some time to figure it out, and—"

"No. We don't have time. If we don't find a credit soon, you're going to end up in the Infirmary!"

Ransom stormed off into the kitchen. He heard Teya pattering after him. He knew he needed to calm down, but for that, he needed some space to think. The last thing he wanted to deal with was Teya trying to make things right. This wasn't the time for it.

He bent down and opened the tiny refrigerator, glaring at scarce offerings on the two shelves. The lack of food brought back the full anger and frustration of the day. He slammed the door and moved to the cupboards, opening them one at a time. Each mostly empty cupboard increased the helplessness he was drowning in. The last cupboard was completely empty. Ransom slammed it as hard as he could and was frustrated that it didn't break.

He turned and saw Teya staring at him with tear-filled eyes as the sharp crack of his slamming reverberated off the walls. Why couldn't she just leave him alone for a minute? What had she been thinking? Keeping this news from him had put their family in danger. How was he supposed to protect her if a team of snatchers came looking for her? He pushed past her, grabbed the conservation card off the counter, and headed for the door.

"Where are you going?" Teya asked, her voice rising in panic.

"Out."

"Don't leave me. Please stay and talk," she begged.

There was enough worry in her voice that Ransom paused momentarily. Then the feelings of betrayal surged inside him again, and he continued down the hall.

Ransom ignored her continued pleas as he tied up his boots. On the way out, he slammed that door too.

six

Ransom stormed across the plaza. At the 'Vard, he crossed the street and entered a small grocery store. A lone clerk stood by the cash register, adding up the day's receipts with a pencil and paper. He looked up as Ransom entered.

"We close in ten minutes," he said before returning to his work.

Ransom walked up and down the aisles, looking for anything that could subdue his anger. The bread baskets and produce aisles were empty. So were most of the other shelves. What remained wasn't anything he could eat without preparation—boxes of pasta, bags of dried beans, containers of honey, and one bag of flour.

He stopped at the refrigeration case. Only eight twelve-ounce bottles of apple soda remained. The glass door was covered with smudges and the handprints of the day's shoppers, and a dank, moldy smell wafted up from the cooler as he opened the door. Ransom grabbed the closest bottle, but it was warm. He traded it, then realized they were all room temperature. The drinks were never ice cold, but were usually kept somewhat cool.

Usually Ransom wouldn't have bothered, but his thirst was strong enough that he headed to the cash register with the bottle in hand.

"The cooler's not working," Ransom said as he fished around in his wallet for the right change and his conservation card.

"It needs coolant," the clerk answered as he rang up the soda and the bottle deposit and punched Ransom's conservation card with perfunctory motions. "Ordered some a month ago. Has to come all the way from Reno. No telling when it will arrive."

Ransom paid the clerk and headed out of the store. He sat on a wooden bench next to the store's entrance, twisted off the bottle cap, and took a long drink. But the soda was over-carbonated and weakly flavored. He angrily spat it out on the sidewalk.

From where he sat, he could see the balcony and kitchen window to his apartment. All the lights were off. He started to mellow, realizing his wife was either waiting on the balcony, worried about him, or in bed crying herself to sleep. He felt a pang of regret for walking out on her and considered heading home. But after a moment, he knew he couldn't do it—not now, anyway. If they started beating that horse again, he'd get too riled up to have a rational discussion. By waiting three months to tell him, she left him feeling trapped and cornered when it came to finding a replacement credit—a process that usually took six months or so to finalize. It wasn't something he could easily obtain in a matter of weeks. He needed some time to think.

Ransom poured the remaining soda on the sidewalk and returned the bottle to the clerk for the deposit money. After pocketing the change, he started down the 'Vard.

Lost in thought, he walked until he realized he needed a bathroom. Looking around to get his bearings, he realized he was just past 17th Street. All the shops were closed, and there wasn't a public toilet in sight.

Then, three buildings down, a door opened and a couple stumbled into the street, arms around each other's waists. They were followed by the loud beat of music and the dim light of a bar. The door swung shut, and the street was quiet again.

Ransom hurried that direction. He wasn't a fan of bars—the dark, cramped atmospheres, the loud music, and worst of all, they were usually packed with people and smelled worse than the trams. But if he wanted to relieve himself, it was the only option available.

He opened the door and was greeted by the smell of alcohol and sweat. Even though ceiling fans were spinning as fast as they could go, it was unbearably hot. Most of the men sitting at the bar or surrounding tables weren't wearing shirts. Their backs glistened with sweat. Everyone in the bar had tired expressions, as though trying to summon the strength to make it through the next day. The jukebox next to the door was playing a remixed version of a pro-earth political song that had been popular twenty years ago. Ransom didn't care for either version and quickly made his way to the back of the bar, but the door to the lone bathroom was locked. He knocked loudly, hoping the occupant would hurry.

A woman wearing a top no less than two sizes too small walked past with a bottle of beer in her hand and shook her head. "You need a key, honey," she said. "Talk to the bartender."

Ransom growled in frustration but hurried to the counter, waving to the petite, brown-eyed bartender.

"What can I get you?" she asked.

"The key to the bathroom."

The bartender leaned forward. "I can't hear you."

Ransom leaned in close enough that he could feel her body heat radiate against his face. "I need the key to the bathroom."

"The bathroom's for paying customers only."

Ransom looked behind the bartender at the different colored bottles lined up on the wall. It was tempting to have a drink, but he was sure he didn't have the money for it. Instead, he asked for a Coke. She rolled her eyes and headed to the far end of the bar. Ransom started shifting his weight from leg to leg, wishing that she'd hurry. She returned a moment later with a tumbler full of dark brown liquid. She placed a small cloth napkin on the bar and set the drink on top of it.

"That'll be two dollars," she said.

The price was outrageous, but Ransom pulled two limp bills from his wallet and placed them on the bar.

"Card," she said.

Ransom slid the card across the counter.

She punched it and turned to leave.

"The bathroom key," Ransom hollered after her.

The bartender turned, grabbed a large ring from a nail above the bottles, and handed it to Ransom. He ran to the bathroom and unlocked the door.

The room was dark and smelled like vomit or even a broken

sewer pipe. He peered up through the dark and could just make out a bulb hanging from the wire. Feeling around in the air until he found the string, Ransom pulled it down, and the room lit up.

The bathroom was slightly larger than a coat closet, as dirty as he imagined, and the sink reminded him of some he'd removed from an elementary school they'd recycled years ago. Maybe this was where one of the sinks had ended up. As he took a step to the toilet, his boots stuck to the floor.

Moments later, Ransom cringed as he washed his hand with cold water and no soap. At least his drink was still waiting for him when he returned to the bar. He set the key ring on the counter and settled himself onto one of the stools. The jukebox started playing another song, one he didn't recognize, as he took a sip of his Coke. Warm and flat. Ransom realized he shouldn't have been surprised, but for what the bar charged, he thought they could at least afford to cool the drinks. Maybe they were waiting for coolant too. Regardless, he felt as though he'd just wasted his money and one of the drink squares on the family's conservation card—make that two squares, thanks to that apple garbage at the store.

After a minute, the bartender approached him. "You look tired," she said. "Would you like something stronger?"

Ransom shook his head.

"If you want, we have some locally brewed stuff that's a lot stronger and cheaper than anything you'll see on the wall," she said. Then she leaned forward and lowered her voice. "And the best part is, we don't have to punch your card."

"Thanks," Ransom said. "But I'm not into that."

"Oh, you don't have to worry about getting busted. The cops come in here all the time and order a glass or two for themselves. In fact, someone behind you is enjoying our local stuff right now." She motioned with her head to a row of booths along the far wall.

Ransom turned. Sitting at the booth directly behind him was the snatcher he'd faced on the tram. He was hunched over a glass of amber-colored liquid, shirtless and sweating profusely. He was talking to another shirtless man who was taller but who had the same large build. Based on the attentive way he sat at the table, Ransom took him to be a snatcher as well. The tall man said something, and they both laughed.

Suddenly, the heat in the bar seemed unbearable as Ransom's heart rate accelerated. He quickly turned back to the bar.

"So, can I get you what they're having?" the bartender pressed.

"Please, just leave me alone," Ransom said.

The bartender obliged, though she walked away in a huff.

Ransom used the napkin to wipe the sweat from his face, then downed the remainder of his Coke, his heart thumping all the way to the door.

He'd taken only a dozen steps down the sidewalk when he heard the sound of heavy boots running up behind him. Before he could turn around, rough hands grabbed his shirt collar and yanked him to the ground. The back of his head smacked against the sidewalk, and for a moment, he saw stars as his vision blurred. Then he felt two strong hands clamp onto his wrists as someone dragged him a short distance from the orange glow of streetlights into darkness. A moment later, he was dropped to the ground.

Slowly, the world came back into focus. Ransom could see a rectangular slice of the night sky above framed by the walls of the nearby buildings. There was a faint smell of rotting garbage. He felt cobblestones pressing into his back.

Ransom tried to sit up, but someone's foot pressed into his chest and forced him back to the ground. He had been dragged into a service alley where no one could see him. Ransom's mind started to race.

"You don't get up unless I say so," the sentinel snarled.

In the dark, just off to his right, he heard another voice. Male, but nowhere near as deep—the tall man.

"Someone might have seen us take him back here."

"Leave, then," the snatcher said. "This won't take long. Besides, even if someone did see us, no one's going to say anything. People don't want to get involved."

"You said he got involved this morning," the tall man countered. "How do you know someone won't come to this guy's aid?"

"If you're going to be a greener, then just get out of here. But I've got some unfinished business."

The tall man was quiet for a moment. "Be quick," he finally said.

The sentinel knelt and placed his knee on Ransom's chest, making it difficult for Ransom to breathe. He moved his face close enough that Ransom could smell alcohol on the man's breath. Flecks of spittle hit Ransom's face as the sentinel spoke. "Sticking up for that breeder friend of yours was the dumbest thing I've seen in years," he started.

"She's not my—"

The sentinel struck Ransom in the face. "I didn't tell you to talk! You keep your mouth shut unless I say otherwise. Got it?"

Ransom nodded, choking out a yes.

The pressure on his chest eased a bit, and Ransom could hear the sentinel fumbling for something in his shorts pocket. Ransom took several breaths while he had the chance.

There was the sound of something scraping the ground next to Ransom's ear. A match burst into flame, bathing the snatcher's bare head and shoulders in pale yellow light. His eyes looked black and empty.

"I got something I want you to see," he said. He reached into his back pocket and brought out a wallet with a silver badge attached to it. He held it inches from Ransom's face. Next to it was a photo ID and the man's name. His hand was covering part of the ID but Ransom was able to read the name DRAGOMIR between the sentinel's fingers.

"I'm a sentinel, in case you didn't notice. My job is to keep the peace through intimidation. You and that breeder made me look like a fool. So now my mission in life is to make you both very miserable every time we cross paths."

The flame reached Dragomir's fingers, and he shook it out. The world went dark, and his knee came off Ransom's chest. Ransom's vision filled with the blue spot where the light had been, and he knew he couldn't count on his eyes to help him escape. He could use the darkness as cover, though, and he inched his body to the left. As he moved, his hand brushed against a loose cobblestone about the size of his fist.

Another match was struck, and he saw Dragomir put the badge in his back pocket.

"I should take you to the Infirmary and continue beating you. No one can hear you scream down there. Maybe that will keep you from interfering with other people's business."

"I didn't realize your business was picking on defenseless women and children," Ransom said.

Dragomir raised his hand, and Ransom flinched. Dragomir let out a short laugh. "You're all bark and no bite."

"Enough," the taller man said. "You've had your fun. Let's go."

"I'm not done, Seamus," Dragomir growled in answer, pushing his friend away. He dropped the second match. It hit the ground and sputtered out.

Ransom again moved his body to the left, his hand clasping the smooth cobblestone.

The sound of another match being struck filled the alleyway. Ransom kept his hand around the rock.

Dragomir handed the match to his friend and started frisking Ransom, pulling a wallet from his front pocket. He riffled through the contents.

"Three dollars in cash? That's all you got? Come on. You owe me." He pulled out Ransom's identification card, reading over the information with interest. "Ransom Lawe. Kaczynski Terrace, Building C, #514. And now I know where you live. Better start minding your own business, or I'll have to pay you a personal visit."

The other sentinel shook the match out.

"What are you doing?" Dragomir demanded. "I'm not done."

"I can't hold it forever."

There was the sound of a matchbox being slid open. "Only got one left," Dragomir said with disappointment.

"Good," Seamus said. "I'm ready to go."

The final match was struck and again handed to the second sentinel. Dragomir continued riffling through Ransom's wallet, tossing the items he wasn't interested in onto the ground. His eyes lit up when he pulled out the green card.

"A family card. For four. And it's only half full! Now this is worth everything you put me through this morning."

Ransom felt dread spreading through his body. Not the card. His family couldn't pick another one up for two weeks, and they barely had enough food to make it through the weekend. Ransom started to sit up, but Dragomir returned his boot to Ransom's chest and shoved him back to the ground, sliding the card into his pocket as Ransom struggled against him.

"Now we're even," Dragomir said cheerfully. "When your wife's forced to walk the streets to keep your kids from starving, remind her that it's your fault. Better yet, I'll be her first customer."

Ransom still clutched the cobblestone, ready to leap up and smash Dragomir's face with it. He knew he couldn't take both men, but they had been drinking. Maybe he could surprise them well enough to get the card back and run down the alley.

Suddenly Dragomir noticed the cobblestone in Ransom's hand. "Don't try anything stupid," he warned. "Remember, I know where you live. I get any blowback from this, your wife and kids are going to pay for it."

Ransom fought back his anger, finally willing the cobblestone to tumble out of his hands.

Dragomir smiled. "That's a good boy." He took a step forward and kicked Ransom in the side. It was the side opposite from where he had kicked Ransom earlier in the day, but it hurt just as bad. Ransom doubled over in pain, gasping for breath.

Seamus dropped the match, and the alley became black. "You've had enough fun," he said. "I need to get home."

"Well, Mr. Lawe," Dragomir said, "you better hope I don't see you riding the tram again. If I do, I'll have to pay a visit to your wife and kids." There was the sound of heavy boots heading down the alley. Ransom rolled to his side so he could look toward the entrance. He saw the silhouettes of the two men stop as they looked both ways before heading left.

After several minutes of trying to catch his breath, Ransom got to his hands and knees and felt around in the dark for his wallet and the contents that had been tossed aside. When he thought he had everything, he stood, brushed the dirt off his knees, and headed for the street. A group of teens made a wide berth for Ransom as he stumbled out of the alley, probably assuming he was drunk.

Ransom looked in the direction Dragomir and his companion had taken. Aside from the teens walking the opposite direction, the sidewalk was empty.

Ransom swore, furious with himself. How would he feed his family? Had he endangered them? After several minutes of pacing and fighting the burn in his side, he surrendered to his fate. There was nothing he could do that night. Slowly, painfully, Ransom turned and started the long walk home.

seven

It was pitch black inside the lobby of the apartment building. Ransom climbed the stairs slowly, pausing on each step and keeping his hand on the wall for balance. When he reached the fifth floor landing, he held his arms in front of him and shuffled down the hall until feeling the door. After fumbling for the keys, he unlocked the dead bolt and stumbled inside.

He stopped at the bedroom door and listened to Teya's slow, regular breathing. He was surprised she was asleep. Usually after a fight, she'd be up half the night stewing, wondering if he still loved her. Ransom was relieved she was okay. He had obsessed over the possibility of finding Dragomir and his friend inside the apartment.

He stripped down to his underwear and eased himself into bed. The mattress springs creaked. Teya stirred and rolled over so she was facing him. He waited for her breathing to resume a slow, steady pace. It didn't.

It was quiet for awhile. Then she spoke. "Where did you go?"

"Can we talk about this tomorrow? I'm tired."

"Just tell me where you went."

"Headed down the 'Vard about a mile or two, near the river." More silence.

"You were gone a long time," she finally said.

"It takes a long time to walk to the river and back."

He could feel Teya staring at him through the dark, so he turned his back to her. His anger had been replaced by fear during the slow walk home. Now that the snatcher knew where he lived, he worried about his family's safety. There was also the missing card. There was so much to tell her, but he didn't know where to start or how to begin. She was under enough stress as it was. As he lay there, he began to sympathize with his wife's struggle to break the news of the pregnancy to him. He should have been more understanding instead of storming out of the apartment.

"What are we going to do?" she said.

"About what?"

"Us. Our family. The baby."

Ransom didn't say anything because he didn't have an answer for her. He had no idea what they were going to do.

After several minutes, he felt Teya roll back to her side. He waited for her to fall asleep. After a few more minutes of listening to her short and irregular breathing, it was obvious she was awake and worried.

"I'm sorry I got upset and left," he offered.

Teya was quiet for a minute, then extended her olive branch. "I should have told you as soon as I was sure. I'm sorry. I trust you more than anyone, and I should have treated you that way once I found out about the baby."

Ransom turned so he was lying on his back. A moment later, Teya rolled over and rested her head on his shoulder, laying her arm across his chest. He smarted as her hand brushed against his side.

"I'm sorry," she said, withdrawing her arm. "I forgot about your bruise."

"I'm fine," Ransom said, hoping she wouldn't realize she'd touched his other side—the new injury.

"So, what are we going to do?" she asked after a moment, her tone softer.

"Well, the most obvious solution is to buy a credit. But since we're down to about a month until someone notices, I don't know if we can find one that quick. And even if we did, I'm not sure how we would afford it. We only have the thousand dollars my mother left me after she died—nowhere near enough. The only way we're going to buy one is to take out a loan, using the apartment for collateral. It would probably require most of my current income just to pay off the loan—even if we did get one of those fifty-year mortgages. Right now, including the stuff I sell from job sites, we barely have enough money to feed the four of us. And we're not even considering the extra taxes that would come with having a third child."

"I could work an extra job. Maybe another clinic would want some help during weekends. Maybe there's something at the Census Bureau. I could talk to Mona next time I see her."

"If either one of us worked more than we already do, we'd never see the kids, let alone each other. It seems like forever since I've spent more than a few minutes with James and Warren."

They were both silent for a minute. Even though he couldn't see her in the dark, he knew she had that worried look on her face—the pursed lips and wrinkled brow that always came when she was trying to solve a complex problem.

Finally Teya spoke. "We can always give someone the apartment in exchange for their credit. That way we wouldn't have to worry about the debt."

"I'd rather save that for our last resort—the city gave us the apartment after a three-year wait, and it's the only thing of value we own. Besides, there's no guarantee that renting will be any cheaper. Remember what happened when the lease at our first apartment expired? I don't want to scramble in the face of another 50 percent rent increase."

Ransom started to move over to be closer to his wife, but the pain from his fresh injury caused him to stop. He took a deep breath, then continued. "And even if we could find a way to pay for a credit, I'm more worried about what kind of person can sell on such short notice. I mean, it can take weeks to negotiate a deal and legitimize the seller's credit. I don't want to be one of those suckers you read about on the news boards who gave everything they owned to a con man. It's bad enough that we're desperate—if someone realizes that, it will be easy for them to take advantage of us."

"So what do you want me to do? Give it up for adoption?" Teya asked, a wary tone to her voice.

"I didn't say that."

"You make it sound like buying a credit is going to be impossible."

"I'm only saying it's going to be extremely difficult," Ransom said, his voice rising again. He sat up and leaned his head against the wall, grimacing as the bump on the back of his head touched the cement. He took another deep breath, and when he spoke again, his voice was level and calm. "I don't want to give the baby up, but I'm saying that maybe we should keep the adoption alternative open if things don't work out in a couple of weeks."

"What? No. I'm not giving up our child."

"It might be the best option for everyone if we have a hard time finding a credit. The baby gets a safe, loving home, and our lives remain the same. I think it would be easier to find someone who can't have children and would take one off our hands than to go through all the red tape and expense of buying a credit."

The bed springs creaked as Teya sat up. "Our lives will never be the same if we give the baby away. Every day we'll wonder what our child is doing or if she's safe. At least *I'll* feel that way. Besides, you've heard the stories of what happens to lots of those kids—there's no guarantee that the child will have loving parents. Too many babies are 'adopted' out to people who smuggle them to the Green States and pollute their minds with extremist dogma."

"I didn't say it was an easy choice. It's just something we should at least consider."

"I'm not going to let someone else raise my baby, Ransom. If the Census Bureau ends up taking her out of my womb, then I'll find some way to live with that—but I will not have some stranger raising my child!"

"You'd rather lose the baby than give it to someone else? Is that what you really want?"

Teya got out of bed and began pacing around in the dark, her feet making a soft padding sound on the cement floor. She stopped by the bedroom window and looked outside. Ransom could just make out her profile in front of the faint orange glow of the city lights.

"I'd like to avoid that, if possible," she said quietly. "But I'm telling you right now, adoption is off the table. I'll do anything to have this child."

Ransom had never seen Teya this adamant about something. She was usually so easygoing. That was one of the things he found so attractive about her. Her carefree manner balanced his workaholic tendencies.

"Why are you so determined to keep it?" he asked, his brow wrinkled.

He saw Teya turn so she was looking at him. He wished he could see her face.

"I don't know how to explain it. Deep down, I feel as though we should have this child. It's—it's just a gut feeling. I'm scared to death of what keeping the baby could mean for our family, but I think she needs to be born."

"She?"

"I think it's a girl."

They were both silent for several minutes.

"Maybe I should ask Mona," Teya finally said.

"You just told me she'd never sell her credit."

"Maybe if she understood the gravity of our situation, she'd change her mind."

"Where'd this burst of optimism come from? You did talk with her this afternoon, right?"

"Yes, but—"

"Do you honestly think she'll come around to our point of view just because our birth control failed?"

"People change their minds. It happens all the time."

"You're right. They do. But on an issue like this, it generally doesn't happen overnight. It takes time and a lot of love and persuasion to make someone see things differently. If we were thinking about getting pregnant a year or two down the road, we might have a chance if we started talking to her about it now. But we're not in that situation. Besides, I can see her becoming extremely suspicious if we even brought up the subject. She'll never agree."

"You don't know my sister."

"Maybe not as well as you do, but I do know that the political implications for her would be enormous. She's a public figure and a vocal opponent of credit sales. If she were to give hers up, it would be a blow to her credibility. It might even end her career." He was frustrated that Teya didn't see this, but he did his best to keep his voice level. "Mona may be bright and capable, but there are still a lot of politics that go into appointments like hers. Odds are she wouldn't be where she is if she'd sold her credit or even had her own child. Selling your replacement credit becomes public record. Even if we never said where the credit came from, it wouldn't take long before a reporter or one of her political enemies came across the information."

"Maybe she could do something else to help us," Teya said.

"Such as?"

"She's very well connected. She knows the governor. Maybe she could call in a favor and see if we could get a state-sponsored waiver. Maybe she knows someone who's willing to part with a credit for a price we can afford."

"It's possible, but there would still be fallout once word spread that you got special treatment because you're Mona's sister."

"Not everything is about politics."

"When it comes to having more than two children, it's all about politics."

"I can't believe how negative you are about this."

"Am I? How many people do you work with who have more than two kids?"

"None, but—"

"But what? You work in a population clinic. You have to set the example. Do you think Dr. Redgrave would ever hire someone who has more than two kids?"

Teya paused before answering. Finally she said, "How would he even know how many kids someone had? It's against the law to ask that in an interview or to refuse to hire someone because of it."

"Dr. Redgrave goes to the Census Bureau every day. It wouldn't be hard to vet a candidate by simply asking the Bureau to run a check. As the head of the clinic, I'm pretty sure he can ask that question without raising any suspicion. He's not stupid—he'd never come out and say that was the reason for not hiring someone. He'd simply hire someone else, claiming the candidate had more experience or education. Besides, in your office, it wouldn't be smart to hire someone with more than two kids—the last thing they need is a tech or a nurse who might sympathize with the women trying to have thirds."

"He wouldn't run a check. He's a good person. He wouldn't break the law."

"Switching pregnancy results is illegal, and *you're* a good person."

Ransom could tell by her silence that she was a little hurt but also skeptical of his dire world view.

He pressed his point. "Look at Dempsey, Teya. He and his wife have four kids. He's been working at the Recycling Center since before it was even called that. He's smart, works hard, and knows more about recycling than just about anyone. But it doesn't matter how smart or talented he is, because he's going to drive that recycling truck until the day he dies. Most of the guys he started with run the place now. They don't go outside and tear down houses or pick up people's trash. They work in comfortable offices. The most manual labor they do in a day is use a pencil or walk from their office to the bathroom. He works under *me*, for crying out loud. Why? They don't want to promote someone who's legally managed to get around the limits. Getting promotions at the kind of places you and I work is all about toeing the government line. Promoting Dempsey would damage the green image of the Recycling Center. If you had a third, Dr. Redgrave wouldn't hesitate to fire you."

Teya sat on the edge of the bed. A quieter voice belied her obstinate tone. "Dr. Redgrave is a kind man. He wouldn't do anything like that."

Ransom sighed in frustration. "Teya, honey, as soon as he knows you're pregnant, you'll lose your job. And don't tell me it's illegal to dismiss someone because they're pregnant. He won't have to skirt that law. He'll realize you've been faking the results of your own blood tests, and you'll be lucky if the state doesn't press charges against you."

Teya stiffened. Ransom instantly regretted bringing up

possible jail time. His wife had enough on her plate. Trying to redirect the conversation, he offered, "If you want, I'm still willing to go down to the Census Bureau tomorrow and check out the baby board. Maybe we'll get lucky and find someone who's willing to sell at a price we can afford."

More silence. Teya shifted her weight on the bed. Even though Ransom couldn't see her face, he could feel her eyes boring into him. "You haven't told me what you want to do with this baby," she said, her voice just above a whisper.

Ransom swallowed and leaned forward. The truth was, he'd never thought about having a third until today. It wasn't that the subject hadn't come up, but he'd always thought the answer was simple. The two-child limit had come into effect soon after he was born, and most of his exposure to the topic just reinforced his belief that families with two or fewer were to be praised. Growing up, he just assumed something was wrong with anyone who wanted more than two. His stance had softened somewhat after James and Warren were born. He'd been surprised by the feeling of completeness each child brought to him. And despite the stress and trials that came with fatherhood, he enjoyed spending time with his boys and teaching them about the world. But a third had never crossed his mind. He was torn about what to do now that the situation was personal. Seeing the pain it was causing his wife made him pause and reconsider everything he had been taught about the population laws.

"I honestly don't know," he finally said. "I think I'm still in shock. I never thought about what I'd do because I thought it would never happen to us."

He waited for Teya to say something.

"Are you upset?" Ransom asked after a minute of silence.

"No," Teya said. "I guess I thought you'd have a stronger opinion, that's all."

"I'm not against having the baby. I just really need to think about the sacrifices it would require."

"You're going to have to make up your mind soon."

"I know."

"If you—" Teya stopped for a moment. She sounded like she

was fighting back tears. "If you decide you can't support me, I need you to be honest. I don't know what that will mean for us, but I need to know where you're going to come down on this, okay?"

He was surprised by the idea that her pregnancy might shake their marriage in some way—Teya's strong feelings still amazed him—but he was so exhausted that he knew he was going to let the comment go. Maybe it was the high emotion of a stressful night. He answered carefully and gently. "Of course I'll let you know. But for now, I'll do whatever it takes to find a credit. You have my word on that."

Teya remained on the edge of the bed for several minutes before climbing under the sheets and gingerly putting her arms around Ransom.

It was hours before either of them slept.

eight

The metal clang of the alarm clock sounded at six-thirty—a half hour earlier than usual. Ransom flipped the switch on top of the clock and wound it ten times. Teya stirred and rolled over, facing away from him. He pulled the sheet back and sat up. It seemed as though he had just closed his eyes. His head hurt and his sides throbbed where Dragomir had kicked him. He thought about taking a sick day, even though he didn't have many left. They were best saved for flu season anyway—especially if a virulent strain made its way through the city. Besides, he had to get to the Census Bureau before work in order to look at the baby board. And if he was going out that far, he might as well cross the street and clock in.

In the bathroom, he examined his newest bruise. Fist-sized and tender to the touch, it was a painful reminder that his family was now without a conservation card. It was a subject he'd have to bring up with Teya after work. He knew it was something he should have brought up last night, but they were so emotionally drained by the time they finished talking, and he didn't want to add to her burden. Maybe it would lessen the blow if he could come home with a few valuable materials to trade at the Station.

He opened the mirror and looked into the medicine cabinet. Next to the half-empty box of baking soda they used for tooth-paste was a bottle of arnica ointment. He shook the bottle until a gob of lotion slid down the glass to his palm and rubbed the cream onto the bruises.

He finished getting ready, then headed for the kitchen. It wasn't until he opened the cupboard where he normally kept his lunch pail that he remembered it too was gone. Not only would this make it difficult to carry any food, it would make it nearly impossible to bring anything home to resell. Ransom bit his lower lip and searched the kitchen for something he could use. Unable to find anything, he unzipped his uniform pocket and put a piece of dried meat and a half dozen apricots inside. It wasn't a lot, but it would get him through the day.

Behind him came the sound of bare feet running on cement. Ransom turned and saw Warren charging toward him at full speed. Catching Warren just before he reached his legs, Ransom picked the boy up and held him high above his head. Warren squealed with delight.

Ransom looked up at his son's beaming face. Warren had captured most of his wife's genes. He had her general face shape and the same black hair, but he had managed to land his father's green eyes. He was three and short for his age. But what he lacked in height he made up in strength and fearlessness. Unlike James, Warren didn't hesitate when it came to physical activities like trying to knock Ransom over.

"You forgot to give me a kiss last night, Daddy," Warren said.

"I did give you a kiss, but you were asleep."

"I was asleep?"

"Yeah, I didn't want to wake you up." He set Warren back down on the floor. "Where's your brother?"

"James is sleeping. He's very tired."

So is Dad, Ransom thought.

Warren looked his father's uniform up and down. "Are you going to work?"

"Yeah, I need to go in early today."

"What about breakfast?"

Ransom tousled Warren's hair with his hands. "I can't do it today, son. Tomorrow I will—I promise."

"But you always fix breakfast for me." Warren looked disappointed enough to burst into tears.

"I'm sorry, but Dad has to leave early today. I'll tell you what—since I can't make breakfast, what if I come home in time for dinner, and we can eat that together? I'll even make it for you."

"Okay," Warren accepted begrudgingly. There was enough disappointment in his voice that Ransom felt guilty, despite his good reason for leaving early.

Looking at the clock, he knelt down so he was eye level with Warren. "If you go sit in a chair real quick, I'll make you some toast."

Warren ran to one of the metal chairs and moved it next to the stove so he could watch.

Ransom pulled the bread from the refrigerator, checking for mold before cutting a thin slice. He buttered one side, then turned on the stove's large burner and put a small frying pan on top.

"Can I have honey on it too?" Warren asked.

"I don't think we have any honey," Ransom said as he placed the piece of bread, butter side down, in the frying pan.

As he was putting out some plates, Teya walked into the kitchen, wearing a threadbare robe. Her eyes were puffy from lack of sleep. "I'll take care of this. You need to go."

Ransom handed her the spatula. "Thanks. Hopefully I'll have some good news tonight."

"I wish you could tell me before then."

Ransom smiled grimly, his sarcasm getting the better of him. "If you want, I'll find a phone and leave a message with the clinic. I bet Dr. Redgrave would love to tell you whether or not I found an affordable credit."

Teya squeezed his arm. "Just be careful, okay?"

"I will," Ransom said, his tone more sincere. "I promise."

The butter crackled in the pan, and the smell of frying bread filled the kitchen. Teya tended to the stove while Ransom went down the hall and put on his boots. He looked up and saw James standing at his bedroom door, staring at him. James always woke to the smells of breakfast cooking, though this morning he didn't look as excited as usual. Like Teya, he had large puffy rings around his eyes. He was tall for his age and two years older than his brother, a younger-looking version of Ransom—though like his mom, he wasn't much of a morning person.

"Aren't you going to eat with us?" he asked.

"Not today."

"Will you be home to eat dinner?"

"Yes. I'll be home for dinner. I promise."

Ransom picked James up on his way back to the kitchen. He sat his son in his chair, then turned to Teya and gave her a kiss.

"I love you," he said and put his hand on her stomach.

Teya put her hand over his and rested her head on his shoulder. "I love you too," she said.

Ransom was headed down the hall when Warren called out after him, "Daddy!"

Ransom turned to find a wounded expression on his son's face. "You forgot to give me a kiss."

"Me too," James said.

Ransom returned to the kitchen and gave his children each a kiss on the head, then hurried out the door, hoping his early morning trip to the Census Bureau would be successful.

* * *

The tram heading downtown was just as packed as the one Ransom normally took to work. The only difference was that this one didn't have a broken window. For once, Ransom didn't care. He kept his eyes open for the woman with the baby, or the snatcher, but saw neither amid a sea of unfamiliar faces.

He got off at 25th Street and headed straight for the Census Bureau. He stopped just as he reached the doors and looked around. No one seemed to be watching the doors or otherwise paying attention to who came and went. He shook aside the nervous feeling in his stomach and entered the building. He hadn't been to the Census Bureau since he'd filled out the paperwork so Warren could be born. Back then the baby board had been located down the hall, just to the right.

The inside of the Census Bureau looked pretty much as he remembered it, except that the teller windows were dark and empty. He paused when he saw two sentinels standing against the far wall by the elevator. Neither looked familiar, and though one gave him a quick glance, he remained more interested in their conversation.

To Ransom's relief, the baby board was where he remembered

it. And it looked the same—half full of handwritten, pink note cards tacked to the cork.

Next to the board was a wall-mounted case of blank cards. Anyone who hadn't used their credit could walk in and fill one out. Ransom glanced over the cards to see how much the sellers were asking. The least expensive cash requests were the equivalent of five years' salary for Teya and him combined—twelve years if they just used his salary alone. Other sellers, however, were willing to trade for apartments in certain parts of town or residency permits in other cities.

Ransom saw a snatcher walk past out of the corner of his eye. His heart skipped a beat as he turned and watched the man make a beeline for the elevators. The guards waved him through. As he turned back, Ransom's eye caught a clock on the wall above the elevators—7:50. In ten minutes, the Census Bureau would be a hive of activity.

He quickly identified the three most promising cards—one accepting cash and two whose owners were looking for apartments in their area of town. He grabbed a pink card from the wall mount and looked for something to write with. Two strings hung limply at either side of the board, the pencils missing. He felt his pockets, then looked around the lobby for an option. Nothing.

Ransom glanced again at the sentinels. They were still absorbed in their conversion, so Ransom pulled the three pink cards from the board and shoved them in his pocket. The metal thumbtacks that had held them to the board clattered to the floor. Ransom peered nervously at the sentinels, relieved to see one of them burst into laughter over some shared joke.

As he headed for the main doors, he nearly bumped into his sister-in-law.

"Ransom," she said. "Didn't expect to see you here this morning."

Ransom swore under his breath. He felt as though Mona's eyes were boring straight into his uniform pocket that held the cards. His mind raced as he forced a smile. It felt fake.

Mona cocked her head to one side and asked, "Is everything okay? You look sick. It's not the flu, is it?"

"I'm fine, just got to bed late last night. It's hard to get going in the morning when you've only slept for four hours."

Mona nodded her head understandingly. "I have those nights once in a while too."

There was a moment of silence that made Ransom feel awkward. "Oh, I was coming to thank you for the apricots," he blurted out. "They were delicious. We all enjoyed eating them."

"Well, I just got lined up with another blind date for Saturday. He's a farmer too. If he brings something good, I'll be sure to share it with your family."

"I'll cross my fingers for tomatoes."

Mona smiled. "Me too."

Ransom looked at the clock on the wall. The big hand pointed to the eleven. "Well, I need to get to work. There's a home we have to tear down by the end of next week."

"I'm glad for what you do, Ransom. You're helping to breathe life back into our world."

Ransom just smiled.

"Tell Teya hello for me," Mona said. She turned and took three steps, then stopped. "Oh, and what did you two decide about the New Earth Day parade?"

"The New Earth Day parade?"

"Didn't Teya tell you?"

Ransom shook his head. "About a parade? No, she didn't. Like I said, we had kind of a long night. We both had other things on our minds."

"I thought she seemed preoccupied yesterday. Oh well." She briefly told Ransom how she wanted their family to be part of the float.

"That sounds fine," Ransom said, even though it was the last thing he wanted to do. "I'm sure the boys will love it."

"I know they will!" Mona agreed. "Oh, I'm so glad you approve. Just be sure you're all there no later than eight. We need you on the float before the parade starts."

"We'll be there."

"Great! I'll put your family on the list when I get to the office." She gave Ransom a half wave, then hurried toward the guards.

Ransom watched Mona until she walked past the sentinels, placed his hand in his pocket to make sure the baby cards were still there, and hurried to the Recycling Center.

He walked in the doors exactly at eight and followed two other recyclers down the hall to the cargo bay. The bay was already a hive of activity. A quick scan showed Dempsey working under the hood of a recycling truck.

Ransom headed straight for his locker. He opened it, and then, looking around to make sure no one was paying attention, he quickly took the pink baby cards from his pocket and stuck them in a training manual he'd had since his first day on the job. He thought they'd be safe there, and he wouldn't have to worry about losing them while working. Wiping the dust from his fingers and satisfied no one had seen him, he grabbed his toolbox and headed for the truck.

* * *

By midday, the garage had been completely dismantled. Piles of shingles, drywall, and beams lay where the garage had once stood. In a smaller pile, carefully placed to the side, was a stack of wiring, electrical outlets, and a few other things Ransom thought he could sell.

Ransom took a seat in the pleasant shade of the cherry tree. It was a shame he'd have to cut it down. He took a long drink from his canteen and leaned his head against the trunk, keeping an eye on the small pile. He'd spent the morning trying to think of a way to sneak the contents into his jumpsuit. The problem was that most items in the pile were too long or bulky to fit into his pockets without being noticeable. The only other place to hide them was his toolbox, but it was so full of tools, he doubted he could fit more than a piece or two in—not enough to make a trip to the Station worthwhile.

He pulled one of the apricots out of his pocket and popped it in his mouth. Then, nestling his body against the trunk, he closed his eyes. The lack of sleep coupled with the heat of the day had left him exhausted. Maybe a short nap would clear his mind and give him the strength to finish work.

He heard footsteps crunch on the dry grass and stop next to him.

"You're not eating?" Dempsey's voice ended any chance for a doze.

Ransom opened his eyes and looked up at his coworker. His face was shiny with sweat, and he held his lunch pail in his hand. Ransom spat the apricot pit out of his mouth. "I am eating."

"Just apricots? I never took you for a greener."

Ransom patted his pocket. "I've got a piece of meat in here somewhere."

"That's it? No wonder you're working slow today. You don't have any energy."

"I'll be fine," Ransom said.

"You didn't bring food yesterday either. What's going on? They not stocking the stores on your end of town?

Ransom shook his head. "I left my lunch bucket on the tram yesterday. Needless to say, it's long gone."

"Lucky for you, my wife made an extra sandwich," Dempsey said. He popped the lid off his pail and held it so Ransom could see its contents. Inside were two sugar cookies and two sandwiches wrapped in wax paper.

"Thanks, but I'm fine," Ransom said, his mouth watering.

"You're hungry and exhausted," Dempsey pointed out again.

"I'll live."

Grunting, Dempsey sat next to Ransom and put the lunch pail between them. "Hard to work when you don't eat. I'm getting old enough that I can't haul all that material to the truck by myself, that's for sure. And I'd like to get home at a reasonable hour today so I can spend some time with the wife. Eat it for me so I'm not working up here after dark."

He took one of the sandwiches, unwrapped part of it, and waved it under Ransom's nose. "It's a roast beef sandwich. Made with real roast beef. Take a look."

Ransom glanced down at the sandwich. Between two thick slices of homemade bread was at least an inch of meat—more than he ever remembered having for one meal. His stomach rumbled with hunger.

"Come on," Dempsey said. "I can't eat all this food by myself. My wife will be real disappointed if she finds out I ended up feeding it to a pack of stray dogs."

Ransom gave the sandwich a long look, then took it from Dempsey. "Thanks," he said. "I owe you one."

Dempsey just smiled as Ransom unwrapped the rest of the sandwich and took a bite. The bread was soft and fresh. So was the meat. He gulped down a few more bites, then noticed something white between the bread and the meat. He peeled back the bread for a better look, then held the sandwich out to Dempsey. "What's this white stuff?"

"Oh, that? It's mayonnaise."

"It's delicious. Where do you buy it?"

"Mayonnaise? Oh, you can't buy it. Not anymore, anyway. My wife makes it. It's not quite the same as the stuff I remember eating years ago, but it's close enough. Makes the sandwich though, doesn't it?"

"It really does. What's in it?"

"Oil and eggs, I think. Used to be you could buy it all the time. Not anymore. I think between the fat taxes and the expense it takes to refrigerate things, no one can afford it, so they stopped selling it."

Ransom finished the sandwich and washed it down with a drink from his canteen. Then he started on a sugar cookie. It was soft and sweet. It was undoubtedly the best meal he'd eaten in months.

When he was done, he pulled an apricot out of his pocket and handed it to Dempsey.

Dempsey's eyes lit up at the sight of the orange fruit. "Where'd you get that?"

"Sister-in-law."

"The Population Director?" Dempsey asked.

Ransom nodded.

Dempsey popped the fruit into his mouth. "I ever tell you that the house I grew up in had three apricot trees?" he asked.

"No," Ransom said. "I don't think you did." He'd heard lots of stories over the years about the house Dempsey grew up in—a small, ten-acre farm that was now the center of town. It was something his friend looked back on with nostalgic fondness, though Dempsey was honest enough to admit he had hated all the farm chores during the summer, like irrigating the fields or stacking bales of hay clear to the roof of an old wooden barn.

"We had these big trees that were at least fifty years old. They were like twenty feet tall, and the fruit at the top was hard to reach. Because I was a good climber, I'd make my way up to those high branches carrying a five-gallon plastic bucket with a rope attached to it. When the bucket got heavy, I'd lower it down to my mom. This time of year, we'd eat fresh apricots until we were sick of them."

Ransom handed Dempsey the rest of the apricots.

"I can't take these," Dempsey protested.

"You just gave me the most delicious food I've had all year. The least I can do is give you these in return."

Dempsey smiled and took the fruit. He ate them one at a time, chewing slowly.

"Can I ask you something?" Ransom said hesitantly as Dempsey ate.

"Sure. What's on your mind?"

"Why did you and Tammy decide to have four kids?"

Dempsey stroked his chin. "Well, that's a question I don't hear much anymore. I mean, with my kids being all grown and out of the house, most people don't know how many we have. Used to be I'd get that question all the time when the kids were younger—usually from complete strangers."

"I'm not trying to be nosy. You don't have to answer."

"Oh, I don't mind. It's just that it's been a long time since someone asked, that's all."

"So why'd you do it?"

"The wife and I like kids. Both came from large families too. Maybe that had something to do with it. Guess since we didn't mind having lots of siblings running around, we thought our own kids would enjoy the same learning experience we got." Dempsey readjusted his position against the tree. "Truth is, we wanted more. A lot more. We would have been happy with six or seven.

But we got married just as the population control laws went into effect. That put a damper on our plans."

"So, how'd you afford it? I mean, buying extra credits is expensive."

"We had some money left over from when the government bought the family farm. My mom never spent any of it. I think she considered it blood money or something, since the government took the land even though she didn't want to sell. The money was divided up between her kids when she died. My share ended up being just enough to buy two credits."

"How'd you afford feeding and clothing the kids, though? Even back then, they weren't giving people full rations for extra kids, right?"

"We cut corners, stretched our budget. Did what we had to do to make things work out. Wasn't easy, mind you, but somehow we did it."

Ransom nodded. He looked at the pile of roofing material in the backyard. Their lunch break was almost over, but he didn't feel like leaving the shade of the cherry tree.

"You get a lot of crap for having four kids?"

"Some. Stares, mostly. An occasional busybody would ask what we were thinking. Wasn't as bad as it is now, though. Back then, people were still used to seeing the occasional large family. Most folks hadn't spent years sitting around in school, learning that having too many kids would unbalance our ecosystems. It's different now."

"Even a little harassment must have been hard, though."

Dempsey shrugged. "You learn to ignore it. Frankly, I never saw how it was anyone's business."

Ransom took another drink from the canteen. "Was it worth it? Having four kids, I mean."

"It was for me and my wife."

"You think people are missing out when they choose not to have kids?"

"I don't think everyone appreciates what kids have to offer. For some people, one or two is all they can handle. Personally, I think people who don't want kids are doing the world a favor by not having any. If you don't want to be a parent, then you probably shouldn't be one. Live your life the way you want to live it, and I'll live mine. Let's just not give each other a hard time about it, and we'll all get along just fine."

Dempsey took a long drink from his canteen and wiped his mouth with the back of his hand. "What's up with all the questions today? You aren't thinking about having another one, are you?" he asked with a wink.

Ransom wanted to tell Dempsey about Teya's pregnancy. Maybe Dempsey would even have some ideas about where to buy an extra credit. But it was a risk he couldn't afford. Even though Dempsey was sympathetic to large families, he couldn't put his friend in a precarious legal situation. It was better to keep things a secret—at least for now. He decided to tell Dempsey only if he ran out of options.

He smiled. "No. The wife and I couldn't afford a credit, even if we did want one. Just curious, I guess."

"Well, if you ever decide to take that step, let me know. Having gone through it twice, I'd be happy to tell you what pitfalls to avoid."

Ransom felt his face blush. He glanced to see if Dempsey had noticed, but his friend was staring at the house, chewing on an apricot.

They both sat in silence for several minutes under the shade of the tree. Ransom could feel his strength returning. Finally he stood and stretched his arms, ready to return to work.

"Oh, I've got one more thing for you," Dempsey said. "Wait here."

He stood and walked over to the far side of the recycling truck. Ransom heard the sound of a side panel being opened and closed. A moment later, Dempsey returned with a dented lunch pail in his hand. "I fished this out of my closet for you," he said, handing it Ransom.

A wave of relief swept over Ransom. It was what Teya would call an answer to prayer. Not only did he have a lunch pail, but he now had a way to carry the valuable parts from the garage. He had to stop himself from grabbing the bucket and letting out an exultant scream. Instead, he shook his head in disbelief. "Dempsey, I can't. This is too much."

"Take it. You can't be spending money on another one when you've got little ones who need to eat."

Ransom took the lunch bucket by its handle and looked it over. Aside from the dents, it seemed usable. "How did you know I needed one? I just told you a few minutes ago that I'd lost mine."

Dempsey shrugged. "I was . . . just cleaning out the closet last night and came across it, then suddenly I remembered that you didn't bring lunch yesterday. Figured maybe something happened to your bucket, so I brought it. Now, the lid's a little hard to get on—you need to give it a good push. Otherwise, it should work just fine."

Something about Dempsey's response seemed rehearsed—as if he'd hurried through it—but Ransom decided not to pursue it. After all, now he had a lunch pail. Maybe his family wouldn't starve after all.

Ransom thanked Dempsey and put the bucket under the tree. He headed over to the pile of shingles on the ground. Dempsey's gift had given him hope that he could work things out. Now all he had to do was make sure the bucket was full by the time they headed home.

nine

Teya emptied the blood from three dozen vials into the sink, watching the pink water swirl down the drain. Then she washed each vial one at a time and placed them on a wooden rack to dry.

She had spent the entire morning going through the motions of drawing blood and running pregnancy tests—all without really thinking about what she was doing. Instead, her mind had been on Ransom and whether he had been able to make any headway with the replacement credit. Right now she was willing to pay any price just to calm her worries.

She leaned against the counter and double-checked the day's paperwork. All the pregnancy results had come back negative. That fact alone made Teya happy. The last thing she wanted was to let another woman experience the same fear and anxiety she was going through.

The door opened and Lia poked her head into the office.

"Your three o'clock is here," she said.

Teya looked up in surprise. "My what?" she asked.

Lia glanced at the patient's chart in her hand. "Eloise Johnston. She's here for a second blood test."

A heavy feeling weighed on Teya's stomach as her actions from the previous day came rushing back to her.

"Oh, yes," she said pleasantly. "Give me a few minutes, will you? I need to ready the room."

Teya took a ring of keys from her pocket and used one to unlock the supply closet against the far wall. She retrieved a large, sixty-year-old stereo from a shelf cluttered with beakers and Erlenmeyer flasks. It was heavy, and it took both hands to lift and set on the counter. She used the stereo system to help calm her patients. Teya had found that women generally came back to her office extremely stressed over the prospect of another test. It didn't help matters that they were escorted by one of the clinic's guards and had to be strapped to a chair during the test. She had seen healthy women go into shock or hyperventilate as soon as they were brought into the room. The best thing to do was provide a relaxing environment for them, and music went a long way in doing just that. The stereo itself was Ransom's gift to her. It had been left behind in a house Ransom had recycled several years ago. Knowing how Teya was looking for a way to calm her patients, he had filled out the paperwork requesting the device be donated to the clinic instead of being taken apart and recycled.

The challenge, of course, was getting it to work. The black power cord was worn and had several holes that exposed the tightly wound copper wiring inside. She usually had to fiddle with the cord in order to get it to work. Searching local shops that specialized in repairing or refurbishing old electronics had proved fruitless—they never had a cord that would fit. Without a cord, she knew it was only a matter of time before the stereo stopped working. She hoped it had another year or two of life before it was finally recycled.

She plugged the stereo into the outlet. Nothing. She unplugged it, wiped the plug's prongs with her fingers, and plugged it back in. Still nothing. She twisted the cord, hoping for a sign of life. Thirty seconds later, a red power light came on, followed by a burst of static. Teya smiled. Now she only had to get a signal. She slowly turned the radio dial with one hand while holding the coat hanger serving as a makeshift antenna with the other. After a minute of work, she was able to clear out most of the static, and the melodic voice of someone identified as Krassimira filled the room.

Satisfied that the signal would hold, Teya picked up the chart and scanned through it, paying special attention to the names and ages of Eloise's two children: Chloe, age six, and Chance, who'd just turned two. The second best way to relax women brought back to her office was to talk about their other children. The tactic was somewhat ironic, considering the circumstances, but most of the women were more than happy to tell Teya how smart, cute, or talented their children were.

There was a quick knock, and Lia entered. She held the door open for a short, rail thin woman with close-cropped black hair and skin so pale Teya wondered if it would glow in the dark. She was followed by Brigham, one of the clinic's two security guards—a tall, beefy man with gray hair and mutton chop sideburns.

Teya was surprised by how young Eloise looked. Though the chart said Eloise was thirty, she could have easily passed for someone in her early twenties. She also looked familiar, but Teya couldn't remember where she had seen the woman before.

She set the file on the counter and walked over to Eloise. "I'm Teya, the clinic's lab technician. You must be Eloise."

Eloise glared at Teya. "You're not a doctor."

"No, I'm not," Teya answered, smiling. "I spend most of my day doing blood work."

Eloise's eyes darted around the room until they came to rest on the Incubus.

"Is that the machine?" she asked.

"Yep. That's it."

"It's small," Eloise said. "I thought it would be bigger."

"The nurse will take a blood sample from you, and I'll run the test. The entire process takes less than a minute." Teya put her arm around Eloise and escorted her to the chair. She could feel the tension in Eloise's muscles as she guided her across the room. She also noted that Eloise never took her eyes off the Incubus.

"Your daughter, Chloe—she's six, right? That means she's in, what—first grade?" Teya asked, hoping to provide a distraction.

"Smart kid, that child," Eloise said as she sat in the chair. "She's already the best reader in her class. Most of them can't even read yet. I don't know what parents are doing nowadays, but their irresponsibility just delays everyone's potential."

Teya took Eloise's right arm and laid it so it was flat against the arm rest. Lia immediately fastened it to the chair, using one of the leather straps. She nodded to Teya when it was secure. Procedure called for Eloise's other arm and legs to be strapped to the chair as well, but since Teya already knew what the result was going to be, she decided to skip that step. She glanced at the guard to see if he was going to say anything. He simply stood there looking bored, arms folded across his chest. Lia tied a piece of rope around Eloise's forearm and began looking for a vein.

"Well, I'm sure her teachers are glad she has an attentive mom," Teya said. "My oldest has just learned the alphabet, so we hope he'll be reading soon." Teya retrieved a clean syringe and vial from the cupboard.

"You have two boys, right?" Eloise said.

Her words stopped Teya cold. The music from the stereo momentarily faded into white noise. She'd never had a patient who was aware of her personal life before. "Yes, I do," she said slowly, hoping her voice didn't sound too agitated as she turned around. "How did you know that?"

"We live in the same building. I see you and your boys occasionally in the play area next to Building C. I've seen you on the stairs a couple times too. You live on the fifth floor. I live on the sixth—the apartment right above yours."

That's why she looks so familiar. "I'm sorry I didn't recognize you," Teya said. "I guess we've never talked."

"It's okay. It's easy to live anonymously in those buildings. I don't even know half the people who live on my floor. I just remember you because you have two very cute boys."

"We're ready here," Lia interrupted.

Teya handed the syringe to Lia. Suddenly Eloise grabbed Teya's arm with her free hand. The beefy guard took a step toward them, but Teya gave him a look indicating that he could relax. The guard reluctantly moved a foot back, but he kept his eyes focused on Eloise.

"Tell me," Eloise said. "When your second boy was born, did they make you plug your ovaries?"

The question took Teya completely by surprise. "What are you talking about?"

"Your ovaries," Eloise said. "Did you have them plugged after you had your second child?"

"No, I didn't," Teya said as nonchalantly as possible, despite the personal nature of the question.

"Why not?"

"It's an optional procedure, Eloise. After a second child, a woman can have her ovaries plugged or take the mandated birth control pills. Didn't anyone tell you that? It should have been explained to you."

"But you didn't do it. Did you forego the procedure because you were hoping for more?"

Blood rushed to Teya's face, and her heart started pounding in her chest. She could feel the stares of the guard and Lia boring into her. "Two is perfect for my husband and me," she said, sidestepping the question.

Eloise pulled Teya close. Her voice was just above a whisper. "Tell me the truth," she pleaded, looking Teya straight in the eye.

Teya met her gaze and said, "Actually, I didn't want the complications that come with surgery."

She shook herself free of Eloise's grasp and stepped out of reach. She nodded to Lia, who walked forward, syringe in hand. Teya noted that Eloise didn't flinch when Lia inserted the needle.

In less than thirty seconds, Lia was finished, and she handed the full vial to Teya.

"Okay, Eloise, I'm just going to place this sample in here, and then you'll be on your way," Teya said pleasantly.

"Only if the result's negative," Eloise said, her voice full of sarcasm.

Teya didn't turn around. She didn't want to talk to this woman. She felt bad enough that Eloise was here, but knowing the woman's private feelings made Teya's dishonesty seem more like a personal betrayal. She just wanted to get back to work and have her lab and her worries to herself.

"The device is a little old and gives out the occasional false positive. Most of the tests we redo come back negative. That's probably what happened to you."

"If it comes back positive, it will be a miracle. There were complications when my first child was born, and the doctors told me I wouldn't be able to have any more kids."

Teya tried to block Eloise's voice out of her mind. She put the sample into the Incubus and counted down the seconds in her head until the red light would appear.

Fifteen . . . fourteen . . . thirteen . . .

"Well, I believed the doctors," Eloise continued. "I went on with my life, and then—much to my surprise—a few years later I found myself pregnant. He came healthy and without problems. I called him Chance because it was such a chance occurrence that he was even born. Now I find myself here again. It's no accident. If I'm meant to have another child, there isn't anything you can do about it."

Three . . . two . . . one.

The Incubus buzzed.

"Well, it looks like we had another—" Teya stopped mid-sentence.

The light was green.

For what seemed like a long moment, everything in the office came to a sudden stop.

Then Brigham moved toward Eloise. "Ma'am, I'm going to need you to come with me."

Eloise gasped, taking in the news and the guard's intentions. Then she suddenly jolted, trying to free herself. "You can't take my child from me!" she said angrily.

Brigham put a hand to his nightstick as he closed in. "Ma'am, I need you to calm down. Everything's going to be just fine as long as you stay still," he said.

Eloise started to panic under the restraints. "I know where you're taking me, and I'm not going to let you!" she screamed. She brought her right foot up and landed it squarely in Brigham's chest, knocking him backward into the door. Lia pushed a red button next to the chair and ducked as Eloise sent her free arm flying.

As the office exploded into chaos, Teya stared at the green light, too stunned to move. A positive result wasn't possible. She had just switched the samples yesterday.

The sound of the door being flung open brought Teya out of her trance. She turned as Dr. Redgrave and the other security guard came through the door. Together, the two guards managed to hold down Eloise's legs.

She writhed like a fish out of water. "Don't take my baby!" she screamed over and over.

Dr. Redgrave ran to the sink and grabbed a syringe that was drying on the rack. He took a glass bottle of clear liquid from his pocket, unscrewed the cap, and put the syringe in the bottle with a series of quick motions.

"Hold her still!" he said to the guards. "This will only take a minute."

"Wait!" Teya suddenly yelled. She was surprised how loud her voice sounded in the small room.

Everyone stopped and looked at her. Eloise's mouth was agape, hope spilling into her desperate expression. Only the soft music from the radio filled the room. Teya yanked the cord from the wall, leaving silence in its wake.

"I want to test her again," she stated.

"Isn't this her second positive?" Dr. Redgrave asked.

"Yes, but the Incubus has been very inaccurate of late. I want to retest her."

"There's no need to do that. The law's very clear on what we need to do next—"

"I know what the law says, Geoffrey," she interrupted. Teya immediately regretted challenging Dr. Redgrave and calling him by his first name. In the clinic, the doctor was to be obeyed, not questioned. No doubt she'd hear about it later. But with those words out of her mouth, she had no choice but to continue.

"And I also know what's going to happen if we've made a mistake. Remember last year when we escorted a woman downtown who wasn't actually pregnant? The Bureau sent their technicians back and took over our lab for a week while they examined the Incubus and our procedures. If we send another false positive down, it will be even worse. Maybe they'll start looking at the management and employees and wonder if we're competent enough to run the place."

Teya hoped he wouldn't call her bluff. They likely wouldn't replace Dr. Redgrave—his clinic was considered the top clinic in the city—but it wasn't out of the realm of possibility either. Occasionally, doctors were replaced by bureaucrats who knew nothing about running a clinic. The Bureau's only concern was shielding their agency from the legal morass that could come from false imprisonment charges, civil suits, bad press, or any of the above.

There was a red tinge to Dr. Redgrave's face. After working with the man for years, Teya knew it indicated his building internal rage, and she knew she was in for a strict reprimand.

Dr. Redgrave straightened his white lab coat before speaking. "Very well, test her again," he said coolly.

Teya handed a clean syringe and vial to Lia. Brigham held Eloise's arm down, even though it was still strapped to the table. The second guard held her legs.

Lia repeated the blood draw and handed the vial to Teya. Everyone waited in silence as the machine did its work.

Twenty seconds later, the green light came on.

Eloise started thrashing and wailing again. Dr. Redgrave immediately injected the clear liquid into her arm. Seconds later, her eyes rolled back, and her body stopped moving.

Dr. Redgrave checked her pulse and listened to her breathe. When he seemed satisfied that she was going to be all right, he looked at the two guards. "Call the sentinels and have them pick her up."

Brigham started to strap Eloise's legs to the chair.

"She's not going anywhere for an hour," Dr. Redgrave said. "We'll be fine."

The guards looked at each other, then left the room.

Dr. Redgrave instructed Lia to check on the patient in room three. Lia gave Teya a knowing glance and quickly left the lab, closing the door behind her.

Once the door was shut, Dr. Redgrave spun around. His face was bright red. "Don't you ever publicly question one of my decisions again!" he yelled. "I run this clinic. What I say goes. In a tense situation like this, I can't afford to have people second-guessing me. There's a clear chain of command around here, and I'm at the top of it. Understand?"

Teya sardonically considered saluting Dr. Redgrave in the traditional schoolchild's pledge to teacher and country but finally opted to look at the floor and mumble a quiet apology.

"If you have a problem with anything I've done, you take it up with me privately in my office. If you ever question me in front of nurses, guards, or patients again, I'll have you dismissed from this clinic and will ensure that you remain unemployed. Got it?"

Teya nodded. She waited for more, but all she heard was Dr. Redgrave's sigh. She looked up. The red in his face was beginning to fade. He walked over to the stool and sat down. He took off his glasses and rubbed where the nose pads had rested. "Look, I'm sorry. I didn't mean to yell. I'm having a bad day. You know I respect your opinion, Teya. You were right about the Census Bureau. We're one of the best clinics in the state, and I want to keep it that way. Next time, just talk to me privately if there's an issue."

"I won't let it happen again," Teya said.

"I really appreciate the job you're doing. You're detailed and extremely accurate, and you're a big reason we always get high marks. It's due to your diligence that I don't have to worry as much as other doctors when the Census Bureau performs an audit or checks our paperwork."

If you only knew how diligent I've been the last three months, Teya thought guiltily. She forced a smile at the compliment. "Thanks," she said. "It's always nice to know my work's appreciated."

Dr. Redgrave smiled, then glanced over at Eloise. "You want me to have one of the guards come back and keep an eye on her?"

Teya looked at Eloise's sleeping figure. "I'll be fine. Like you said, she's not going anywhere."

Dr. Redgrave turned to leave. He stopped as his hand touched the doorknob.

"Out of curiosity," he said, "what made you want to retest the patient today?"

"What do you mean?"

"Well, in all the years you've worked here, you've never asked for a retest after a second positive. I'm curious as to why you were so insistent this time."

Teya felt as though someone had just punched her in the stomach. "I . . . uh . . . the Incubus has had problems lately," she answered, motioning to where the green light still shone brightly. "We really need to upgrade."

Dr. Redgrave nodded and put his glasses back on. "Yes, well, I'll see what we can do to get you a new machine. It might take a while, considering they have to be shipped in from California. We only have so many transportation credits allotted each year, and shipping even one in would use up most of them. Anyway, I apologize again for yelling. Just be sure to talk with me first next time."

After Dr. Redgrave left, Teya leaned against the counter, breathed a sigh of relief, and let the adrenaline subside. She looked at Eloise and wiped a sudden tear from her eye.

What had she done? Her attempt to hide her pregnancy had now involved an innocent third party. If she hadn't swapped the tests, Eloise wouldn't be here right now. She'd probably be playing with her kids or working or doing whatever she did during the day. Instead she was strapped to a chair and would wake up in the Infirmary.

Teya tried to rationalize away her guilt. After all, Eloise's pregnancy would have been discovered sooner or later. Maybe the Incubus really was broken and would only give positives from here on out. Maybe in the twenty-four hours between the first and second test, Eloise really had become pregnant. There were a thousand things that could explain the negative result yesterday and the positive today. But no matter how Teya tried to explain it away, she couldn't assuage her guilt.

Her eyes went from Eloise's face to her arm. The leather bands pressed into her skin, the lack of blood flow turning her arm purple. Teya loosened the bands and rubbed Eloise's arm to get the circulation going again. When Eloise's arm was stark white, Teya retrieved her purse from the supply closet and ate her remaining salt crackers. She turned on the faucet at the sink, cupped her hands to get a drink of water, washed the remaining vials in the sink, and put them on the rack to dry.

As she worked, Teya thought back to Eloise's question about getting her ovaries plugged. Ransom had never insisted that Teya undergo the procedure, and she'd never insisted that Ransom get a vasectomy. Cost wasn't an issue, since both operations were completely paid for by the government after the birth of seconds. Instead, they had gone on birth control, and Teya had agreed to be subjected to the mandatory, monthly pregnancy tests.

Why had they agreed so easily? It wasn't that she dreamed of having a large family or even a third child. But for some reason, she wanted the option of having another child if the population laws were ever to be relaxed or—heaven forbid—something happened to one of her children before he turned eighteen. The freedom to decide for herself how many or how few children she wanted to have was appealing—she wanted control over her body and her family.

She looked up to make sure the door was shut before she pulled back her lab coat and placed her hand on her stomach. The thought of not being able to protect this child made her sick, and as she looked at Eloise, the tears welled up again.

* * *

Teya leaned against the reception desk, chatting with Nevaeh. The last of the day's patients were back in the examination rooms being seen by Dr. Redgrave and the nurses.

"Fifteen minutes and we can go home," Nevaeh said, looking at the clock above the door.

"You can. I'm stuck until the snatchers show up," Teya said. "We called an hour ago, and they still aren't here."

"Oh, they'll be here," Nevaeh said. "They probably got a more important call to take care of first. Snatchers never miss a call."

"Oh?"

"Yeah, I dated a snatcher once. Making every call is a point of pride with them. Did I ever tell you about him?"

"No. I didn't know you dated one."

"Yeah, we were together about six months."

"How was it? Dating a snatcher, I mean."

"Well, they're all super intense. I almost wonder if they're on something, you know?"

"Why'd you end it?" Teya asked. She was thinking of Mona as she asked the question, wondering if Nevaeh could shed any light on why her sister's marriage had ended so suddenly.

Nevaeh looked down at her desk and drummed her fingers on the wood thoughtfully.

Teya immediately regretted raising the subject. "It's okay," she said. "I shouldn't be prying."

"No. It's better if more people know what they're really like," Nevaeh said. She stood and leaned across the desk so she could lower her voice. "At first he seemed like a nice guy. I mean, there were some things to get used to—the phone always ringing in the middle of the night and stuff. Sometimes he'd just up and leave without telling me where he was going, then come back four or five hours later without saying where he'd been. He said it was all part of the job. But I could have lived with that. Then, a few months after we started dating, his shine wore off, and the real him emerged. He had a violent streak in him. Not with me, mind you, but with complete strangers. Acted like he could get away with anything. One night, we were in the park, and he didn't like the way a guy looked at me, so he shoved him into a cactus garden, then just laughed, like it was some big joke. I left him soon after that. But the funny thing is, his snatcher friends were all really callous like that—even the female ones."

Before Teya could say anything, the door opened and Brigham walked in, followed by a sentinel.

Teya's breath caught. He was the same one she had seen talking to Mona during her visit yesterday. His eyes locked on her, and the same feeling of dread welled up inside her.

"He's here for the patient," Brigham said.

Teya couldn't take her eyes from the sentinel's dark gaze.

"You want me to show him where she is?" Brigham said.

Silence.

"Teya?"

Teya snapped out of her trance. "I'll take care of it," she said.

"Follow me."

The snatcher followed her down the hall. She walked fast, not liking the way she sensed his eyes boring into her back.

"You've got a great body," the sentinel said.

Teya felt the blood rise to her face in anger, but instead of responding, she chose to continue down the hall.

"A woman like you could really go places. How about after I'm done here, I come back and we get to know each other a little better?"

"I'm married," Teya said stiffly as she continued down the hall.

"You shouldn't let your husband come between the two of us," the sentinel said. "I know I won't."

Just as Teya reached the door to the lab, he spun her around, pushed her against the wall, and pressed his body against hers. He flashed Teya a wicked smile and put a finger to his lips.

Teya's heart raced. She struggled to free herself, but he was too strong.

"The exam room to my left. Is anyone in there?"

Teya glanced along the wall. The clipboard on the door where the nurses hung patient files was empty. She looked down at the floor, not daring to make eye contact with him.

"I'll take that as a no," the sentinel said, his hot breath tickling her face.

Out of the corner of her eye, Teya saw him look over his shoulder as if making sure they were alone. Then he turned back, lowered his head, and locked eyes with her. "We're going into that exam room together for a few minutes, just the two of us. You try to scream or yell or do anything else stupid, and I'll break your neck." He placed his free hand on Teya's neck and gave it a little squeeze.

Teya wanted to run screaming down the hall, but her legs wouldn't move.

"Let's go," the sentinel said, putting his hand on her hip and giving her a little push.

Suddenly there was a sound of a door opening down the hall. Lia walked out of one of the exam rooms, a vial of blood in her hand. She took a few steps before she noticed them. "What's going on?" she asked.

The sentinel took a step back. "Your pretty lab tech is taking me to the breeder."

Lia gave Teya an anxious look. "Are you okay?"

Teya forced a smile. "Everything's fine. Just go back into the room and stay with the patient. I'll come get you in a few minutes."

Lia opened her mouth to speak, but Teya shook her head. "I'm okay. Just go."

Lia's eyes moved to the sentinel, then back to Teya before retreating into the exam room.

"I guess we'll have to wait until next time." He put his hands on her shoulders and spun her around so she was facing the door. "Open it."

Teya didn't move.

The sentinel reached around her, turned the knob, and gently pushed her inside the lab.

She was still in shock from the sentinel's actions, and it took her a moment to realize that the chair where Eloise had been sleeping was empty. She took a step back and placed her hand against the wall in surprise.

"Where is she?" the sentinel growled.

"Dr. Redgrave must have moved her to a different room. I'll be right back."

Teya hurried down the hall, glad that her legs finally felt like moving again. She wanted to put as much space between her and the sentinel as possible. She opened the door to the last exam room, where Dr. Redgrave and a nurse were talking to a patient. Dr. Redgrave started up from his chair as she opened the door.

"Teya, you can't just—"

"Eloise is gone."

"Who?"

"The woman who was back in my lab. She's missing."

Dr. Redgrave stood up and excused himself. He grabbed Teya by the arm and hurried her out of the room, shutting the door behind him.

"What's going on?"

Teya motioned with her head to the sentinel who was standing at the end of the hall. She couldn't bear to make eye contact with him, so she stared at the floor. "I took him back to get the patient. She wasn't there. I thought maybe you moved her."

"Moved her? Why would I do that? She was fastened to the chair. Even if she woke up, she shouldn't have been able to leave."

Suddenly Teya remembered loosening Eloise's restraints. She bit her lower lip, unsure of what to say.

Dr. Redgrave ran toward the lab. Teya reached the room just in time to hear him swear.

"Where's the breeder?" the sentinel demanded.

"Everything's fine, Dragomir," Dr. Redgrave replied.

"Then where is she, Geoffrey?" Dragomir growled.

"She must be in one of the other rooms."

"I have a van waiting out front. We're in a hurry."

Dr. Redgrave looked at Teya and motioned for her to follow. He went down the hall, looking in every exam room and the bathroom. He also opened the doors to the closets inside each room. He stopped in the last exam room, said something to the nurse and patient inside, and stepped back into the hall and closed the door. He looked back at Dragomir, then pulled Teya into the waiting area. It was still empty, save Nevaeh, who was confirming an appointment with a patient on the phone, and Brigham, who stood by the door.

"When was the last time you saw the patient?" Dr. Redgrave asked.

"Twenty, twenty-five minutes ago. I finished cleaning the vials and filling out the day's paperwork, then I came up here to talk with Nevaeh."

"Was she asleep when you left?"

"I think so. Her eyes weren't open. She hadn't moved—"

"There's no other way out of this clinic except the front door. Tell me exactly what you did after you left the lab."

"I told you. I walked to the desk and talked to Nevaeh."

"Straight to the desk? No stops in any of the exam rooms?"

Teya paused before answering. For the first time since she had known Dr. Redgrave, she could detect fear in his voice. "No, I didn't come straight here," she said. "I stopped in the bathroom. I was only there a minute at the most."

Dr. Redgrave pushed the glasses up the bridge of his nose. He turned to Nevaeh, took the phone from her hand, and hung up. "Nevaeh," Dr. Redgrave said, "when did you last get up from the desk?"

Nevaeh paused for a moment. "About an hour ago. Why? What's going on?"

"How many patients have left the office in the last thirty minutes or so?"

"Two," she said. "Mrs. Rose and another woman."

"What did the other woman look like?"

"Dark hair—oh, and the palest skin I've ever seen. She looked like a ghost."

Dr. Redgrave turned to Brigham. "Get Terence and look for the woman who had her blood drawn. She couldn't have gone far."

Brigham got out of his chair and hurried out the door.

"Where's the woman, Geoffrey?" Dragomir's deep voice filled the whole room.

All three of them turned.

"She's not available at the moment."

Dragomir took a step forward. "What does that mean?"

"Well, the patient is . . . missing."

Dragomir's expression soured. "Missing? You mean she escaped?"

"Apparently she walked out about twenty minutes ago. I'm sure—"

Dragomir lunged forward and grabbed Dr. Redgrave by his lab coat, picked him up, and swung him against the concrete wall. Dr. Redgrave's head smacked against it hard enough that his glasses flew from his face. One of the lenses shattered on impact with the floor.

Nevaeh screamed.

"Where does she live?" Dragomir roared.

Dr. Redgrave's eyes fluttered open briefly, then closed.

Dragomir smacked him hard across the face. "Wake up! I need to know where the breeder lives!"

Dr. Redgrave's eyes opened again. "Lives? I don't know. I'll have to get her file." The doctor said each word slowly, as though it required great thought.

"Then get it!"

"I know where she lives," Teya said, suddenly remembering that the woman lived one floor above her own apartment. For the doctor's sake, she hoped that what Eloise had told her was accurate.

Dragomir turned his hateful gaze directly on her. Teya shuddered internally. "Kaczynski Terrace. Building C. Apartment 614. It's three blocks north of here."

"Are you sure?"

Teya nodded.

"You better be." He let go of Dr. Redgrave and strode out the door.

Dr. Redgrave fell to the floor, collapsing on his side. His eyes had a glazed look to them.

"Find Lia!" Teya directed Nevaeh.

As Nevaeh hurried to find Lia, Teya raced out the door just in time to see Dragomir get into the passenger side of a black Census Bureau van. Before the door was even shut, the van pulled away from the curb. Dragomir's eyes locked menacingly with hers as the van headed north.

ten

As Dempsey backed the recycling truck up to the conveyor belt, Ransom went to gather his things. After placing his gear in his locker, he reached for the training manual on the top shelf. He pretended to look something up in the manual, casually opening the front cover, ready to turn his back protectively as he slipped the baby cards into his lunch pail. But the cards were gone. He shook his head, thinking he must have placed the cards somewhere else in the book, then flipped through its pages.

No cards.

Looking around, he held the book by the spine and shook it. Nothing fell out.

Ransom set the book on the bench and searched the top shelf.

Panic welled up inside him as he searched the rest of the locker. When that yielded nothing, he turned his pockets inside out.

Empty.

He slammed the locker door. It hit the lock and bounced back open, hitting the locker next to it. The sound echoed throughout the bay. Out of the corner of his eye, he saw Dempsey and several of the conveyor belt workers turn to look at him.

Calming himself, Ransom replayed the morning from the moment he entered the Recycling Center. He clearly remembered putting the cards in the training manual. Had he forgotten to secure the locker? He wasn't sure. It was such a routine activity, he never gave it a second thought.

Lockers were sometimes searched to make sure employees weren't taking items home. The law, however, required that the employee be present when the search was conducted. But that didn't ensure that someone hadn't rifled through it. The combination to the lock was kept on file somewhere. Someone with access to that information could have opened it easily while he was gone.

Ransom tried to calm the churning in his stomach. Getting caught with the cards wasn't illegal, but it would certainly raise suspicion. If the person who now had the cards placed an anonymous call to the Census Bureau, Teya would have to undergo a pregnancy test she couldn't fabricate the results of.

The clock on the wall read 4:40. Teya should still be at work. He could call the clinic and give her a heads-up. She was rarely busy this late in the day. He hurried to the phone on the wall near the sink. It was against the rules to use it for personal calls, but right then, Ransom didn't care. Cradling the receiver on his shoulder, he dialed the clinic's number, twisting the phone cord while the ringing went on and on. No one answered.

After fifteen rings, he hung up, waited a minute, and tried again. While it was ringing, he noticed Dempsey walking in his direction.

"You okay?" Dempsey asked.

"Yeah, fine. Just trying to get a hold of Teya."

"Everything all right with her?"

Ransom nodded and waved Dempsey away.

The phone kept ringing.

On the twentieth ring, he hung up and made for the door.

* * *

When the tram arrived just before five o'clock, Ransom was the first one off. He hurried down the platform and ran the two blocks to the clinic.

The door was unlocked, but there was no one in the lobby or behind the desk.

"Hello? Teya?" he called out.

Silence.

He walked swiftly to Teya's lab. The light was on, and vials were drying on the rack. Knowing she would never leave the lab without everything in its place, Ransom started checking the doors to the examination rooms. Inside the last room, he found Dr. Redgrave sitting in one of the chairs. An auburn-haired nurse was stitching up a cut on the back of the doctor's head. Her fingertips were red with blood.

"Where's Teya?" Ransom asked.

The nurse flinched as she looked up, then recognized him. "Gone," she said.

"Where'd she go?"

The nurse shrugged. "Ran out the door after—"

"That's enough, Lia," Dr. Redgrave said. He rolled his eyes so he could see Ransom. "Your wife's not here. She left about fifteen minutes ago."

"What happened?"

Dr. Redgrave didn't answer.

"It's really important that I find her," Ransom pressed.

"I'm sorry, I don't know."

Ransom looked back at the nurse. "Lia, do you know where my wife went?"

"Lia can't discuss what goes on in the clinic with anyone other than those who work here," Dr. Redgrave said evenly before Lia could open her mouth.

In an instant, Ransom moved across the room. He grabbed Dr. Redgrave by his lab coat and hauled him to his feet. He moved so fast that Lia didn't have time to let go of the suture in her hands. One of the stitches in the back of the doctor's head pulled out, and he winced in pain.

Ransom pulled the doctor close so their faces were just inches apart. "Where's my wife?"

"I—I don't know. She just ran out."

"Why?"

"She ran after a sentinel. I don't know why."

Ransom froze. "What was a sentinel doing here?"

"I can't tell you. That would violate doctor-patient—"

"If it involves my wife, I have a right to know."

"It—" The doctor winced again. "It has nothing to do with your wife."

"Where was she going?"

"I can't say. Again, that would violate—"

"I don't give a—" Ransom paused and took a deep breath. "I just want to know where my wife went."

"I can't tell you."

Ransom grabbed the suture attached to the doctor's head and pulled. Another one of the stitches came out, followed by a trickle of blood. Dr. Redgrave screamed.

"Don't hurt him!" Lia cried. "She went to the apartments around Kaczynski Terrace. Building C, I think. A patient who's wanted by the Census Bureau fled there. I don't know why Teya followed her."

Ransom let go of the doctor and raced out of the clinic. He weaved his way through people on the sidewalk until he reached the alley. As he entered the plaza, his heart leaped in his chest. A Census Bureau van was parked in front of his apartment building.

Suddenly the wail of a siren blurted out behind him. He turned just as a police car sped down the alley. It was followed by a second boxy Census Bureau van. Ransom stepped to the side as the vehicles raced past.

The vehicles parked in front of his building next to the first van. The back door of the second van popped open, and five sentinels jumped out. They wore black helmets and ski masks over their faces. Each held a shiny black nightstick in his hand. They headed straight to the entrance of Building C.

A moment later, two additional masked sentinels emerged, dragging a large, bunched, white cloth that was ten feet square and at least five feet high. They headed to the balconies on the side of the building.

Four police officers emerged from the car and grabbed wooden barricades out of the back of one of the vans. Before Ransom could reach Building C, they had a perimeter set up in a fifty-foot semi-circle around the entrance.

Ransom stopped in front of the newly erected barricade. He glanced up at his apartment. It looked dark and quiet. A police officer walked by on the other side of the barricade, keeping an eye on the crowd that was beginning to form.

"I live in the building!" Ransom shouted at the officer. "I need to get inside."

"Sorry, sir, you'll have to wait."

"What apartment are you searching?" Ransom asked, this time with a tinge of anger in his voice.

The police officer stopped and looked at Ransom. He rested his hand atop his nightstick and took a step toward him. "I can't tell you that."

Suddenly there was a loud pop, followed by a hissing sound. The gathering crowd watched as the white canvas began to self-inflate. In less than a minute, it had turned into a large white cushion about twenty feet high and thirty feet wide. A sentinel grabbed each corner and pushed it so it was resting against the lower balcony.

Ransom looked around the plaza at the sea of faces. Some of them looked familiar—people who lived in his building but whose names he didn't know. Glancing up, he saw that people in the surrounding apartments were standing on their balconies, watching the show. But there was no sign of Teya.

"Come on," the man standing next to Ransom complained to the officer. "Go up and get her already. I live in the building. I have things to do."

Ransom glanced over at the man. Mid forties, dressed in a worn polo shirt and slacks that were at least two sizes too big for him. The man noticed Ransom looking at him and took the opportunity to gripe. "Some people have no self-control. They just go out and reproduce like rabbits without a thought for anyone else. They should all be rounded up and kept in cages, if you ask me."

Ransom clenched his fists, but he turned his attention back to the building, forcing himself to stay calm and focused on Teya. He looked up at the empty balcony, then scanned the crowd again, hoping to see his wife's familiar face.

He looked through the windows on each landing as black-clad sentinels ran up the stairs, stopping on the sixth floor. He breathed out a sigh of relief. It wasn't his apartment they wanted to search. The sentinels removed their backpacks and started unloading their equipment. A minute later, a sentinel on the ground sporting captain chevrons on his sleeve pulled a white handkerchief from his pocket and waved it in the air. One of the sentinels near the sixth floor window waved his in return.

The crowd grew quiet. The sentinels on the sixth floor moved down the hall, out of sight of the people on the ground. Thirty seconds later, there was the sound of a metal door being forced open. A woman ran out to the balcony. She was up high enough that for a split second, Ransom thought it was Teya. His heart skipped a beat before he noticed the woman had the whitest skin Ransom had ever seen. He unclenched his fists, relieved that it wasn't his wife.

"You're not going to take my baby!" she screamed, trying to climb the railing.

A sentinel grabbed her from behind and pulled her back into the apartment. Someone slammed the balcony door, and its large glass window shattered. Then all was quiet.

A minute later, a sentinel walked out to the balcony and gave the thumbs-up sign to the sentinels and police officers below. A cheer arose from the sentinels on the ground and several people in the crowd. A few minutes later, with the aid of several sentinels, the woman was carried down the stairs, followed by two children and the remaining snatchers. Ransom felt relieved that Teya wasn't among the group.

Obviously panic-stricken, the two children watched as their mother was loaded into one of the vans. The oldest one—a girl Ransom thought looked to be six or seven—had her arm around her much younger brother. Both children had tears running down their cheeks. One of the sentinels stopped, bent down, and said something to the children. Ransom couldn't hear what he said, but it made the girl cry harder. A few moments later, the children were escorted to the front of the van. A few sentinels jumped in the back, and the van slowly made its way through the crowd.

With most of the action over, the onlookers began to disperse, except for those waiting to get back into Building C. Ransom watched the crowd and spotted Teya standing in the middle of the plaza. Her shoulders were slouched forward, and a tear ran down her cheek.

Ransom ran to her, relieved. "Are you okay?" he asked as he embraced her.

Teya looked up at him for a long moment, then nestled her face into his chest.

Ransom kissed the crown of her head. "I thought you were up there with the woman they brought down."

"I should have been. . . . It's my fault," Teya said, sobbing.

Ransom took a half step back so he could look her in the eye. "What are you talking about?"

Teya's body shook from another sob. Ransom hugged her until she stopped crying. Finally Teya lifted her head, her eyes nervously scanning the crowd. Ransom followed her gaze. Even though the crowd had dispersed, there were still plenty of people milling about. He took a step toward Teya and pulled her close so no one could hear them.

"What is it?" he said.

"That woman they took away," Teya said in a shame-filled whisper. "It's my fault they came for her."

"What do you mean?"

Another sob welled up inside her. "If it wasn't for me, she wouldn't be in that van. Her kids wouldn't be—" She buried her face in Ransom's neck.

Ransom just held her. He knew she'd clarify when she calmed down. After a minute, Teya stopped crying. She wiped her nose with her sleeve and took several deep breaths. Quietly, she told Ransom that she had switched Eloise's test yesterday and about Eloise's subsequent escape from the clinic that afternoon.

"It's not your fault," Ransom assured Teya when she was done with her story. "If this woman was already pregnant, the test would have confirmed it the next time she came in anyway. A trip downtown would have been inevitable."

"You don't know that. She might have tested negative again. Maybe she would have miscarried before coming in. Maybe she would have found out on her own and gone into hiding. If I hadn't fudged her results, she would have had more time—wouldn't have gone through this nightmare—" Teya's voice quivered again in sorrow.

"You're being too hard on yourself."

Teya looked up at him. "Did you see the look on her children's faces? They were terrified. And it's all because of me."

Ransom gazed at his wife. She had always been prone to guilty feelings if things didn't turn out just right, but he couldn't use that fact to comfort her now. She apparently did bear some responsibility for what had happened. He didn't know what he could say to comfort her.

Teya wiped a tear sliding down her cheek and said, "I don't ever want our children to experience what her children did today."

"I don't either."

"I mean it, Ransom. Our boys can't see snatchers breaking into our house to haul their parents away. We have to find another way to solve our . . . problem."

"Don't even talk about it. It's not going to happen. Everything's going to be fine. We'll have a credit and a new baby before you know it." His earlier feelings of panic, when he hadn't found Teya at work, momentarily returned, and he fought to stay calm for her sake.

Teya wiped her eyes with the back of her hand. "Did you go to the Census Bureau this morning?" she asked. "Did you find one we might be able to afford?"

Ransom didn't answer immediately, unsure how to bring up the subject of the missing cards.

"Ransom?"

"I got three leads."

"Three," she said, her mood brightening. "It's so hard to find affordable credits, I would have been happy with one. That's good news. What are they asking? Can I look at the cards?"

Ransom was tempted not to tell Teya that the cards were missing. She had enough stress and worry in her life right now. But not telling her could be even more dangerous. Someone could be watching them, trying to determine if Teya was indeed pregnant. Knowing about the lost cards would keep her alert to a possible threat.

He put his arm around his wife and led her to a part of the plaza with fewer people nearby. Then he told her about putting the cards in his locker but finding them missing after work. "As soon as I realized the cards were gone, I called your office, but no one answered. When I saw that black van parked in front of our building, I thought . . . they'd come for you. I thought they were going to take you away. I thought—" He stopped, trying to fight back the tears.

Teya put her arms around him and hugged him. "Do you think someone knows?" she whispered, fear in her voice.

"I don't know."

As they stood there in each other's arms, Ransom glanced over at Building C. He wanted to get off the plaza and away from prying eyes. The police had taken down several of the white barricades and loaded them into the back of the remaining van. Ransom guided Teya toward their apartment building with the rest of the impatient crowd.

Twenty feet from the barricade, Ransom froze. Dragomir walked around the van and bumped elbows with another sentinel in congratulations. They reenacted busting down a door, laughing together. All at once, Ransom's fear from the previous night returned.

"Ransom, are you okay?" Teya asked. "You look pale."

"I'm fine," he replied. "Hey, maybe we should go get the kids."

Teya shook her head. "I don't want them seeing this and asking questions. Let's wait until the snatchers are gone. We still have half an hour before we need to pick them up, and right now I want some alone time with you."

Teya continued to talk, but her words blurred into the background. Ransom had to get out of there before Dragomir saw him. He pulled Teya away from the sentinels.

"Where are you going?" Teya asked.

Ransom grabbed her arm more firmly and was about to escort her to the far side of the plaza when Dragomir glanced in their direction.

Their eyes locked. A flicker of recognition played across

Dragomir's face. He smiled and started toward them.

"You just can't get enough of me, can you." Dragomir bellowed. His deep voice echoed across the plaza as he stormed toward Ransom.

Ransom heard Teya let out an audible gasp and watched her face turn pale. She took a step back as if getting ready to run.

Ransom was tempted to grab Teya and flee, but he knew Dragomir could probably outrun both of them. Besides, Ransom had learned as a kid that running from bullies never did any good. Fear inspired them to hunt you down more often.

"Come to watch real men work?" Dragomir mocked, stopping just a few feet in front of Ransom.

Ransom held his tongue, not wanting to inflame the situation.

"Nice to see you finally know when to keep your mouth shut," Dragomir smirked. He looked more closely at Teya, eyebrows rising as if he'd suddenly placed her in his memory. Then he laughed with sick delight. "This is too good. You know this one's married, right? Better stay away."

"She's my wife," Ransom said, eyes narrowing.

"Really?" Dragomir sounded incredulous and laughed even harder at the apparent absurdity. "Seems to me you and I already discussed your wife." He turned to Teya. "Why don't we finish what we started?"

"You touch me again, and you'll regret it."

Dragomir smiled. "I don't think your husband will rush to your aid. I've already bested him twice."

"What are you talking about?"

Dragomir looked at Ransom. "You haven't told her?"

Ransom's jaw clenched. He felt his world falling apart.

"This is why you need a man like me," Dragomir said, turning his attention back to Teya. "We've run into each other before. In fact, just to make the second beating stop, your husband gave me your family's conservation card. He practically begged me to take it."

Teya shot Ransom a look that demanded an explanation. Ransom just shook his head. He'd meant for her not to push it. Instead, she read it as a "no."

"I don't believe anything you've said," she retorted.

"Fine. I'll show you."

Dragomir whipped out his nightstick. Before Ransom could react, he struck Ransom behind his left knee. Ransom crumpled to the ground. Dragomir flipped him on his back, unzipped Ransom's jumpsuit down to his waist, and pulled it back. Ransom felt a warm breeze blow across his stomach, then heard Teya's gasp.

"This is what I did to him the last two times we met. If I ever see him again, I won't be so gentle." Dragomir stood and took a step toward Teya. "You enjoy being married to a liar?"

Teya didn't respond. Ransom couldn't tell what she was thinking. Apparently Dragomir couldn't either, so he chose only to wink at Teya. "As soon as you need some food for your family, let me know. I'll pay you hourly for a little personal attention."

Teya just stared at him.

"And if you don't come to me, I'll come to you," he said, an evil grin spreading across his face. "After all, I know where you live."

Lying on the ground, Ransom watched Dragomir walk back to the van. The sentinels who had observed the incident from afar bumped elbows with Dragomir and slapped him on the back before piling into the back of the van, laughing.

eleven

Ransom winced as Teya rubbed the last of the arnica ointment on his bruises. Neither had spoken since the incident with Dragomir on the plaza. It was as if both were waiting for the other to blink first. The voice of the narrator from a nature show drifted into the kitchen, describing the eating habits of blue whales. Ransom listened for the sounds of James and Warren, who were watching the show, a little surprised they hadn't come into the kitchen wanting to spend time with him.

Teya tossed the lotion bottle in the recycling bin and washed her hands. She turned, arms folded, and stared at Ransom. Her face was pale, and she looked as though she was about to cry.

"How's your knee?" she asked.

"A little sore, but it'll be fine."

"Were you ever going to mention the card?"

"Yeah, I was planning on doing it tonight after the kids were in bed."

"Why didn't you tell me as soon as you got home?"

"If I remember right, we had other things on our minds. Something about a pregnancy you forgot to mention."

Teya looked away at his reminder.

Ransom sighed. "Sweetie, I'm not trying to make you feel bad. . . . I'm sorry I said that. I was going to tell you. It just didn't seem right under the circumstances."

"What are we going to do about food? Tomorrow's the day the stores get most of their supplies. If we can't buy anything tomorrow, it may be another week before we can eat."

"We're not going to starve. I'll figure something out."

"We only have two or three days of food at the most," Teya said. "We're going to need something before that. At the very least, something to keep the kids' stomachs full."

"You too. There's no way you're going without food."

Teya picked up Ransom's shirt from the table and handed it to him. "Did that snatcher really give you those bruises?"

"Yeah. Except the first time we met, he didn't win. It was more like a draw."

"What are you doing fighting with a snatcher, anyway?"

Ransom told her about the incidents on the tram and at the bar. While he talked, Teya listened in silence.

"He wasn't afraid to get rough with Dr. Redgrave today at the clinic," Teya said when he was done. "For a moment, I thought he'd kill Geoffrey."

"Well, don't worry. I plan on staying as far away from him as possible. Hopefully our paths will never cross again."

"The woman on the tram—did you know her or something?"

Ransom shook his head. "I've never seen her before."

"So why'd you jump in?"

"He could have killed her baby. If someone were threatening James or Warren, and you couldn't help them, wouldn't you want someone—even a complete stranger—to step in and do something?"

"Yes," Teya said. "But I guess that's not what I'm asking. You've always seemed . . . I don't know . . . willing to rock the boat. There's the stuff you take from recycling sites, and that time you climbed the fence to pick peaches from the city orchards. Helping this woman just seems like more of the same."

"Is it a problem? All that stuff has helped us survive. It just doesn't sit right with me that someone can blatantly threaten the life of a baby and get away with it. A whole tram full of people, and no one stepped forward." Ransom stood and walked to the door of the balcony. A woman's laugh came from somewhere on the dark plaza below. "Sometimes I feel this whole city is on the brink of chaos. We live cramped together, stacked on top of one another like rats in a lab. We spend most of our weekends standing in line to buy half-rotten food. People treat each other like animals in a survival-of-the-fittest contest. Sometimes I wish we lived in one of those homes I recycle—one with more living space and a yard." He turned so he was looking at Teya. "Wouldn't it be nice to have an extra bedroom, a fruit tree or two, and maybe a little garden? There's a huge cherry tree at the house I'm taking down now. I don't think I've had a cherry since James was born. I want a giant orchard with enough peaches, cherries, and apples to feed our family and share with others. Doesn't that sound good to you?"

Teya shook her head. "You're dreaming about something we'll never have."

"Says who?"

"Things may have been like that for our grandparents, and maybe for part of our parents' lives, but look around you. The world's changed. We're not going back to how things were. At least, not anytime soon."

"I still think we could improve our family's situation."

"You're not talking about improving it. You're talking about transforming it in a way that's just not possible," Teya said. "Maybe you feel we're repressed because you're one of the few people who spends time outside the city walls. But it's like spending too much time watching those old movies on TV—the ones where everyone drives cars and has more food than they know what to do with. You watch too many of those, and your perception of reality gets warped."

"Even so, sometimes it feels like I'm running in circles. It doesn't matter how hard I work—our family's going to be stuck in this tiny apartment for the rest of our lives. Aside from raising the kids, what else can I accomplish?"

"What about your job? You work hard. You'll get promoted."

"Yeah, until number three's born." Ransom immediately regretted the comment, even before a pained look crossed Teya's face. "That's not what I meant," he said apologetically. "It's just that I don't want to be a recycler my entire life, or even one of the office managers. They might have a little more food and sweat a little less, but you can tell they're not any happier than the guys on the ground. I just feel like there has to be something else to life, but I don't know what. I have this feeling I should be doing something different, but deep down, I know I can't do it. Not here, anyway."

Teya moved toward Ransom and slid her arms around him. "I'm sorry you feel like that. I don't know how to make it better."

"You can't," he said. "Though it helps knowing you want to support me."

They were quiet for a minute, then James and Warren came running into the kitchen. "We want some water!" the boys cried in unison, thrusting their empty glasses toward Ransom.

He took their cups and pushed the button above the faucet, filling each glass with a burst of water. Handing them to the boys, he said, "That's all you're getting tonight. I don't want either of you wetting the bed."

James took a sip of water and put his glass on the counter. "Dad, come watch TV with us. They're showing big whales."

"Yeah," Warren said. "You can sit by us on the couch."

"I'll be there in a minute," Ransom answered, smiling. "I just need to talk to your mom a little bit more."

"But the show's almost over," James pleaded. "Besides, you didn't take us to the park like you promised."

The burden of guilt that came with the responsibilities of fatherhood seemed to press down upon Ransom. "

know. We'll do it soon, though. Maybe tomorrow."

James frowned as he usually did when he didn't get his way.

"Son, I'll be in to watch the rest of the show with you after I finish talking to Mom. I promise. And if you're good, maybe we can find another show to watch or something to read when it's over."

James eyed his father suspiciously. "Okay," he said with a trace of reluctance in his voice before heading down the hall.

"Okay," Warren said in the same tone as he hurried after his big brother.

"Those boys miss you," Teya said when they were out of sight.

"I wish I could spend more time with them. It just seems impossible sometimes."

Teya rested her head on Ransom's shoulder. "Were you able to salvage anything from work today?"

The lunch pail. Ransom had forgotten all about it. He told Teya about the gift from Dempsey and what he'd gathered from work. "There were a few things I could salvage. Outlets and wiring, mostly. They're a little old, but they should bring some money. I left the pail in my locker. I'll get up first thing so I can get it from work and take it to the Station."

Teya sighed. "Well, that's one thing that's gone right," she said as Ransom pulled her close.

"Our kids won't go hungry," Ransom said. "I won't let that happen. And you'll have that baby, I promise."

Teya laid her head on Ransom's chest. "Thank you," she said.

They stood like that for several minutes before Ransom went into the living room.

* * *

Ransom turned off the alarm clock seconds before it rang and eased himself out of bed. In the kitchen, he ate the last of the bread and a piece of cheese. Then he filled a canteen with water and, on a whim, grabbed last month's conservation card, putting both in his backpack. Ransom reached to the top of the cupboards, going on tiptoe and searching around until his fingers touched a jar containing change Teya had been saving over the last two years. As he put the jar in his backpack, he was a little surprised by how heavy it was. He realized he should tell Teya he was taking it, but in the end, he decided against it. He didn't know if he'd even use it—besides, he couldn't afford an argument right now. He had to get some food before the good stuff was gone.

Teya walked out of the bedroom as he was lacing up his boots. "Do you need to leave so early?"

"I want to get the first pick of stuff at the Station. I don't want to settle for leftovers."

"If you wait an hour, the boys will be up. Then we can all go together."

"The Station's no place for them," Ransom said. "Besides, I won't be gone long. Two hours, tops. And most of that will be riding the trams."

"It's Saturday. They're going to be disappointed when you're not here to make them breakfast."

"I know. Tell them I'll take them to the playground when I get back—or maybe even the park."

Teya nodded, disappointed but understanding, before leaning forward to give him a kiss. "Be careful," she said with a sigh as he walked out the door.

* * *

There was only a handful of people on the street at six in the morning—the calm before the Saturday shopping storm. A newspaper boy was hanging up the morning edition at the tram stop's news board. In preparation for the next day's parade, two city workers stood on ladders against the street lights, a banner in hand. As they shouted instructions across the street to each other, Ransom glanced at the banner: "New Earth Day 2065." He shook his head at the irony, wondering if anything in their tired old city was actually new.

The trams were just as empty as the sidewalks, and Ransom had his choice of twenty seats when he boarded. It was a rare pleasure he normally would have enjoyed, but he was so preoccupied, he didn't think much about it.

Getting off at 25th Street, he headed for the Recycling Center. Ransom didn't recognize the guard who looked over his ID and waved him through. He hadn't worked the weekend shift since he had started out as one of the guys on the conveyor belt, and he'd forgotten how quiet the place could get with the office doors dark and the squeak of his boots on the tile floor the only sound.

In the cargo bay, a skeleton crew unloaded one of the trucks that had come in the night before. Glad that they were distracted, Ransom hurried to his locker and was relieved to discover that his lunch pail was sitting at the bottom. He popped open the lid. All the contents were still there.

He turned to leave, bucket in hand, when the door to the cargo bay opened and Dempsey stepped through. Ransom squinted to make sure his eyes were working. Barring an emergency project, recycling crews never worked on weekends, and Dempsey had more than enough years on the job that he wouldn't be tasked with picking up garbage on Saturday.

Dempsey was halfway across the room when he noticed Ransom. He stopped, and they both stared awkwardly for a beat.

"Didn't expect to see you here," Ransom finally said.

"I could say the same for you."

Ransom held up the lunch pail. "I forgot this."

Dempsey nodded. "Oh, yeah. Don't want to forget that. I only had that one. You'd be on your own if you lost it too."

Awkward silence again. Ransom decided not to break it—maybe Dempsey would feel he needed to explain. Ransom had to admit his curiosity was at the brim.

"I had some free time and thought I'd give our truck a once-over. You know she's been having a hard time holding a charge lately."

"Need some help?"

"No. I'll be fine. Really. Thanks for asking, though."

Dempsey moved toward the trucks, keys in hand.

Ransom followed. "Where you going this early?"

"Nowhere. I'm just working on the truck."

"Well, the battery kit is sitting on the other side of the bay, and you're holding the keys like you're ready to leave. You don't need keys to check out the battery."

Dempsey spun around so he was facing Ransom. "I'll tell you what. How about you don't ask what I'm doing with the truck, and I don't ask for a peek inside your lunch pail."

Ransom held up his hands. "Hey, take it easy. I'm not here to bust you or anything. I just want to know which direction you're going."

Dempsey peered skeptically at Ransom, who smiled. "Just tell me which direction on the compass—no details."

Dempsey rolled his eyes. "West. I'm heading west."

"Perfect," Ransom said. "Can you drop me off at the Station?"

* * *

The Saturday morning shoppers were just starting to arrive

when Ransom climbed down from the truck. Wary of pickpockets, he took the backpack off his shoulder and carried it in his hands as he entered.

The Station was an old train depot at the end of 25th Street—one of the few remaining buildings left over from the pre–New Earth Day era. It had once been a busy train hub. Now the interior was divided up into a labyrinth of hundreds of booths that sold anything from watches to shoes to books. It was the most expensive place in the city to shop. It was also the only place you could buy items from other states brought in on the weekly supply train. It was a widely known secret that most of the sellers didn't make their money from their legal imports, but rather, from black market items.

A dozen large skylights had been cut into the roof, and the light cast sharp shadows on the booths, the vendors, and the crush of people. Ransom ignored the cries from vendors hawking their wares and quickly made his way to a small booth on the back row, slipping behind the dark green canvas walls. New and used shoes of various sizes and styles covered the table. Behind the table sat a squat man with slicked-back black hair, reading glasses, and a goatee. He was tipped back in his chair, reading a worn paperback. He looked over his glasses at Ransom.

"May I help you?"

Ransom gave the man a wary look. "Where's Evan?"

"He took the day off. Said he was getting ready to celebrate New Earth Day with his family. My name's Castor. And you are?"

"Ransom."

"Is there something I can help you with, Ransom? Shoes, perhaps?"

Ransom assessed the man. "No. I'm fine."

Castor put the book down and, in a low voice, said, "Perhaps I can interest you in something other than shoes?"

Ransom looked around at the nearby people and vendors.

"What do you need?" Castor prodded quietly.

"Food," Ransom said in the same low tone.

"How much?"

"Enough to feed a family of four for two weeks."

Castor looked up at Ransom. "That's a tall order. And an expensive one. What do you have to trade? There's an acute shortage of steel, and I could make you a good deal if you have some."

Ransom ignored Castor's question. Years of bargaining with people such as Castor had taught him it was better to force an opponent to reveal his hand first. "How much food do you have?"

"Not much, I'm afraid. The guards have been getting better at their searches. Two of the last three runs were seized. All I have right now are some ears of corn and some potatoes."

"That's it? Corn and potatoes? I can't feed my family on that for two weeks."

"Like I said, I'm a little low right now. Are you interested in them or not?"

Ransom looked into Castor's dark eyes to see if he was bluffing. The man had a good poker face—which could be a red flag in itself. Nevertheless, Ransom needed food, and he had to bargain somehow. It couldn't hurt to see what Castor had. "Show me what you got."

Castor pulled the table to the side and motioned for Ransom to come into the tent. "Let's try on some shoes," he said rather loudly, picking a worn pair of work boots from the table. "I think I have some that are just your size."

Ransom moved into the dim interior of the booth. The man handed Ransom the boots. "Try these on. I'll be back in a moment."

Ransom set the boots on the cracked tile floor. He watched a few people walk by and glance at the shoes before moving on their way.

A minute later, Castor emerged from the back with a bulging burlap sack in his hands. He set it on the floor next to Ransom. "Have a seat," he said.

Ransom sat on the chair and put his backpack on the floor. Castor pulled an ear from the bag and handed it to Ransom. Ransom began to peel back the husk.

"Do it out of sight, or someone will see."

Ransom lowered the corn into the shadows. He removed the silk and pulled the husk halfway down. The kernels were large but pale. It was hard to tell in the dim light whether the corn was actually ripe. He moved to hold it up so he could get a better look, but Castor slapped his hand down. "What are you trying to do? Start a food riot?"

Ransom glared at Castor and opened the ear of corn, examining it as best he could. A few of the kernels were gone from the top—perhaps eaten by a worm. Aside from that, the cob looked good and full.

"Let me see a potato," he said.

Castor reached into the bag and pulled out a large potato. "Idaho's best." He grinned.

"This came all the way from Idaho?"

"Of course not. We'd never get them across the border. This one came from a farm near Mead, I think."

Ransom examined the potato. Its skin was covered in a fine layer of dirt and had an earthy smell to it. It felt a little soft, but otherwise it looked okay.

Ransom looked at the burlap bag on the floor. "How much food do you have in there?"

"A dozen ears of corn and ten pounds of potatoes."

"I need more."

"This is all I can give you at the moment. If you need more, come back on Monday. Evan should be back then, and we might have more food in stock."

"How much do you want for it?"

The man looked at Ransom's backpack. "What's in the pack?"

"Outlets and wiring, mostly."

"Let me see."

Ransom pulled the lunch pail from his backpack. Castor sat on the floor of the tent and examined the contents.

"This is good, but not enough for all the food," Castor said. "I could give you more if you had some steel or even some copper."

"That's all I have right now."

"Well, this is worth half the food in the bag."

"I have some money," Ransom offered.

"Money's not good for much. I want something else. Something of real value."

"I don't have anything else—at least, not now."

Castor hesitated. "Then I'll have to take the money, I guess. Gotta help a brother, right? I'll need fifteen dollars, along with the contents of your bucket."

Ransom had to stop the rage from erupting inside of him. "Fifteen dollars? That's highway robbery. I could buy all this food for a fifth of that at any store near my house."

"Then why don't you?"

Ransom pursed his lips. He was lost without his card. His gut told him to leave and try the seller on the south end of town. But it was a long ride out, and there was no guarantee they'd have more food or that their prices would be any more reasonable. Besides, if he had to come back, Castor would just jack up the price even more. What his family needed was some good food. It was expensive, but Ransom could always recoup some losses once he recycled a house with something more valuable in it.

"Look," Castor interrupted the silence, "if you want, I'd be happy to set this aside if you have something else to give me. Like I said, for ten pounds of steel, I could give you all this food and more."

Ransom grabbed Castor by the collar. "I thought you didn't have any more than this!"

Castor held up his hands. "I meant if I had some food later—you could try back Monday when another shipment is scheduled to arrive. Honestly, this is all I have right now, and these are the prices I have to charge to run this business. If the business stays strong, I can get access to better food. You know how it works."

Ransom let go of Castor and looked at the bag. "Ten dollars for the bag."

"Twelve," Castor countered.

Ransom looked back at the bag of food. "Fine," he grunted. He reached into his bag and pulled out the jar of coins.

"You're going to pay me in coins? What do I look like? A bank?"

"If you can't take the time to count out some coins, then I'll take my business to someone who will."

"No, no, no. I'll take them."

Castor changed his tune a little too quickly, and Ransom regretted not threatening to go elsewhere earlier. He might have gotten a better deal if he had. Usually a good negotiator, Ransom knew the pressure to feed his family was putting him off his game.

While Castor counted the money, Ransom returned the jar to the backpack. It felt only half as heavy as it had that morning, and he dreaded the prospect of telling Teya how much he'd paid for a few days' worth of food.

But he also felt relieved at solving at least one problem—even if it was just a temporary fix. It was buying him some time, if nothing else.

Castor pulled a small leather bag from under his shirt and slid the coins from the table into the bag. "It was a pleasure doing business with you, Ransom. Come back anytime."

Ransom turned and headed out of the booth and down the crowded aisles, then walked up 25th Street to the tram stop. As he boarded the first tram that arrived, he glanced at the stop's clock tower. Barring a power failure, he'd be home earlier than he thought. He smiled as he envisioned the kids eating a good meal and enjoying a day at the park.

As the tram started forward, his thoughts were interrupted as someone tapped him on the shoulder. He turned around and found himself face-to-face with the woman whose baby he'd saved.

"Hello, Ransom," she said.

twelve

How do you know my name?" Ransom asked.

"I know a lot of things about you," the woman said. "For instance, I know you work as a recycler, have two darling little boys, and a beautiful wife who works at the Paul Ehrlich Clinic."

Ransom felt panic rising inside him as the woman rattled off each fact about his life. As though everyone on the tram could hear what she was saying, he glanced over his shoulder as she spoke. At the far end of a car, a uniformed police officer stood holding the handrail. The cop was looking their direction, but he didn't appear to be focusing on them.

"Who are you?" Ransom hissed.

"My name is Esperanza." She extended her hand.

Ransom looked at her hand, then back up at her face. Her right eye was blackened and swollen halfway shut. "What do you want?"

"To thank you for saving my baby."

"You're welcome," Ransom said. "Next time, try not to bring her on a crowded tram—especially when there are snatchers on board."

"Lesson learned," she said. "As you can see, I'm baby-free."

"That gold cross you're wearing isn't doing you any favors either."

There was a noise from the back of the car, and Ransom glanced in the direction of the cop.

"Nervous?" Esperanza asked.

"Yeah, well, I can't say I really want to be seen with you. Saving your baby might have worked out for you, but it hasn't been so great for me."

"I'd like to make up for some of the problems you've experienced since we last met. Why don't you come with me and meet some of my friends? There'll be food to eat and good conversation."

"Thanks, but I've got more pressing matters."

"Tell you what—you come with me, and I'll give you enough food to feed your family until you get a new card."

Ransom's head snapped back so he could look at Esperanza. "What did you say?"

"I know your family is short on food. I'd like to help rectify that problem. Think of it as a more formal thank you."

Fear tripled inside him, and Ransom felt violated that she knew so much about his family's situation. "Who told you?"

Esperanza just smiled.

Ransom took a step toward her and spoke in a low voice. "I haven't told anyone about my family's needs. How do you know?"

"Are you interested in feeding your family or not?" Esperanza brushed aside the question. "I'm only asking for twenty minutes of your time."

"Actually, our needs have been met for a few days," Ransom said, readjusting the backpack on his shoulder.

"Been to the Station this morning?"

Ransom shrugged, not wanting to share any more information than necessary. "I've been shopping."

"Let me guess. Corn and potatoes?"

Ransom's eyes narrowed. Before he could ask her if she had been following him, the tram came to a sudden stop. He tightened his grip on the handrail to avoid falling into Esperanza. Somewhere on the opposite end of the tram, a woman let out a little scream of surprise. He turned and saw the cop helping the woman to her feet.

Ransom moved past Esperanza and looked over the conductor's shoulder out the front window. The next stop was thirty yards down the road. The conductor pushed a few buttons on his panel, then shrugged and leaned back, hands behind his head.

Power failure, Ransom thought. He looked at Esperanza and decided he was through with her. Moving to the closest doors, he gave them three strong pushes and had them open. He hurried across the street to the sidewalk. Out of the corner of his eye, he saw Esperanza right on his heels. He stopped and spun around so they were standing inches apart. "I'm glad you and your baby are okay, but that doesn't give you the right to delve into my life and learn everything about my family. Leave me alone."

"I don't mean to seem threatening. I just wanted to know more about a man who would save my baby at his own risk—so I could best decide how to help him in return."

"Help me? With what?"

"Your family's food situation, for starters."

"I told you, I already took care of it," Ransom said, motioning again to the bag over his shoulder. He turned to leave.

"Ransom, wait." Esperanza grabbed his arm. "I'm here to help. Please, let me explain myself. If you don't want anything to do with me when I'm done, I'll walk down the street, and you'll never see me again."

Ransom stared at her. He didn't know if he should run or listen. "Who are you?"

"I can't discuss that. Not in public, anyway. There's a place about a mile from here where I'll answer every question you have. Just come with me, meet some friends of mine, and listen to what we have to say. At the end, no matter what you think, we'll give you enough food to feed your family for a month. I promise. And it will be fresh food too—not that rotten stuff in your backpack."

"What's wrong with the food I have?"

"I told you—rotten."

"I don't believe you."

"Take off your backpack."

"No."

"Just hand me a potato. A small one, if you want. I'll prove it to you."

Ransom stared angrily at her for several moments, then finally gave in, hoping she would leave him alone. He took the pack from his shoulder, unzipped the top halfway, then reached into the back and handed a potato to Esperanza.

Before he could react, Esperanza threw it on the sidewalk as hard as she could. It hit the sidewalk with a loud smack and broke in half. The inside of the potato was black and rotten. The smell of decay wafted up from it. Ransom put his hand over his nose and took a step back.

Esperanza squatted next to the potato and opened it up more. "It's rotting from the inside out," she explained. "Probably some kind of blight. The potato fields by Mead and Fairwood all have it. The farmers can't stop it from spreading. It's just a matter of time before it makes its way throughout the state. My guess is no one's going to be eating potato soup until they get this thing under control."

Ransom took another step back to get away from the smell.

"Now look at the corn," Esperanza instructed.

Ransom rummaged through his bag and pulled out a large ear. He peeled back the husk. Small, white worms moved over the pale yellow kernels. They had already eaten about half the ear. He looked up at Esperanza, questioning.

"They can't stop the worms either. They're going to be lucky to get half the yield they got last year. A lot of people will go hungry this winter."

Her words put a heavy feeling in Ransom's stomach. If what Esperanza said was true, it really would be a long winter. He remembered when a bug had killed off most of the wheat crop five years previous. Bread had been scarce and even nonexistent at times. When it could be found, it was prohibitively expensive. The potatoes and corn posed a bigger problem. They were the staples that got people through the winter. If there was a shortage, people could starve. It was the downside of living in a sustainable community. If enough of something wasn't produced, you had to go without.

"What do you say, Ransom?" Esperanza said, interrupting his thoughts.

Ransom looked her up and down. The food was tempting, but there was something about the woman that made him nervous. He didn't like that she knew so much about him and his family. There was a good chance she was a Green State terrorist or some other rogue group that used food as a ruse to get others to join them. He had helped her once, and as a result his family had suffered. Going with her wherever she wanted to take him was just asking for more trouble. His family needed food, but he was sure there were other ways to feed them.

Suddenly he caught a whiff of freshly baked bread from the bakery two doors down. He had an idea.

He turned to Esperanza. "I appreciate the offer, but I can take care of my family." Before she could protest, Ransom turned and hurried down the street.

* * *

Fifteen minutes later, Ransom reached Topper's Bakery, sweating and out of breath. He looked over his shoulder to make sure Esperanza hadn't followed him. There was no sign of her.

He turned and counted a few people lined up in front of the store. The door was obviously locked. He felt relieved he'd made it to the bakery before it opened. Things would be a lot easier this way. Moving past the crowd at the door, Ransom ignored the yellowed sign that read CLOSED and knocked on the glass.

"No cutting in line," said a brusque female voice.

Ransom turned and looked at the middle-aged woman, who held a shopping bag in each hand.

"I've been here for an hour. You need to get in the back of the line."

"I know the owner," Ransom said. "I need to talk to him."

"Doesn't matter. I was here first."

Ransom cupped his hands around his eyes and pressed them to the glass. Inside was a small waiting area, surrounded on three sides by glass counters. It had been years since he'd last seen the place, and he found himself surprised at how little it had changed. The far shelf was full of fresh bread. Each oval loaf was about eighteen inches long and delicious-looking. Steam from the bread fogged the glass, hiding the loaves on the top shelf.

Ransom again knocked loudly on the door, keeping his face pressed to the glass. No one came out from the kitchen. He waited for a moment, then pounded a third time.

A young man with blond hair, dark eyes, and a Roman nose walked in from the kitchen. His yellow T-shirt was covered with a white apron and a thin layer of flour. He wiped more flour from his hands as he mouthed the words, "We're closed."

Ransom knocked again, hard enough to make the door shake.

The young man walked around the counter to the door, and Ransom took a step back, but the young man only pointed to the closed sign, held up five fingers, and mouthed the words, "Five minutes."

"I need to speak to Chauncey," Ransom said loudly.

The kid paused and unlocked the door, opening it an inch. Ransom noticed he kept most of his body behind the door, probably afraid Ransom might try to force his way in. "We don't open for five more minutes," he said, sounding annoyed. "If you want bread, you can wait in line. From the looks of things, you'll be the first one."

The woman standing behind Ransom said something about being first. They both ignored her.

"Is your father here, Harden?" Ransom asked.

"Excuse me?"

"I'm looking for your dad."

"What do you want with him?"

"I'm an old friend. I used to work for him—back when you were a kid. I just want to talk with him for a minute."

"How do you know my name?"

"I told you. I worked for your dad. Last time I saw you, your father had you taking out trash and running the cash register."

"What's your name?"

"Ransom. Ransom Lawe."

Harden looked Ransom up and down. "You look sort of familiar."

"Is it possible to speak to your dad?"

Harden shook his head. "He's not in today—not doing well."

"I'm sorry to hear that. Is he at home? I'd like to drop by and talk to him for a minute or two."

Harden looked down at the floor. "He's not home. He's at the Roosevelt hospital. He's been there about two weeks now."

"Is it serious?"

"Yeah. Colon cancer. He's over sixty, so they won't do anything to treat it other than pain meds."

Ransom bit his lower lip. "I'm sorry, Harden. I didn't know."

"It's okay. I mean, we all have to go sometime. Besides, his death will mean more food and water for everyone else, right?" His eyes looked down at the ground. "At least, that's what the doctors say."

"How long does he have?"

"A month. Maybe two."

"I'm so sorry. Is there anything I can do for you?" Ransom said, not sure how he could help. Once you were put in the hospital, there wasn't much anyone could do.

"No. I'm fine." A female voice called Harden's name from inside the bakery. He took his eyes from the ground and looked at Ransom. "Look, I have to get the last loaves ready. The power went out for a few minutes this morning and screwed everything up. We're running behind. I'll open up in a minute, and you can have first pick."

Harden went to close the door, but Ransom jammed his foot in the space.

"What are you doing? Move your foot."

"I'd like to help you get things ready. If you're running behind, you could use an extra hand."

They stood staring at each other for a long moment. Finally, Harden held the door open, a bell ringing above it as he did.

It was twenty degrees hotter inside the bakery. Ransom hurried in and locked the door behind him. The middle-aged woman stuck her thumb between her middle and index finger and yelled something at him. Behind the door Ransom couldn't hear her, but he could read her gesture just fine.

He followed Harden back to the kitchen. A girl with a narrow face was pulling the last of the loaves from the oven. She paused when she saw Ransom, then continued her work.

Harden stopped in front of eight wooden crates filled with loaves of bread.

"Delivery boys should have been here twenty minutes ago to get these out," he sighed. "The old man used to talk about you. If you're the Ransom who used to help out here, you were by far the best delivery boy he ever had. Better than me, and a lot better than the two I have working for me now. When I finally got old enough to deliver, he used to compare me to you all the time."

"I enjoyed working for your father. He always treated me well and was honest with the customers. I never saw him cheat anyone or cut ingredients just so he could make more money. That was rare, even back then. It smells like you're upholding his values."

"I try," Harden said. He paused as if recalling a pleasant memory, then he picked up a box and handed it to Ransom. "Put these on top of one of the empty glass cases. If those boys aren't here in a minute, I'll pay you to deliver them."

Ransom spent the next few minutes stacking the boxes on the counter. As he lifted the last one in place, there was a knock at the door. Ransom looked up and saw two teenage boys with long, unkempt brown hair and brown eyes. They wore wrinkled T-shirts and dirty blue jeans. Both had bags under their eyes and were obviously brothers.

"You're late," Harden said as he opened the door.

The taller boy shrugged and motioned with his head to the bike leaning against the bakery window. "I got a flat."

Harden shook his head and motioned to the crates of bread. "Get these out as fast as you can. One crate per store today."

"Only one?" asked the younger boy.

"I only make as much bread as I have flour. And don't short the store on their loaves—each box has twenty. I have your pay and a fresh loaf for both of you when you get back—providing the stores don't call and complain about missing bread."

The boys looked at each other, shrugged their shoulders, grabbed a crate, and carried it to their bikes.

Ransom watched as they put the crates in metal holders that went over the front and back of each wheel. They came back for a second crate each, then a third. Soon four bread crates were loaded on each bike, and the boys pedaled down the street.

Harden stood in the entrance of the bakery to watch the boys, but the crowd moved forward. He had to apologize for running late and shut the door again. Then he hurried back to the counter and retrieved a loaf of bread from the shelf. He set it in front of Ransom but put his hand over it before Ransom could touch it.

"Sorry, but I can only give you one loaf," he said. "My flour ration was cut last week, so I'm only able to make half of what we usually make."

"One loaf's fine," Ransom said, gratefully.

"And look, I won't charge you for it, but I do need to punch your conservation card."

Ransom opened his wallet and pulled out the old conservation card, handing it to Harden.

Picking up a punch from the counter, Harden was about to use it when he stopped and took a closer look. "This one's expired," Harden said. "I need your current card."

"This one still has a spot for bread," Ransom said casually.

Harden's eyes narrowed. "Look. I need to punch a valid one. It's the law. You know that."

The heavy feeling in Ransom's stomach returned. He looked down at the bread and thought about how much his family needed it. He thought about grabbing the bread and running out the door. It wasn't as though Harden could stop him. The problem was that Harden already knew his name. If he called the police and filed a complaint, they'd be at Ransom's apartment that afternoon. The penalty was a reduction in rations for the next month. His family couldn't afford that.

"I don't have a current one," Ransom said with a sigh. "Some guy beat me up in an alley the other night and took it."

"Then I can't give you the bread, Ransom. I'm sorry."

"Come on, Harden. Your father would make an exception. I saw him do it all the time."

"Times change. The city would shut down this bakery for a week if they learned I gave you a loaf without punching your card. My sister and I are barely keeping up with my dad in the hospital."

"I'm not going to tell anyone."

"I can't take that chance. Now look, I've got to open the store. Those people waiting have more places to shop. I can't hold them up."

"Harden, I owe your father a lot. He gave me a job when things were scarce. I'd never do anything to hurt his business. I swear I won't say anything to anyone."

"I can't. Just get me a current card—beat up some other guy and take his. I don't care where it comes from."

"I have two kids at home. They're hungry."

"Everyone's kids are hungry." Harden let out a deep breath before continuing. "Making less bread than we used to, I can barely afford to stay open. A week's closure for illegal food sales would take food out of my family's mouths. Just don't take this personally."

Ransom looked down at the loaf of bread. He decided to give pleading one more try. He was about to open his mouth when the door to the bakery opened.

Harden swore. "How'd they open the door?"

Ransom turned around and saw a crowd surging into the bakery. Esperanza was at the front of the pack. She hurried to the counter and stood next to Ransom.

"Hey, no cutting!" the middle-aged woman cried. "I was here first!"

"I'm with him," Esperanza said, glancing at Ransom. She reached into her back pocket and pulled out a conservation card. She walked to the counter and slid it across with some money.

"Two loaves, please," she said. "One for me and one for him."

Harden just stared at the card.

"The law says nothing about using your card on another's behalf," Esperanza prodded. "Punch my card and give Ransom one of the loaves. I'll take one for myself."

Harden shrugged, took the card, and made two punches.

"Thank you." Esperanza laid some coins on the counter, then turned and headed for the door. The middle-aged woman treated Esperanza to one of her more expressive hand gestures.

Ransom picked up his loaf of bread. It was still warm. He nodded to Harden and pushed his way through the now-crowded waiting area.

Esperanza was standing just outside the door. She broke off the end of her bread and popped a piece in her mouth. "There's nothing like fresh bread, wouldn't you agree?"

Ransom just shook his head. "We're even now, okay?"

Esperanza swallowed. "Why did you come to my aid on the tram the other day?"

The question caught Ransom off guard. He thought back to the tram and his anger at the sentinel's behavior. "It doesn't matter why I did it," he finally said.

"Yes, it does," Esperanza replied. "A car packed full of people, and only one of them cares to help a child whose life is in danger. That's the kind of person who deserves my help."

"The bread is thanks enough." He turned and started down the sidewalk.

Esperanza called quietly after him, "Your wife's pregnant."

Ransom stopped cold. He turned and strode back angrily. "What did you say?"

"Are you finally ready to listen?" she asked pleasantly. She reached into her front pocket and produced one of the pink cards Ransom had taken from the baby board at the Census Bureau.

Ransom's heart pounded in his chest. "How did you get that?"

As he spoke, a woman hurried past with a full shopping bag in her hand, distracting Esperanza. Ransom lunged for the card, but she gracefully moved her arm and took a quick step to the side.

"Put that away," he hissed, his eyes darting around to the people standing in nearby food lines.

"Why? It isn't illegal to carry this around."

"It makes people suspicious."

"And if you have nothing to hide, it wouldn't matter if you had a whole stack of them, would it?" She slipped the card into her pocket. "You know where the Columbia Repair Shop is?"

Ransom nodded. It was located on the 'Vard about a half mile south of his apartment.

"I have a solution for your growing problem."

"What if I don't like your solution?"

"You're free to go. And you can still take all the food I promised you."

Ransom looked down at the loaf of bread in his hands and thought about Esperanza's offer. Bread was a start, but it wasn't enough to feed his family for two weeks. He'd give her twenty minutes and take her food. If it worked out, he'd be rid of her forever.

"Okay," he finally said.

Esperanza smiled. "Follow me."

thirteen

Teya stood on the balcony, watching a flock of magpies jump around the branches of a cottonwood tree. Since her balcony faced west, it was covered in the morning's shade—the perfect temperature for a T-shirt, shorts, and bare feet. She glanced at the clock in the kitchen and thought that Ransom should be at the Station about now. At least, she hoped he was. With the trams, it was impossible to know exactly how long it would take to get across town.

Teya was about to go inside and check on James and Warren when she heard the balcony door above hers creak open, followed by the sound of someone walking on broken glass. She took a step back, surprised anyone was home. There was silence for a moment, then the sound of a broom sweeping. Every few moments, someone dumped shards into a metal bucket.

A man cleared his throat from inside the apartment above. "You should be wearing gloves. You'll cut yourself."

"I'll be careful." The second voice was deeper and came from directly above her. There was a sad, hopeless quality to the reply, as if the man was struggling to control his emotions.

A heavy silence followed, and Teya realized she was intruding. She debated going inside, but, in the end, she felt she had to know what had happened.

The man in the apartment stepped closer to the balcony door, his voice carrying more clearly now. "I'm going to head out to the repair shops. If I can find the parts, I should be able to have your front door fixed by the end of the day."

"You don't have to do that. I'll take care of it."

More silence. Teya imagined the two men looking awkwardly at each other, trying to find the right words.

"You don't have to stay by yourself again tonight. You're welcome to stay with us until—"

"I need my kids to feel like this is a safe place." The deep voice cracked at the end of the sentence, making the last words barely audible.

"I'm still amazed you kept them here last night. How'd they do?"

"I had to stay with them in their room. They were terrified. They kept asking what happened to Mom."

"What'd you tell them?"

"That she'd be home soon."

Glass was dumped in the bucket again.

"You look as though you could use some sleep." The friend's tone was concerned but not pushy.

Teya's neighbor sighed. "I'm fine. I just want to clean this mess and straighten up the place."

"What about this door? You need me to find some plywood to cover the broken window?"

"I know where I can find some scrap wood until we can afford some glass. I have time . . . we won't have to worry about the cold until October."

"I know someone who works at the Recycling Center. Maybe he can find a piece of glass in those houses he's always tearing down."

"Really?"

"Yeah. He's a neighbor. Name's Dempsey. I'll see if he can hook you—"

The phone rang in the apartment above, and footsteps hurried across the balcony, freezing the conversation. Teya could hear only mumbling for a minute, then silence as heavy feet returned to the balcony above.

"What'd they say?"

The previous quiet continued for a moment, then her neighbor's deep voice filled the small space above. "They'll wait until Wednesday morning."

"That long? Really? I thought it was something they did rather . . . uh . . . quickly."

"Five days. She told me that accidents happen, and they're willing to give me some time to buy a credit."

The other man swore. "Five days might be longer than you'd expect, but it's impossible to find another credit that fast."

"That's what I said."

"What are you going to do?"

The silence made Teya sick to her stomach. She had caused this suffering.

There was a choking sound above. Finally, an "I don't know" broke through.

Teya couldn't stay on the balcony any longer. She ran to the kitchen and quietly shut the door, then put her face in her hands and slid down the balcony door until she was sitting on the floor. The sobs were big and heavy. She cried for what she thought Eloise was experiencing in the Infirmary, for the broken-hearted husband and father on the balcony above, and for their two terrified children. She wished she had told Ransom about her pregnancy earlier. The guilt was crushing and seemed to get heavier by the minute.

"Are you all right, Mom?"

Teya looked up. James was leaning against the kitchen doorframe. His mouth was curled into a frown, and a worry line appeared across his forehead. Teya wiped her eyes with the back of her hand and stood up. "Mommy's fine," she said.

"Why are you crying?" James asked, enough skepticism in his voice that she had to face the fact that he was growing up and wasn't so naïve anymore.

"I'm just very tired," she said. "I'll be okay." She stood, grabbed a rag from a drawer next to the sink, and wiped her eyes and nose with it.

As she rinsed it off, James said, "Your hair looks crazy."

Teya touched her hair. It felt big and puffy. She realized she had forgotten to do anything to it after showering. "Mommy's not done getting ready for the day," she explained.

"Is Dad here?"

"No, he's gone."

"Did he go to work?"

"No, he's out getting food."

"I'm hungry."

"I know. I am too."

"Can I eat breakfast?"

"Not right now. Let's wait until your dad comes home. He might have something really good for you to eat."

James frowned. "But I'm hungry now."

Teya grabbed a salt cracker from the box on the cabinet and offered it to James. "I'll tell you what," she said. "Eat this and go play with your toys. If your dad doesn't come home soon, then I'll make you breakfast."

James's face brightened. He grabbed the cracker and scampered off to the living room.

Teya returned to the bathroom and looked in the mirror at her red, puffy eyes. She washed her face, brushed her hair, and pulled it into a ponytail so she'd look halfway presentable. While she worked, she was unable to get her mind off Eloise. She imagined the woman sitting in a cell with her knees against her chest, waiting for the doctors to come and get her. Teya tried to focus her mind on Ransom and the food he was getting, but her thoughts kept drifting back to Eloise and her shattered family. Finally she took a deep breath, knowing she had to move on with her duties so the boys wouldn't suffer.

Forty-five minutes later, she knew she couldn't wait any longer to fix breakfast. She opened the last can of peaches and put half a peach in each boys' bowl.

On a normal Saturday, she'd be out standing in line at one of the stores, splitting up the weekly shopping list with Ransom. It felt weird to be home. It also made her feel helpless. She didn't like the idea of depending on smugglers to feed her family.

She glanced at the clock. Ransom should have been home by now. After checking on the boys to make sure they were okay, she slowly opened the door to the balcony. A warm breeze moved through the kitchen, and she paused to listen for any sounds from above. Not hearing anything, she stepped onto the balcony, hoping to see Ransom hurrying across the plaza with a backpack full of food.

Nothing.

Teya bit her lower lip. Before her mind could focus on the fear, a soft knock at the door startled her out of her reverie. She hurried to the door and looked through the peephole. A wrinkled face under a mop of white hair looked back at her.

Oh, no, Teya thought. *I forgot about Eve.*

Eve was an elderly neighbor who lived in apartment 501. She had also been Ransom's fifth-grade teacher. When they'd moved into their apartment and found her living on the same floor, Ransom had been delighted to meet her again. At seventy-five, Eve did her best to be self-reliant, but she'd broken her leg in a fall the previous year, and that had started the tradition of Ransom knocking on her door and doing her shopping every Saturday morning.

Teya took a step back from the door and tried to put on her best smile. "Eve, please come in."

"I'm sorry to bother you. I thought maybe you already left to go shopping."

"Actually, we haven't started," Teya said as she took Eve's arm. "Ransom had to run to work this morning, and I'm just feeding the boys."

She glanced into the kitchen as she guided Eve to the couch. James was standing on his chair, trying to fish more peaches out of the can with a spoon.

"I don't mean to intrude," Eve apologized. "I didn't know Ransom had to work."

"Don't worry about it," Teya said. "I'd be happy to take the boys and do the shopping for you."

"No, I can go. You've been so kind to do all the shopping for me since the accident."

"Don't be ridiculous. I can do it."

"Then at least let me watch the boys. They'll get bored and hot standing in line."

Teya wanted to protest, but she knew Eve was right. She was also glad for the opportunity to get out of the apartment and do something instead of waiting for Ransom to come home.

"Sounds like a great trade. Where's your list?"

Eve held out a shaking hand with a canvas bag and a small change purse. "The card, list, and money are all in the purse. I hope it's enough. Sometimes the city changes prices without telling you. If it costs more, let me know, and I'll pay you back."

Teya looked through the list. It seemed like the same list Eve gave them every week. She should be able to get everything at one store if the shelves weren't too picked over.

"I haven't read about any price increases," Teya said reassuringly. "I'm sure you have enough."

She hurried to the kitchen to tell the boys that Eve was going to watch them and to behave but stopped short when she saw that the can of peaches had been knocked over. Two peach halves lay upside down in a puddle of syrup that spread over most of the table and was dripping onto the floor. James and Warren both stood on chairs with guilty looks on their faces. Even though the mess was the last thing Teya needed right now, she fought the urge to yell.

"Eve's in the living room," she said. "Maybe she'll read you a story."

The boys pushed their chairs away from the table and ran to the living room.

Teya placed the peaches back in the can and scooped as much syrup into the boys' bowls as possible with her hands before wiping up the rest with a rag.

Teya moved a chair to the sink and stood on it to grab some change from her savings jar—in case the prices for something on Eve's list had changed. Even though the city was supposed to give residents a thirty-day notice before increasing the price of food, it rarely happened. After feeling around for a second, she was surprised not to find the jar. Thinking she wasn't looking in the right spot, she stood on the counter and peered over the top of the cabinets. The change jar was gone. A circle in the dust marked the spot where she usually put it.

A wave of panic washed over her. Had someone broken into the apartment and stolen it? She remembered putting change in it after their shopping trip last Saturday. Maybe Ransom grabbed it on his way out the door and hadn't told her. That wouldn't have been like him, but maybe he was in a hurry or simply forgot. She debated whether to do the shopping with just the money Eve had given her and decided she at least would buy what items the money would cover.

Teya put on her shoes and looked into the living room. Eve was reading from a worn children's book. The boys sat on either side in rapt attention.

"I'll be back as soon as I can," Teya called as she headed out the door.

* * *

Even though the stores had been open for half an hour, long lines still stretched out their doors, and Teya wondered if there was going to be anything left by the time she was allowed inside.

She decided to stand in line at Safeway. It wasn't where she normally did her grocery shopping, but she knew Eve preferred it. Since it was Eve's list and money, Teya might as well see what the store had to offer. Slowly, the line moved forward as people came out of the store with bags of food. Teya watched them enviously, wishing she could bring just one of those bags home to her family.

A tram stopped, and she watched eight passengers get off. Ransom wasn't among them, but moments later, as the tram pulled away, she happened to glance across the street and was surprised to see him. He was heading in the opposite direction of their apartment, seemingly with a petite Hispanic woman. The woman said something, and Ransom gave her a half-smile. Teya's eyes narrowed at the way the stranger looked at her husband. It was more than a friendly exchange between passersby or even work associates. There seemed to be an almost secretive quality to it. She watched Ransom tear a piece of bread from a loaf in his hands and continue down the street with the woman. Why in the world wasn't he bringing it home to the family? And where was he going?

Teya looked down at her pregnant belly, a sick clenching

starting up in her stomach. From the moment she had fallen in love with Ransom, she had never given a second thought to the possibility he'd be unfaithful. He had always been a good husband and father—he worked hard and spent pretty much all his free time with her and the boys. He'd never, ever given her a reason to think that he wasn't in love with her or that he'd consider another woman on the side. But how would she know? She'd heard about lots of men who led double lives. But lately he'd been angrier, less cautious—unsettled.

Maybe the baby was the reason. Ransom had verbally supported her in having it, but he'd hardly seemed enthusiastic about it. It might have been shock, or perhaps it was something else entirely. Maybe the fact that she'd hidden it from him for months had caused a chasm between them. It wasn't beyond the realm of possibility. She had friends whose husbands and boyfriends had cheated on them for less. And Ransom would have no problem getting a divorce and custody of the boys once he proved she'd concealed a third pregnancy. Then he could settle down with another woman and not have to deal with the mess they were in now.

Teya's heart was beating erratically, and she forced herself to calm down—for the baby's sake, if nothing else. She told herself Ransom would never do anything like that. She knew him too well—at least, she thought she did. Maybe the woman was a food smuggler and Ransom was working with her.

She watched until they were nearly out of sight before stepping out of her grocery line. Shadowing them from the opposite side of the street, she walked slowly until they stopped at the Columbia Repair Shop. She was familiar with the shop since she had visited it on several occasions to have the clinic's stereo repaired.

Teya watched the woman knock on the door, then motion for Ransom to enter. Her husband hesitated before walking into the shop. Right before the door closed, Teya caught a brief glimpse of the man who had opened it. He was also Hispanic, thin, and wore a green shirt.

She waited for several minutes to see if Ransom would come back out, but the shop windows remained dark. She couldn't imagine why they'd had to knock on the door, unless the shop was a front for a brothel. This idea was even more repulsive than the first, and she had to sit down on the curb and breathe deeply in order not to vomit. But after a few minutes of mulling it over, she decided to cross the street. All she had to do was walk past and look in the windows. The sidewalks were crowded enough that she wouldn't be noticed.

She waited for two donkey carts to pass, then headed across the street at an angle so she ended up in front of the butcher shop to the right. She slowly walked past the repair shop. The glare from the sun made it impossible to see inside the windows. She walked a quarter block, then stopped and headed back. This time she paused and feigned interest in some wiring placed in the window. The shop behind was dark and empty. Just to make sure, she cupped her hands around her eyes and pressed them against the glass. Aside from shelves full of old tools and parts, the place was deserted.

Teya took a step back from the door and looked around for a place to wait. The butcher shop and cobbler shop on the other side didn't offer much of a cover, and there was no telling what direction Ransom would head when he left. Across the street was a café. Six wooden tables, each with four matching chairs, sat under faded red-white-and-blue-striped umbrellas on the sidewalk.

She crossed the street again and sat on a chair directly across from where Ransom had disappeared. It didn't matter what the truth was, she was going to face it. She was tired of running scared. Leaning forward and resting her forearms on her legs, Teya waited.

fourteen

Ransom followed Esperanza to the doors of the Columbia Repair Shop. Of all the repair shops in town, this was the only one that didn't buy parts from recyclers—interesting, as it was also known for having the most quality and diversity of parts. When he needed to fix or replace something at home, this was the store Ransom usually tried first.

Esperanza knocked on the door, and while they waited, Ransom looked at the products in the display windows. There were high-quality electrical outlets, some wiring, light bulbs, a faucet, and various plumbing supplies. It was a nice-enough display to let the discerning eye know the place sold quality parts but nothing valuable enough to entice those willing to pull down the black iron bars in front of the window.

The door was finally opened by a thin man with a green shirt. He unlocked the iron gate in front of the door before motioning them inside, and he pulled it off smoothly, without gaining further attention from the crowds.

"Where have you been?" he said to Esperanza once they were in. "The baby's hungry. She's been crying for half an hour."

"Ransom here was a little stubborn," Esperanza replied, encouraging Ransom to come deeper into the room.

Ransom looked the man up and down. He was around five foot seven and couldn't have weighed more than a hundred and twenty pounds. He had suspicious brown eyes and a scar across his left cheek.

Ransom looked away, feigning interest in his surroundings. Along with the usual fare, old computers, stereos, and other electronic devices that he didn't recognize were on display in a glass case near the cash register. Most of the items were in better shape than the stuff from the buildings he recycled.

The man slid the gate back into place and locked the door behind them.

"Where do you get all this stuff?" Ransom asked.

"Follow me," Esperanza said, ignoring the question and walking behind the counter.

Ransom waited for the thin man to move. He didn't. Ransom shrugged and followed Esperanza through the door along the back wall and down a short, narrow hall. One door at the end had a thin beam of yellow light coming from the crack along the bottom. He could just make out the faint cries of a baby.

He followed Esperanza through the door. Unlike the front of the store, the back room was neat and orderly. A workbench ran along the far wall, where a radio and a television lay open, their electronic guts spilled open, along with a stack of circuit boards and various other components. A floor lamp was placed in each corner of the room, sending light up to the ceiling and down the sandstone-colored walls. Ransom wondered how they could afford to keep the place so well lit.

Against one of the walls was a crib where a red-faced baby lay crying. Esperanza grabbed a pink blanket from the crib, spread it over her chest, and started unbuttoning her shirt under the blanket. Ransom looked away until he could hear the baby sucking. When he looked back up, she was sitting on the couch, a blanket covering the left half of her body and the baby.

In the left corner of the room sat a Samoan in front of two television monitors. A gray glow from the screens washed over his face. His black hair was cut so short, Ransom could see his scalp. He turned toward Ransom and crossed his arms, eyeing him suspiciously.

What's with these guys? Ransom wondered. *They're the ones running a shady operation—not me.*

In the middle of the room sat a plush green couch and two leather chairs. On a coffee table between them lay a bowl of peaches, slices of fresh bread, and a jar of what looked like strawberry jam. A ceiling fan spun noiselessly on the ceiling overhead. He wondered again how they were able to afford the power.

She motioned to one of the leather chairs. "Have a seat, Ransom."

"Wait," the Samoan said. He walked over to Ransom and began to frisk him.

"Hey!" Ransom said, taking a step back. "Get your hands off me."

"Is that really necessary?" Esperanza sighed.

"Yeah, it is. Either he consents to a search or he goes back outside. We can't afford to have him back here without knowing if he's broadcasting."

Broadcasting? Ransom thought. *What are they talking about?*

"Please let Nauleo search you," Esperanza said "He's in charge of our security around here, and, as you can tell, he's a little paranoid. But it makes him good at his job."

Ransom gritted his teeth but held out his arms. Nauleo ran his hands over Ransom's arms, legs, and waist, then nodded to Esperanza. "He's clean."

The man returned to his chair in front of the television monitors, and Ransom's gaze followed. His irritation turned to surprise when he noticed the grainy black-and-white images on the screen.

"I thought surveillance cameras were illegal," he said. He felt himself getting increasingly nervous. If these people were terrorists, not only would he be charged with associating with them, but the cameras might bring up violation of privacy charges.

"Sit down and I'll answer your questions," Esperanza said. There was the click of a door shutting behind him. Ransom whirled around and saw the thin man standing by the door with his hands behind his back.

"I'd rather stand," Ransom said, keeping his eyes on the seemingly perturbed Hispanic who had let them in.

"There's no need to guard the door, Jorge," Esperanza said. "Why don't you get our guest some water?"

Jorge grunted and retrieved four glass bottles of water from a refrigerator. Before he shut the door, Ransom saw that it was stocked with water, milk, and juice, along with apricots, peaches, and tomatoes. He hadn't seen a refrigerator that full since childhood. And the six-foot-tall refrigerator itself was something he'd only seen in the oldest homes he recycled. Even without the fridge, the environmental and transportation taxes made bottled water extremely expensive, and these people had tons of it. With whom, exactly, was he dealing?

He looked back at the door to the room. If necessary, he could leave without anyone stopping him. Then he remembered that Jorge had locked the front door. He was trapped.

He noticed a rectangular device mounted in the corner above the door. It had some sort of lens protruding from the middle of it.

"What's that?" Ransom asked.

"Another camera," Esperanza said.

Ransom looked over at the screens where Nauleo was sitting. "Why is he watching us?"

"He's not," Esperanza said, dismissing the question with a wave of her hand.

She picked up her bottle and gave it to Jorge. He twisted off the cap and handed it back without looking at her.

Esperanza took a long drink, then leaned forward and set the bottle on the table. "Sure you don't want some? You won't find colder water anywhere in the city." When Ransom shook his head, she continued. "Jorge is my husband. Gabby here is our daughter. She's our first." She took a peach from the table with her free hand. "Help yourself to some food. You've already had some bread, but the peaches are perfect."

Ransom's stomach growled, but he refused again, not wanting to obligate himself in any way. "Who are you—I mean, really?" he asked.

Jorge said something to Esperanza in Spanish. Ransom didn't understand what he said, but based on the tone of the man's voice and his angry gestures, it was obvious he wasn't thrilled with Ransom's presence.

Esperanza interrupted him. "If you're going to say something, Jorge, make sure Ransom can understand you."

Jorge looked at the floor, as if embarrassed at being cut off.

Ransom smiled. It was obvious who wore the pants in this relationship.

"You'll have to pardon my husband," Esperanza said. "He's a
little overprotective, but he's often right. He didn't want me going
out on the tram the day you saved Gabby, but I went anyway. I'm
going to listen to him a bit more, but not right now. I feel we can
trust you."

Esperanza reached into her pocket and retrieved the three
pink cards Ransom had left in his book. "You can have these
back," she said.

"How'd you get inside my locker?" Ransom asked.

"I want to preface my comments by telling you we have absolutely no intention of turning in you or your wife. The courage
you displayed on the tram the other day was appreciated. As a
result of your actions, we'd like to help you out your third."

"Do you have a credit you're willing to sell?"

Esperanza shook her head. "No. But we can offer you something better."

"Yeah? What?"

"A new life for you and your family. A chance to start over."

"Start over? What do you mean?"

"How would you like to live somewhere else?"

"Like Seattle?"

Esperanza smiled. "I mean a real city. One where you can
have a home of your own. One like you started recycling last
week—only bigger—with a yard. And a garden, if you want. A
place where you and your wife can have as many children as you
see fit without having to worry about neighbors or the Census
Bureau butting into your bedroom."

Ransom paused before answering, trying to remember everything he'd ever heard about such places. There were rumors of
small, independent communities in Wyoming, Idaho, Montana, the
Dakotas, and western Nebraska. Though they were technically part
of the United States, these areas governed themselves and refused to
acknowledge the authority of the federal government. They were
called the Green States because military maps shaded those areas
green. No one was quite sure how these areas operated. Discussing

the Green States was discouraged in classrooms and books. But some thought the states themselves were broken into regions controlled by tribes. Others said there was a governor over each territory who ruled with an iron fist. The news boards had to acknowledge their existence but referred to these areas only as "terrorist enclaves" and occasionally carried stories about the government making a raid into those areas. It was the general conclusion that resources didn't exist to bring this area of the country back in line, as once had been done with the states of Mississippi, Alabama, Georgia, and the Florida panhandle, who'd declared independence around twenty-five years previous. The Green States were too rough, vast, and hostile. So long as those groups stayed in their area and left everyone else alone, the federal government mostly didn't bother with them. If caught outside their boundaries, however, Green State citizens were immediately imprisoned.

Finally, Ransom spoke. "Cities like that don't exist—not in this country, anyway."

"They do," Esperanza countered. "I was born and raised in one. I still have a home there. They've been around longer than people think."

"Then why are you living here?"

Esperanza smiled. "My husband's work required me to temporarily relocate. But Gabby's birth has caused a change in plans. We're heading back next week. We want you and your family to come with us."

"Who are you associated with? Freedom Liberation? Sons of Jefferson? John Gaulters?" Ransom asked, trying to name off as many terrorist groups as he could.

"Does it matter?

Ransom let out a laugh. "Does it matter? Yes, it matters. You want my family to leave their home and join with a bunch of fanatics in some forsaken part of the country?"

"We're not extremists," Jorge said, speaking for the first time since Esperanza had reprimanded him. "We're just people who want to live our lives in peace."

"That's what the government calls you."

"The government calls anyone who doesn't agree with its

policies a terrorist group," Jorge replied. "It gives its citizens an enemy to fear in order to maintain power."

"Well, you're not just trying to live in peace. Last time I looked, you and people like you raid the houses I'm supposed to recycle. Your actions make the lives of everyone in this city that much harder. There's a limited amount of resources as it is, and when you steal them, there's even less to go around. As far as I'm concerned, you're not only a bunch of terrorists, you're a den of thieves too."

"We're not thieves!" Jorge yelled. "You're the ones who steal from the dead!"

"Enough, Jorge!" Esperanza interrupted.

Ransom saw the baby jump under the blanket. A moment later, she started to cry. Esperanza hushed her, then repositioned the blanket up on her other shoulder, shifting the baby.

"We don't do anything to make life here any harder than it already is," Esperanza said. "In fact, we help the people in this town and others by stocking stores like this so people can get the things they have no other way of getting. The government doesn't share what it takes, my friend. Its goal is keeping the citizens as helpless as sheep."

"If you're in any way connected to an illegal group, I don't want anything to do with you," Ransom said firmly. "You're the last people I want my family to hang around."

"Ransom, don't be hypocritical. You don't follow every rule either. Are you willing to lose your unborn child over misplaced loyalty?"

Ransom angrily scooped the pink cards from the table into his hand. He was confused. "I thought you said you could help me. If you've got a credit to sell, then I'll be happy to work something out. But I didn't come here to be recruited."

He stood to leave.

"Wait, don't go," Esperanza said. "We need people like you and your family."

"And what makes us so perfect? The unplanned pregnancy?"

"No. The fact that you stood up to a sentinel on the tram. The fact that you and your wife are trying to figure out a way to have the baby she's carrying. You helped a complete stranger. You don't take the easy way out of your problems. That's a rarity these days—but the courage you're exhibiting is exactly what we're looking for. You're the kind of people who can make our community stronger."

Ransom let out a short laugh. "You think we're being courageous? Oh, please. We're running scared. Courage would be publicly announcing our pregnancy to the world and then fighting the sentinels as they busted in our door to haul my wife away."

"Don't confuse courage with stupidity. It's not smart to take on the Census Bureau directly. They have more people and more resources. They'll beat you every time. But if you can find a credit before they learn about the pregnancy, then you've beaten them. If you have to pick your battles, then fight ones you know you can win, as you're doing. And what you're doing takes real courage, Ransom, because if word gets out before you find a credit, your whole family is going to suffer. Not only will you lose the baby, but you and Teya could be locked up for concealing the pregnancy. If that happens, your two boys will be doled out for someone else to raise, and you may never get custody of them again. You're showing amazing courage to risk so much for your freedom to choose. But there's a smarter way to preserve that freedom. That's what we can offer."

"I'd rather take my chances here than head off to the wilderness," Ransom argued, the ground seeming less firm beneath him. "Besides, you didn't mention what would happen to my family if the government found out I was talking to known terrorists. That's about the only thing that will give you more prison time than hiding a pregnancy."

"I told you this was a mistake!" Jorge erupted. He stood and pointed a thin finger at Ransom. "You'd better not say anything about us, or we'll turn your wife in!"

Ransom took a step toward Jorge. "If someone turns in my wife, I'll make the government a deal and reveal everything I know about you. That might even get me a government waiver for the kid."

There was a creak from a chair, and Ransom felt something

whiz by his ear and hit the wall. A small object clattered to the ground. It was a metal dart like the one Esperanza had used to take down the sentinel on the tram.

Ransom whirled around and saw Nauleo coming toward him with something that looked like a two-foot metal straw in his hand. He was quickly trying to shove another object into it. Suddenly, Jorge leaped across the room and threw all his weight into Ransom. Caught off balance, Ransom tumbled to the floor, but he managed to grab Jorge by the shoulders, using his body as a shield in case more darts were coming.

"Get off him!" Esperanza screamed. "Nauleo, put the gun away!"

"But he's—"

"I said, put it away!"

Ransom looked over Jorge's shoulder. He watched Esperanza snatch the blowgun from Nauleo with her free hand. She gave it a quick shake, and the dart gun collapsed into a two-inch tube. Esperanza shoved the tube into her front pocket. Then she pulled Gabby from her breast and set her in the crib.

The blanket still over her shoulder, she buttoned up her shirt and turned her attention to Ransom and Jorge. "Get up, both of you."

Jorge gave Ransom a long, hard look, then struggled to his feet. "He's going to tell the authorities about us."

"No, he's not," Esperanza said. "He's not going to say a word to anyone about us or this conversation."

"You can't be sure of that," Jorge protested.

"Ransom has just as much at stake as we do. Turning on each other isn't going to help anyone."

Ransom got back on his feet. "Don't worry. I'm not going to tell anyone about your secret meeting room," Ransom said sarcastically as he looked back at Jorge. "As your wife said, we've both got too much on the line." He reached down and picked up the metal dart that had nearly hit him. "What is this?" he asked, looking at Esperanza for an answer.

"A sleeping dart. It contains just enough fast-acting sedative to knock someone out for ten minutes. We like using them.

They're quieter than guns—and they aren't lethal, which is the more important distinction."

"I've never seen one before," he said.

"If you come with us, I'll show you how to use one."

Ransom shook his head, looking down in frustration. "For the last time, no."

"You could also learn how to drive."

Ransom glanced up. "What did you say?"

"You could learn how to drive a car. As soon as next month. Jorge could start teaching you. Beats waiting for one of the current recycler drivers to die or retire, doesn't it? Maybe you could even have a car of your own. Admit it—that's something you've always wanted."

Ransom felt fear rising inside him. There were only a handful of people with whom he had shared his desire to drive. "How do you know all this?"

"I told you. We do our homework before we bring someone in. You're a good person, Ransom. You and your family deserve a better life than you have."

"There's nothing wrong with my life now."

"You're like a caged animal."

The words stopped him cold. He'd felt the same recently, but he forced himself to retort, "I'm not living in a cage."

"Really? What do you call these walls that surround the city?"

"The only way to protect the environment."

Esperanza threw back her head and let out a laugh. "Oh, yeah. That's right, I forgot. We're still this close to burning the place up." Suddenly her tone became more serious. "Have you ever asked yourself why people don't drive cars anymore?"

Ransom rolled his eyes. "Everyone knows the answer to that."

"I'm not from here, remember? Enlighten me."

"Too much carbon dioxide in the air. We used too much oil. The planet was getting hotter. But people didn't care. They still drove. So when I was a kid, cars were banned—end of story. Why are you even asking this? Don't they teach that wherever it is you're from?"

"I learned that story too. Only we didn't learn it in an

environmental science class like you. It was part of our history and political science curriculum." Esperanza paused and looked at Ransom as if she expected him to ask a follow-up question. He said nothing.

"Think about it," Esperanza pressed. "Through most of the world's history, traveling great distances was difficult and expensive. It was rare for people to live or travel more than twenty miles from the place of their birth. Then cars were invented, and suddenly people had the freedom to go wherever they wanted, whenever they wanted. Traveling long distances was suddenly something just about anyone could afford. People spread out. If they wanted to visit a part of the country they'd never seen or to visit a family member a thousand miles away, all they had to do was get in the car and drive. Cars became synonymous with freedom. Of course, people took it for granted after a generation or two. For them, cars became a birthright—driving was just something you did when you turned sixteen.

"Years ago, it used to be a three- to four-hour drive to Seattle from here. Now it's a four or five day journey by horse. Weeks if you walk. And you can't just leave town. You need a travel permit. You have to tell the government where you're going and how long you'll be gone. Now, to get across town, you're forced to take public transportation. You run on some bureaucrat's schedule instead of your own. Cars were banned because they offer too much freedom.

"And it's not just cars," she said, waving her free hand in the air. "You're rationed on how much power you can use. Go over the limit, and they shut it off the next month. Same with the water you drink and the food you eat. To top it off, they tell you how many children you can have. Does that sound like you're free? You're not. You're dependent on the graciousness of your captors to stay alive."

"Did you listen to a word you just said?" Ransom said. "You're crazy. You're all crazy. You don't like the way the world is, so you have to spin some wild conspiracy theory to live with it. Tell me, if this city is like a cage, why do you even bother with it? Why not live where you're free to drive cars and have dozens of children?"

"Because we care about other people, Ransom. We want to find those who want out. That's why we run this shop. It's a great way to find people who are dissatisfied with their lives and looking for something more, a different way to live. And when we find the right people, we ask them to come with us. That's why we're here talking to you right now."

"I'm not going to join your army."

"We're not raising an army. We're starting over with those who believe in freedom. Don't tell me you haven't been questioning the two-child limit since you found out about your wife's pregnancy. You wouldn't be the first. Most people don't think twice about it until they find themselves in the exact position you're in. Then they have to choose whether to make a new life for themselves or go along with the status quo. It's something you're struggling with right now."

Ransom said nothing for a long moment. Finally he spoke. "Yes, I've been struggling with the law, but the current system isn't as rigid as you think. It allows for flexibility. All I have to do is find a credit, and Teya can have her baby. It's going to take a lot of effort, but it's something I can do. Talking to you is taking me away from what I should be doing—and that's taking care of my family."

"We're offering you a chance to start over, Ransom. A place where you can raise your family however you want."

Ransom shook his head and tossed the dart to Esperanza. She caught it and set it on the table. "I'm sorry. I can't. At least not with you."

"This is a one-time offer," Esperanza said. "It won't be extended again."

He shoved the three pink cards into his pocket and picked up the key ring that had fallen from Jorge's pocket. "I'll let myself out," he said as he opened the door to the hallway.

No one tried to stop him.

fifteen

Ransom tossed the keys inside the repair shop and slammed the door. He didn't bother with the metal gate.

As he hurried down the street, he felt anger building inside him. He was angry at himself for buying rotten food and even angrier that he had let a bunch of terrorists get his hopes up. Halfway down the block, he realized he'd left behind his loaf of bread. Worst of all, he felt like a failure as a husband and father. He was going home without food for his family and had no idea how he was going to get some. For a brief moment, he entertained the idea of going back and asking Esperanza for the food she had promised him. But he couldn't do it. Part of it was pride, but the bigger reason was that he didn't want to be in their debt. Giving him food in his time of need wasn't an act of charity. It was their way of sinking their claws into him. In a couple of weeks or months, they'd come back and ask him to do a small favor for them. He couldn't get himself involved in whatever they were doing—in the end, it would come back to bite him.

He shoved his hands into his pockets and felt the three baby cards. A small bit of hope cut through his discouragement. Even if he couldn't come home with food, maybe he'd have good news to offer. At the entrance to a service alley, he turned his back to the sidewalk and quickly looked at the address on each card. One address was about half a mile from where he stood. The other two were on the south side of town. He could hit all three places and be back home in a couple of hours.

He looked around for a phone to call Teya and spotted one a

few blocks down. At the phone, he reached into his backpack and pulled out a nickel from the jar. He put the nickel in, picked up the handset, and waited for the dial tone.

Nothing.

He hung up and inserted another nickel before noticing that the handset felt lighter than usual. Ransom unscrewed the earpiece. The receiver was missing. He unscrewed the mouthpiece. The transmitter was gone too. He threw the handset against the phone in frustration and started down the street in the opposite direction, hoping he'd find a phone on his way.

As he rounded a corner, his eye caught sight of a familiar image, and he squinted, sure he must be wrong.

Then Teya startled, realizing he'd seen her.

They stared at each other for a moment, then Ransom started across the street. "What are you doing here?" he asked.

"I was out shopping for Eve," Teya said, her voice icy.

Ransom grimaced. "I forgot about her."

He could tell Teya was mad, but before he could apologize, she said, "Yeah, well, that makes two of us."

Ransom looked around. "Where are the boys?"

"They're with Eve. She's watching them."

"Are you sure that's a good idea? After the accident, I don't know if she can keep up with them."

"She taught school for thirty years—including putting up with you. I think she'll be fine."

Ransom found himself smiling for the first time that day. A witty comeback was on the tip of his tongue when he noticed Teya wasn't smiling back. A dark feeling returned to the pit of his stomach. He waited for Teya to say something, but she just stared at him. "So, why are you shopping all the way out here?" Ransom finally prodded. "Was there something different on her list this week?"

"No. It was the same list she usually gives us."

"Did she want you to go to a different store?" He wished Teya would just say what was on her mind.

"What are you doing, Ransom? Where's the food you were going to bring home?"

He fought back the urge to lash out at Teya for her criticism after his morning's efforts and failures, but he remembered that she was under stress too.

Taking several calming breaths, he finally spoke—only a little defensively. "What's wrong?"

"Who was that woman you were with?" Teya said quietly.

"What woman?" Ransom's voice rose, all efforts at calm extinguished.

"The pretty Hispanic woman I saw you walking down the street with half an hour ago. Who is she?"

A wave of relief rushed over him. Teya must have seen the two of them on their way to the repair shop. He was glad there was a simple explanation.

"That was the woman whose baby I saved on the tram. Her name's Esperanza."

"What were you doing with her?"

"We ran into each other as I was leaving the Station."

"You weren't anywhere near the Station when I saw you."

"Teya, calm down. We went to Topper's. She bought some bread for me—us."

"Why is she buying you bread?" From the look Teya gave him, Ransom could tell she wasn't putting the pieces together, and she hadn't calmed down.

Ransom spent the next few minutes telling her about going to the Station and running into Esperanza, how she knew about the rotten food and what happened at the bread store. He was careful about the details of what went on in the shop—he knew she would be upset he'd fought again. As he talked, he could see her relax a little, but a new kind of tension filled in for every bit that left.

"Terrorists? They're terrorists?" Teya said, her voice teeming with worry. "If anyone else saw you two together, you could be arrested. What were you thinking?"

"I got out of there as fast as I could, Teya," Ransom said, trying to keep as much emotion out of his voice as possible. "At least they gave me back the three cards they took from my locker. I thought I'd go and follow up on the leads."

"They know I'm pregnant?" Teya said, her eyes growing large. "They could turn us in."

"But they won't," Ransom said. "They know if they say anything, I'll turn them in."

They stood there, looking at each other for several moments. Finally, Teya looked at the empty shopping bag in her hands. "What about food? Our cupboards are empty."

Ransom shook his backpack. "I still have some of that money you've been saving." He hoped she wouldn't ask how much money he'd lost that morning.

He watched Teya bite her lower lip. It was obvious she was calculating how long they could live on the coins they had left. He knew it wasn't the time to burden her with the details of how few they actually had.

"I think Mona could help," she finally said.

"Mona? No. She's the last person I want involved in this problem."

"But she might have some food."

Ransom shook his head. "Involving her is simply asking for trouble. She'll start nosing around as to why we don't have a card, and who knows where that will lead. We can't afford to let her investigate. If she found out you're pregnant—"

"People lose their cards all the time. I'm not worried about her putting the pieces together and coming up with a pregnancy."

Ransom sighed. "I'll tell you what. If I can't find anything by tonight, then you call Mona and see if she can help."

Teya nodded. "Agreed."

Ransom looked at the clock over the tram stop. "You need to shop for Eve and get back to the boys. Who knows what they're doing to that poor old woman."

He bent down and gave Teya a kiss as the next tram pulled up. He had to run to catch it, and he barely had time to make eye contact with Teya before it snatched him away.

sixteen

Teya hurried up the stairs with a bag of groceries under her arm. By the time she'd returned to Safeway, most of the shelves were empty. She had stopped at two other nearby stores, but was only able to get about half the things on Eve's shopping list.

When she returned home, she found the boys stacking up their wooden blocks into a big tower. Eve was sitting on the couch, encouraging them in her soft voice to make it higher. Warren noticed their mother and jumped up to greet her, sending the stack of blocks crashing to the floor.

After Teya hugged the boys, she told them to wait while she walked Eve back to her apartment. On her way, she apologized for not being able to find everything on the list. If Eve was disappointed, she hid it well. She took the bag and thanked Teya for doing the shopping.

Back in the apartment, Teya herded the boys to the bathroom, took off their pajamas, and gave them each two icy blasts of cold water from the shower. Then she dressed them and led them down to the playground.

"I'm hungry," Warren said as they headed down the stairs.

"I know, sweetie," Teya answered. "Your dad should be back with food soon."

"I hope he comes back with a lot," Warren said.

"Me too," Teya said. "Me too."

James and Warren had never gone to bed hungry, and Teya wasn't about to let that happen now. She hadn't told Ransom this, but she'd been adamant about turning to Mona at some point because her sister was storing food in her apartment. Teya doubted anyone else knew about it.

She had found it by accident over a year ago while helping her sister clean. She'd opened a wardrobe in a spare room and found it full of bottled and canned food—a couple of months' worth at the average daily consumption rate. She had shut the door and gone about her business without saying a word to anyone, not even Mona.

Hoarding more than two weeks' worth of food was illegal. If word got out about her sister's stash, she'd lose her job. Even if the authorities didn't find out, it made her apartment a prime target for thieves. If Teya had to, she could throw herself on Mona's mercy, or—worst case scenario—request food in exchange for not turning Mona in. She couldn't imagine betraying her sister like that, or that her sister wouldn't freely offer, but she had an option to keep them all alive, either way.

✳ ✳ ✳

Surprisingly, the play area was unoccupied, and the boys didn't have to wait for a turn on the swings. In glee, the boys let out a cheer and ran toward the playground. Teya stood behind Warren on the swing, pulled him back, and gave him a gentle push. Then she did the same for James. Both boys squealed in delight as they swung back and forth.

Usually, she encouraged them to kick their legs and swing on their own. But she was too tired to do that today. After several minutes, she got lost in the rhythm of pushing them, and her eyes wandered. She saw Eve walking across the plaza, the grocery bag tucked neatly under her arm.

Teya took a deep breath to stop from crying. It was her fault Eve had to head out in the heat of the day to find food. It seemed like everyone she came in contact with lately was worse off for knowing her.

"Mom, we're done swinging," James said, breaking into her swirling thoughts. Teya stopped the swings, and the boys hurried to the corner of the playground where they each found a stick.

Teya sat on a bench near the boys and watched them digging

in the hard black soil. A moment later, a young girl walked out of the apartment complex and headed toward the playground. Her long brown hair was uncombed and shooting out in different directions. There was something familiar about her, but Teya couldn't place it. Then the girl looked directly at Teya, and her heart skipped a beat—it was Eloise's daughter. What was her name? Teya thought back to her conversation with Eloise at the clinic. Chloe. That was it.

Now that she could see her up close, the girl clearly took after her mother, only without the ghost-white skin. The child sat on the swing but didn't move. Instead, she kept her hands folded in her lap, eyes on the ground.

Teya glanced at the boys. Satisfied they were playing nicely with each other, she sat on the swing next to Chloe's. "Do your parents know you're down here?" Teya asked gently, worried about the child.

The girl glanced up at Teya momentarily, then dropped her eyes again. "I'm not supposed to talk to strangers," she said, turning her head and looking across the plaza.

"I know your mom. Her name is Eloise—I live in the apartment below yours."

"My mom's in jail," the girl said. "Men wearing black came and took her away."

Chloe's words tore at Teya's heart. The guilt she kept trying to put aside came flooding back. She blinked back the tears, looking up to stem the flow. "I'm sorry to hear that. Where's your dad?"

"He's helping my brother sleep. Chance couldn't sleep at all last night—Dad had to hug him the whole time. They're both sleeping now."

"Maybe you should go back to your apartment. Your dad might worry when he wakes up and realizes you're not home. I'm sure he'll let you come back down later."

Chloe looked up at her balcony as if to see whether her father had noticed she was missing. Teya followed her gaze. The balcony was empty. Chloe shook her head. "I don't like being up there. I keep thinking someone's going to come and take my daddy away. I want to stay with my aunt and uncle. I feel safer there."

Teya didn't know what to say. Her throat tightened, and she turned her head so Chloe couldn't see her emotion. She wiped a tear with the back of her hand and waited to speak until she'd regained her composure.

"I still think you should let your dad know where you are," she prodded, holding out her hand toward Chloe. "Why don't you let me take you to your apartment? Maybe we can ask your dad if you can come down and play with my boys."

Chloe looked over at James and Warren. "No. I'm okay."

From somewhere above them, a man called Chloe's name. Both Teya and Chloe looked up. A man stood on the balcony of her apartment, looking down at them. Teya couldn't get a good look at the man, but she could hear the worry in his voice as he called out to his daughter. "Chloe! Don't move! I'm coming down!"

Teya immediately recognized the deep voice as the one she had overheard on the balcony that morning.

Chloe's father ran back inside the apartment.

"That's my dad," Chloe said.

A minute later he was out of the building's entrance, wearing holey jeans and a stained T-shirt. His straight brown hair ran past his shoulders, unkempt like his daughter's, his eyes red and puffy. Teya couldn't tell if it was from crying, lack of sleep, or both.

"Chloe!" he yelled. He ran to his daughter and picked her up off the swing. "How many times have I told you not to leave the apartment without telling me?"

"I don't like it there," Chloe whined. "I want to stay with Aunt Marita."

"We're staying at our house for now. I told you we have to stay together and wait for Mom." The man gave his daughter a hug and wiped his eyes with his fingers.

"She wasn't gone long. She just came out a moment ago," Teya reassured him.

He gave Teya a suspicious look.

"She's nice, Daddy," Chloe said. "She wanted to take me back to you."

The man glanced at Teya, then put Chloe down to shake Teya's hand. "I'm Owen. I'm sorry if my daughter was bothering you. The last twenty-four hours have been hard on our family. I should have kept a closer eye on her."

"Your daughter was fine. I was actually more worried about you, once you realized she was gone. I have two boys of my own. It's just a matter of time before the oldest learns how to unfasten the dead bolt."

Owen smiled and, for the first time since he'd come running down the stairs, seemed to relax.

"Come on," he said to Chloe, holding out his hand. "Let's get upstairs before your brother wakes up."

"I don't want to go," Chloe pouted. She sat on the swing and folded her arms.

Owen knelt in front of his daughter. "They're not coming back. I promise. You're safe there."

"I want to go to Aunt Marita's."

"Your aunt will be over later. You can see her then."

"But I want to go there now!"

"Right now you need to be inside the apartment with me where you'll be safe. I can't have you running around outside."

"Maybe I can stay with her," Chloe said hopefully, pointing to Teya. "She lives right below us."

Teya felt her heart skip a beat. She shouldn't have told Chloe who she was. She looked up at Owen—his head cocked to one side, giving her a quizzical look.

"Is that true?" Owen asked. "Do you live right below us?"

Teya could feel her heart pounding in her chest. "Yes," she said, her voice just above a whisper.

With one quick motion, Owen picked up Chloe and took a step back. "Stay away from my daughter!" The anger and fury in his voice took Teya by surprise. "I don't want you anywhere near my family!" he yelled. "Chloe, I don't ever want you to go near this woman again. She's the reason your mom was taken away."

Chloe looked at Teya with confusion.

Teya opened her mouth, but the man continued his tirade. "Yeah, I talked with my wife last night. She mentioned that the woman who tested her the second time lived in the apartment below us. So don't sit there and act all innocent, like you don't know what I'm talking about. You and everyone else at that clinic are responsible for what my family's gone through. If anything happens to her or her baby, the blood will be on your hands. Go back to the office and tell your doctor that. You'll all pay for what you've put my family through!"

He spun around with Chloe in his arms and headed back toward the building.

"I don't want to go back!" Chloe screamed, trying to wriggle her thin body out of her father's grasp. "I don't want to go home! I don't want the men in black to get me!"

"You'll be okay. I'll protect you," Owen said as they entered the building. The door slammed behind them, and there was only silence in its wake.

Teya stood in shock. She'd seen the husbands or boyfriends of patients come to the clinic before and similarly berate the staff, but she'd never taken it personally. It was all part of the job. In this case, every word Owen slung at her went straight to her heart.

Suddenly she noticed a handful of people on the plaza, bags of food and other supplies in their arms, who'd stopped to watch the commotion. Several people in the surrounding buildings were standing on their balconies looking down at her.

The guilt Teya had struggled to control all morning reached a breaking point. She grabbed James and Warren by their arms. They seemed afraid to go with her. Ignoring their howls of protest, she carried them both up the stairs and into the apartment. Once inside, she turned, wanting to lash out at them for making her escape even more humiliating, but when she saw their tear-stained faces, she ran to her bedroom and slammed the door behind her instead. The boys followed her.

"What's wrong, Mommy?" James begged, his voice coming from the crack between the door and the floor.

The sadness in his voice pierced Teya more than anything else that day. She felt like a horrible mother. She wished she had never switched those tests. Facing the sentinels seemed better than enduring her current crisis.

The sobbing from James and Warren intensified, and Teya put her hands over her ears to block out their cries.

It didn't work.

She flung open the door and carried the boys to their room.

"Play with your toys!" She knew she was going to regret yelling at them, but she was too worried and scared that Owen might act on his rage and try to do something. She wished Ransom was home to keep her and the boys safe.

"But I'm hungry," Warren whimpered.

"Why are you mad at us?" James added, his lip trembling.

Teya shut their door, knowing they couldn't open it, then ran to the living room. She fell on the couch and cried until her head hurt and the tears wouldn't come anymore.

She lay there for what seemed like hours until she heard the sound of the front door opening and closing. Her heart skipped a beat as she thought of Eloise's husband coming to take revenge on her and the children. She clambered up from the couch just as a tall figure walked into the living room.

Teya let out a scream.

"Teya."

It was Ransom's voice. She looked up at her husband and started crying again, this time from relief.

"What's wrong?" he asked. He pulled her close and ran his fingers over her hair soothingly.

Teya could smell his sweat. Usually the smell was something she didn't like, but now she found it comforting.

She leaned into him and wrapped her arms around him. She didn't feel like talking—at least right now. If she opened her mouth, she wouldn't be able to control herself. She knew he'd probably assume it was just the stress of the day, so she'd let him think that for a while. Instead, she just held him tight until her heart stopped racing.

"Where are the boys?" Ransom asked.

The boys. Teya hurried down the hall and stepped into the bedroom. Both boys were curled in fetal positions on top of their beds, sleeping.

"Have they eaten anything since this morning?" Ransom asked, following.

Teya shook her head. "Did you find any food?"

"A little," Ransom said. He took the backpack off his shoulder and showed her. "It's not much, but it should be enough for dinner and breakfast tomorrow. The boys won't have to go to the parade hungry."

He opened the backpack and put a bag of apples and several packages of dried noodles on the table. "I stopped at a parts buyer I use occasionally and traded the rest of the money for this. It's not much, but at least it will keep our stomachs full another day."

Teya put away the noodles and apples, glad to be able to give the boys something to eat when they woke up. "Did you have any luck with the cards?"

"No." Ransom sighed, his voice tired and sounding defeated. "The first person changed her mind and had a baby. The second one had moved. No one was home at the last house. I left a note on the door for the person to call."

"We still have one, then," Teya said.

"I'm not overly optimistic about it." Ransom moved to a chair and sat down. "Now, you want to tell me what happened while I was gone?"

Teya told him about meeting Eloise's oldest child on the playground and her husband's reaction.

Ransom stood. "I'll go talk to him," he said. "We can't have him threatening you like that—especially when he knows where we live."

"No, Ransom, please don't!" Teya said desperately, clutching his shirt. "I don't want any more trouble with him. This happens all the time at the clinic. He's just frustrated and venting. I don't think he'll hurt us."

"I'm not willing to take that chance."

"It's fine. Really. The man's wife was just dragged down to the Infirmary, and his children are terrified. I think we can give him a break—just this once. If something else happens, you can take care of it."

Ransom looked at her for a long moment.

"Please," Teya pressed.

"Fine," Ransom said after a long pause. Then he turned and headed down the hall.

Teya knew he was going to the bedroom to lie down—the way his shoulders slumped made it obvious he was physically and mentally exhausted. Though he would never come right out and admit it, he didn't know how to save their family. The handful of food he'd been able to bring home was a small victory, but he didn't know how to solve their problems any more than she did.

She went to the balcony, now directly in the sun, for relief and something else to focus on, but after a few moments she knew she wouldn't be able to stay. It felt as though she were standing in front of an open oven. As she was about to turn and head back into the kitchen, she saw Eve laboring back across the plaza. Her bag was still tucked under her arm—a sign she hadn't found anything. The sight of her dear friend walking home empty-handed added another brick to the crushing load of guilt.

Teya quickly went inside, closing the balcony door behind her. How she wished she could shut it all out as easily.

seventeen

Teya lay on her side. Out the window, the sky turned from gray to blue. She hadn't slept all night, but she wasn't tired. Instead, she felt the peace that sometimes accommodates the resolution of a hard decision.

Her father had once told her how to make hard decisions, and she'd spent the whole night thinking about him. She didn't have many memories of her father—he'd died when she was ten, and even when he was alive, he hadn't been home much. He had joined the Army at nineteen, and the military had become his life. He had spent the first part of his military career in Afghanistan, and later, he'd led one of the first battalions into Iran. Her father rarely spoke of that time. He didn't meet and marry her mother until after the war. Mona and Teya had come soon after, so her parents didn't discuss gloomy topics. A few years later, states started seceding from the Union, and that was the end of her father's involvement in her life. Stationed at a military base near town, he was gone for weeks at a time, then home for only two or three days before being redeployed.

Maybe because he was home so rarely, Teya listened carefully to whatever he told her. They had been playing a card game once when he was home on leave, and in the middle of it, she asked if he'd killed anyone. It was more childish curiosity than anything. The other kids in the neighborhood had bragged about how tough their fathers were, and she wondered where her family stood in their patriotism. The boy two doors down claimed his father had killed more rebels than anyone else. Were the soldiers really killing people? When he was home, her father never discussed what he did while serving in the Army. He focused on getting to know his kids, which Teya didn't realize until later. She'd always thought his job was just top-secret or something.

So that day, after she had blurted out the question, she didn't know what to expect. Her father had looked away, and for the first time, she noticed that the war made him sad. Even though he was sitting across the table from her, he wasn't really with her—he was years and thousands of miles away. She immediately regretted asking the question, but there was no way to take it back, so she waited uncomfortably for the answer.

When he did speak, his voice was soft and tinged with deep sorrow—something she had never heard in his voice before. He seemed to know why she was asking. "Yes. I've killed other men. I don't know how many, exactly. I killed some of them thousands of miles away. Some were just across state lines."

His comment was followed by a deep silence. Teya kept her eyes focused on her cards. She wanted to go back to playing the game and pretend she hadn't asked the question.

"Look at me, Teya," her father commanded gently.

Teya stared even harder at the cards in her hands.

"Teya."

She looked up and saw that her father's eyes were red and glistening. "I'm not telling you this to brag. What I did was simply part of my job. If there was a way to take back every kill, I'd find some way to do it. I'm telling you this so you'll learn one lesson: there are going to be times in your life when you're presented with a no-win situation. It's not going to be easy to decide what to do. Sometimes you'll only have a split second to make your choice. Other times, you may have days. But it doesn't matter how long you have, because whether it's just a moment or weeks, you're going to have to live with your decision for the rest of your life. If there was any way I could have saved those people, I would have made that choice instead. But that's not the choice I was given—it was either my life or theirs. I'm not proud of what I've done, but I've learned to live with it. I hope you never have to make the decision whether or not to kill someone, but I know one day you'll have to make a decision where both answers seem wrong. If that's the case, you need to make a choice you can live with for the rest of your life. Because if you can't live with it, your life will be hell."

Two days later, her father had been redeployed. He'd returned a week after that in a flag-draped casket.

Teya wiped the tears from her eyes and rolled onto her back. She was facing the same kind of no-win decision her father had talked to her about all those years ago.

She lay in bed until the sun rose over the mountain and filled the room with yellow light. Then she got out of bed and pressed her fingers against the screen. A woman stood on a balcony of building B and shook a rug out over the railing. Below, a couple hurried past, probably on their way to secure good seats for the parade.

She looked back at Ransom's alarm clock. Seven-thirty. Sighing, Teya showered and dressed in a short-sleeve green dress with small white flowers. Then she did her hair before adding some blush and lipstick. Looking herself over in the mirror, Teya went to wake the boys and Ransom. They couldn't be late for Mona—not today, anyway.

* * *

By the time they arrived at the 'Vard, people were packed five deep. Teya held James's hand and followed Ransom and Warren down the sidewalk.

"How much farther, Mom?" James asked.

"Three more blocks," Teya said, looking down at her son. "We'll be there before you know it."

"I'm thirsty."

Teya looked down at James. His cheeks were flushed, and the sweat along his hairline glistened in the sun. It had to be at least ninety degrees. "I know it's hot, sweetheart, but we're running late. Aunt Mona will have something to drink as soon as we get to the park."

A cheer went up from the crowd. The parade was starting.

"Can we watch?" Warren asked, ahead of them.

"We need to hurry," James said, parroting his mother. "Or

else we can't be in the parade." He looked to his mom for confirmation of his last assumption.

"Please, Dad," Warren said. "Just for a minute."

Teya bumped into Ransom, who had stopped and was looking over the heads of the crowd. He heaved Warren up on his right shoulder.

"We need to go," Teya said, giving Ransom a gentle push.

"I see the parade," Warren said excitedly, pointing to the street.

"I want to see the parade." James's expression showed his displeasure at the injustice.

Ransom picked up James and placed him on the other shoulder.

"We're going to be late," Teya prodded.

"We'll just be a minute," Ransom replied. "The Census Bureau float is always one of the last. I doubt they've even lined up yet."

Teya tugged at Ransom's arm. "Mona's not going to be happy."

If Ransom heard her, he didn't do anything to acknowledge it.

A moment later, both boys called out, "Horses!"

Teya stood on her tiptoes and looked over the shoulders of the two people in front of her. Two horses pulled a trailer bearing painted wooden cutouts of apricot and apple trees, corn stalks, and a variety of other plants. Several waving farmers stood next to the trees with hoes, shovels, and rakes over their shoulders. A wooden sign on the float's side read

Sponsored by the Farmers Union of Washington State

It was an old float. She remembered first seeing it in a New Earth Day parade probably twenty years ago. The wooden cutouts looked just as she remembered. Even the people seemed to be dressed the same.

"Ransom," she tried again.

"One more float and we'll go," Ransom promised.

"More horses!" Warren squealed.

Following the farmers' float was the horse-drawn float of the New Earth Society—also one Teya had seen numerous times. At the front was a fifteen-foot replica of Mother Earth. She had long, flowing red hair and piercing green eyes. She was looking down near her feet, where three-foot-high models of various animals and plants were congregated. Her mouth was painted in a half-smile, her left arm outstretched toward the back of the float in a defensive manner, as if trying to protect the animals and plants near her. A banner on the side of the car, in big green letters, read

Earth before Greed

Another float followed. Twenty people waved to the crowd below a raised platform on which stood a woman wearing a white dress. She held two dolls in her arms. Underneath her dress she wore something that made her appear to be nine months' pregnant. Across her dress was printed the word, THIRD. She held a sign that read

Three's a Crowd.

The crowd cheered.

Teya felt sick to her stomach. "We need to go. Now!"

"Okay, okay," Ransom said, grimacing. He set James and Warren back on the sidewalk. "Come on. Let's find your aunt."

* * *

It took them ten minutes to make their way to the park. Another thirty or so earth-themed floats snaked around the trees, sagebrush gardens, and rusting playground equipment. Teya traced the line of floats with her eyes, trying to find the entry from the Census Bureau.

James tugged on Teya's hand and pointed to a tall metal slide. "I want to play."

"After the parade. Right now we need to find Aunt Mona. And watch out for the horse poop!" She grabbed James's arm and moved him away from a pile he'd almost stepped in.

"I see the float," Ransom said.

Teya looked up, her eyes following where Ransom pointed. The Census Bureau float was near the back of the park. It was about thirty feet long and consisted of a large wooden platform painted in brilliant white. There were two levels to the platform.

The higher level was partitioned in the middle and had a Census Bureau logo painted on either side. Under the logo were the words

Families Come in Different Sizes

About a dozen adults and a handful of children sat on the float. There were also two single parents, each with one child, and several single people. Two black horses stood in front of the float with feedbags over their mouths.

Ransom took Warren off his shoulders and set him on the grass. The boys ran toward the float.

Mona was standing by the front, talking to the driver. She looked up and smiled when she saw them, breaking off her conversation as the boys reached her. "I'm so glad you made it!" she said. "I was getting worried. I thought I'd have to find a family off the street to stand in for you."

"It took a little longer than usual to get the boys ready," Teya said.

"How are my favorite nephews?" Mona asked, kneeling down and giving each of them a hug.

"We saw horses!" Warren exclaimed.

"I know. Isn't it fun?" Mona agreed. "And there are two more right behind me!"

"They're black!" Warren noted excitedly.

Mona looked into her nephews' eyes and asked, "How would you two like the horses to pull you down the street?"

The boys let out a loud cheer, and Mona took them by their hands to help them onto the float.

As Teya watched them climb up with their aunt, she could feel Ransom staring at her. "What?" she asked.

"You look sick. Are you feeling okay?"

"I'm fine."

"Are you sure?"

"I think it's the heat and the . . . you know. They don't go well together."

"Are you sure you'll be able to handle the float? It's pushing ninety-five. And there's no shade once we get out on the 'Vard."

"I'll drink plenty of water."

An excited whoop came from the float. "Mom, Dad, look. I'm in a parade," James called.

"Come up and join us," Mona said, motioning for them to come. "We're going to leave any minute."

"You sure you're feeling okay?" Ransom pressed. "I'm sure Mona will be fine with you stepping aside if you tell her you're ill."

"No. I'm good. I really need to be in this parade."

Ransom was about to counter, but Teya brushed past him. She climbed up the tiny, metal steps on the side and made her way to the front of the float where the boys were sitting.

"Stand here and wave," Mona instructed. She gave her sister a brief hug. "I'm so excited that you're here. I'll be back in a second. I need to check on everyone else before we start."

Teya watched her sister until she felt Ransom's arm around her waist. He pulled her close and said, "Just a few hours, and everything's going to be over."

"I know," Teya replied, a chill running down her spine.

Mona came back just as the driver shook the reins and let out a short whistle. The float slowly moved forward, the horses following the pace of the float twenty feet in front of them.

"Okay, everyone," Mona said, climbing to the top of the platform. "Smile and wave!"

The float wound its way through the park, then pulled out of the trees and onto the 'Vard.

eighteen

Teya felt as though she was standing behind a piece of glass, watching the world pass her by. Ransom was talking to her, but she was so absorbed in her own thoughts that his words barely registered.

She watched him kneel down next to the boys and realized he had stopped talking. He pointed to the crowd, the horses, the New Earth Day banner hanging across the street. He waved at the crowd. The boys waved too. Then Mona's voice sliced through Teya's thoughts, sharp and clear.

"You're not waving."

Teya didn't respond. She just gazed at the faces in the crowd as the float moved past.

Mona stepped down from her platform and stood next to Teya. She grabbed Teya's hand and started waving it for her.

"Come on," Mona cajoled. "Join the fun."

Teya let Mona wave her hand. Normally she would have jerked it away, but right then, she was too numb to care what her sister did.

"What happened to Eloise?" Teya asked.

"Who?" Mona said.

"Eloise Johnston. The woman who was brought to the Infirmary two nights ago."

"A lot of things go on where I work, Teya. I can't possibly know everything that happens there."

"I thought you had to approve all raids on private property. Was the raid on her house unauthorized?"

Mona let go of her sister's hand. It fell limply to Teya's side.

When she faced Teya, her smile was gone.

"Sentinels don't enter homes without my authority." Her voice was short and crisp. "Why are you so worried about that woman, anyway?"

"Her name's Eloise."

"What's with the sudden concern for Eloise?"

"It's my fault she's sitting in a cell right now."

"You're not indulging in another guilt trip, are you? I thought we talked about this in my office the other day. All you did was run the test, Teya. You did your job. It's not your fault she decided to have unprotected sex."

Teya looked over at Ransom. He and the kids were having a good time. For a moment, she forgot about all their troubles. They were one big, happy family enjoying the New Earth Day parade. Then the heat and the way her stomach pressed against her dress increased her discomfort, and her mind slipped back to Friday night and the tearstained faces of Eloise's children. She wondered what they were doing right now. She doubted they were part of this jubilant crowd. They were probably in the apartment with their father, asking when their mother was coming home.

"I switched the test." Her voice was just above a whisper, just loud enough for Mona to hear.

Out of the corner of her eye, she saw Mona's body jerk. But a moment later, she was waving again with a big smile on her face. Her reaction was so subtle that Teya wasn't sure if her sister had actually heard her. However, after a moment, Mona took a step closer to Teya, though she still didn't look away from the crowd. "What did you say?"

Her eyes made it clear she hadn't misunderstood. Mona's voice was also low, but Teya heard her over the din of the crowd and the hooves clattering below them.

"I switched Eloise's pregnancy test with my own."

Mona's eyes grew wide. "What are you talking about? I had the internment paperwork signed by Dr. Redgrave, stating that she got a second positive."

"Not *that* test, Mona," Teya said. "The first one."

Teya watched Mona's face intently. It took a second for what

Teya had said to register. When it did, the smile on Mona's face disappeared. But it was only for a moment. "How long have you known?" she asked between smiles and waves, but there was shock and disbelief in her voice.

"Does it matter?"

"Yes, it matters," Mona said, her voice rising and taking on an edge.

Ransom turned and looked back at the two of them. "Everything okay?" he asked.

Teya nodded. Ransom stared at the two of them doubtfully but returned his attention to the boys when James grabbed his hand and pointed to something in the distance.

There was silence between Mona and Teya for over a minute. The float continued down the 'Vard. Teya stood with her hands at her side, staring straight ahead. Finally she got the courage to look at Mona again. Despite the smile on her face, Teya knew she was anything but content.

Finally Mona spoke. "Answer me," she said. "How far along are you?"

"Three months. Maybe a little longer," Teya said.

"Have you acquired a third credit?"

"What do you think?"

"What I don't understand is why you're telling me this now. You've managed to hide it this long. Why not conceal it until you can find a credit or something?"

"Because of Eloise. I should be in the Infirmary right now. Not her."

Mona was quiet for only a moment.

"You know what this means, don't you?"

Teya didn't reply. She was quite sure she knew what it meant but wanted to hear it from her sister's mouth.

"By law, I need to report you. Immediately. When this parade ends, I'll find the nearest sentinel and have him escort you to the Infirmary."

There was a part of Teya that didn't think Mona would actually do it—or maybe a part of her that hoped she wouldn't. But looking in her sister's eyes, she knew Mona was trapped. If it ever came out that Mona broke protocol regarding her sister's pregnancy, the job she had worked so hard for would be over. There was no point asking Mona to treat her differently. She had already ruined enough lives. Still, there was something she had to try.

"I'll go on one condition."

"There are no conditions. You broke the law. You have to live with the consequences of your actions. No exceptions."

Teya ignored her. "I want to trade places with Eloise."

For the first time since Teya's confession, Mona turned and looked at her. "You want to what?"

"I want to trade places with Eloise. I'm the one who should be in there, not her. I want you to release her and put me in her place."

"I can't do that."

"You're the director of the Census Bureau. I'm sure you could arrange it."

"Letting a pregnant woman out on the street without a credit is something only the governor can do. Besides, if I did it, I'd be out of a job."

"You could say her test got mixed up with mine. It wouldn't be the first time that happened. Besides, you know she's pregnant. You can put her name on a travel ban so she can't leave the city. Then next month, when she goes in for her pregnancy test, you can be right there to take her back."

"I'm not doing that."

"Please, Mona. I need you to do this for me. It's the only way to make things right."

Mona brushed her hair out of her eyes. Teya could tell she was at least considering the idea.

"I can't make any promises."

"That's fine."

Teya picked up Ransom's canteen and took a drink.

"I have one more request."

Mona looked at her, then turned away.

"Don't ask for any special treatment once you're in the Infirmary. You're not going to receive any," she said coolly.

Teya hadn't expected any favors once she was locked up,

but to hear her sister say it made her feel as though she'd been slapped in the face. She fought back the tears that were welling up before making her request. "I don't want my children to see me get arrested," she said quietly. "I won't run or do anything stupid when the parade is over. I just don't want it done when they're around. I don't want them to see their mom being led away."

"If you want to spare your kids, tell your husband what's going on and have him take them away before I come with the sentinels."

Teya looked at Ransom. He and the boys were enjoying themselves. She watched them and wondered what they'd remember best at the end of the day—the parade, or that their mother didn't come home with them.

She stared at Ransom's taut muscles and tanned arms. She hadn't noticed the tan. They'd had so little time together lately. Telling him what she'd just done was going to be difficult—he'd have a hard time understanding her decision and probably a harder time accepting it. Only now did she focus on how hurt he'd be. She just hoped that when it was all over, her marriage would survive it.

"I'll let him know," Teya said. She wanted to say more, to tell Mona how sorry she was for dumping this on her and putting her in a bind and complicating her life. She knew her actions had left Mona feeling betrayed. But the apology would have to come later—after she was out of the Infirmary. It might even be months or years before they could speak civilly again.

She moved down a level and stood next to Warren. Her confession to Mona had brought with it a strange feeling of peace. Hiding the truth the last three months had been stressful and exhausting. She ran her hand through Warren's hair.

"Look, Mom, horses," Warren said, pointing to the animals that were pulling the float.

"I see. What color are they?" Teya asked.

"Black," Warren said excitedly.

"You're not waving, Mom," James said.

Teya looked at her son, then at the throngs of people on either side of the street. She was up high enough to see the park that marked the end of the parade route in the distance. That's where everything would come to a head. She fought back the tears and started waving to the crowd, telling herself everything was going to be all right. Somehow Ransom would forgive her for telling Mona, and somehow he'd be able to find a credit before it was too late.

* * *

Thirty minutes later, the float came to a stop under the shade of a giant pine tree. The driver put on the brake and headed to a trough of water with two silver-colored buckets in his hand.

Teya looked down at her boys. Their faces were sunburned, but they radiated happiness. Ransom gave the boys the last of the water from the canteen, then told them to stay put while he went to get some more. Teya reached to stop him, but he jumped down before she could say anything.

She turned and looked for her sister. She wasn't anywhere on the float. Teya's heart skipped a beat. Mona had been standing behind her only moments ago when they entered the park. Moving to the top level of the float, Teya scanned the people milling around for any sign of her sister.

A police officer walked past the float and nodded to Teya. She managed to smile back, even though she felt her legs were about to give out.

Ransom had returned with water from the trough and was helping the driver carry one of the buckets for the horses. Then he hoisted himself back on the float and handed the canteen to the boys.

She watched as they passed the canteen among themselves, then took turns filling their mouths up with water and spitting it out on the grass.

Suddenly Ransom was standing beside her. "Where's your sister?" he asked. "Are we heading straight to her place, or should I let the kids run around the park for a while?"

"I don't know," Teya said. "I'm looking for her."

Then she saw her across the park. Mona was making a beeline

toward the float, followed by two sentinels.

"I don't think we're going to be having dinner with my sister," she said.

Ransom gave her a confused look, then glanced over his shoulder to see what caught Teya's attention.

"Why not?" he asked.

Teya grabbed his arm and looked him right in the eye. "I need you to take the boys away from here."

"Why? What's going on?"

"I just need you to do what I say. I don't want them to see what's about to happen."

"What's about to happen?"

Teya looked back over the crowd. Mona and the sentinels were thirty yards away and closing fast.

"Please, just do as I ask. I'll explain everything later. I promise. Just take the kids and go."

Ransom gave Teya a long look. "I don't understand."

Teya pointed across the park. "Look. Over there by the rain-forest float. My sister and two snatchers are coming. They'll be here in a few minutes. Get the boys out of here now."

Ransom followed her gaze. He studied the scene for a moment, then his eyes grew wide. He turned back at Teya. "You told Mona? Why did you do that? What were you thinking?"

"There's no time to explain. Take the boys away from here now. I don't want them to see me being led away. Please, Ransom. Please." A tear ran down her cheek.

"Teya, I—"

"Don't argue. Please, just go."

Ransom didn't move.

Mona was fifteen yards away. Then ten.

Ransom jumped down from the float, facing Mona and the approaching sentinels.

"Don't!" Teya screamed.

She scrambled down the float and stood by Ransom's side just as Mona reached them.

Mona pointed to Teya. "This woman is in violation of the population laws. Take her to the Infirmary immediately."

One of the sentinels took a step toward Teya, but Ransom blocked his path.

"Move out of the way," the sentinel said, looking up at him.

"No. I'm not letting you take her."

The sentinel placed his hand on the top of his nightstick. "If you don't move, you'll be arrested for obstruction," he said.

Teya moved to step around Ransom, but he pushed her back behind him. She shrieked as the sentinel withdrew the nightstick from his belt and raised it threateningly.

"Last warning," he said.

Suddenly Mona moved between the two men. "Put the stick away," she said forcefully.

The sentinel paused. His eyes went from Ransom to Mona.

"Sentinel, put your weapon away now," she repeated.

The sentinel gave Ransom a hard look, then slid the stick back in his belt, though he kept his hand on top of it.

Mona looked up at Ransom. "This isn't the time to play hero. I understand that you're upset, but don't blame me for this. I'm not the one who let your secret out of the box. I'm simply doing what the law requires. But you're being stupid. If you interfere, you'll go to jail while your wife will be taken to the Infirmary, which means your kids would be placed in state custody. The last thing they'll see is their mom and dad being dragged away in handcuffs. Is that what you want? To leave your kids in the hands of the state until they can figure out what to do with you?"

Ransom looked back at the boys. Teya followed his gaze. James and Warren were standing on the edge of the float with confused, frightened looks on their faces.

Teya stared at Ransom. "Please," she said. "Let them take me."

Ransom's shoulders slumped, and he stepped to the side.

Quickly the sentinel grabbed Teya and spun her around. She heard the clink of metal. "Place your hands behind your back," he said.

Teya complied. The sentinel grabbed her arms and snapped cool metal cuffs tightly around her wrists.

"This way," the second man said. He pushed her between the shoulder blades, and she started walking forward.

Suddenly Ransom was walking by her side. "I'll figure something out," he said. "I promise. I'll get you out of there."

"I'll be okay," Teya said, fighting back the tears.

The other sentinel moved between them.

"Stay back," he said. "No more warnings."

Teya got another push on her back. She turned and saw Ransom watching as she was led away. On the float, both James and Warren were crying and calling out for their mom to come back.

nineteen

With the trams not running due to the holiday, it took Ransom almost three hours to get the boys back home. When they arrived, the boys were dehydrated and tired, so Ransom gave them water and the last of the noodles and apples. After cooling them off with a quick, cold shower, he put them down for a nap.

Since the moment the snatchers had taken Teya, his mind had been racing, searching for a solution. The only thing he'd come up with on the long, hot walk home was to call Dempsey. He'd said something the other day about being able to get a credit, so maybe he could help. Besides, Dempsey was the only person Ransom felt he could trust anymore.

No one answered the first call. He waited for a while, then called again. After the third attempt, Ransom slammed down the phone and headed to the balcony. He took a drink, then set the cup on the balcony's ledge. He looked out over the plaza, the heat rising over the cobblestones, and listened to the faint chatter of someone in an apartment several stories above. He didn't know and didn't care what they were talking about—he felt like he should be doing something to help his family. But with no one to watch the kids, trying to find a credit or more food was impossible.

He turned and headed back into the living room. He dialed Dempsey's number again. Still no answer. He wished he knew where Dempsey lived. He had an apartment somewhere near the Recycling Center, but despite working alongside the man for years, Ransom had never had occasion to get an address. He picked up the phone to try Dempsey's number again but was interrupted by three quick knocks at the front door.

Ransom looked through the peephole and saw Mona standing back from the door. He squeezed the doorknob, trying to keep his anger in check. "What do you want?" He kept his voice flat and level.

"Please," Mona said. "Just open the door."

"Why are you here?"

"Do you really want to have this conversation in front of the neighbors?" she asked, her voice echoing down the hallway.

Ransom paused. He'd overheard many conversations that took place in the halls. He took a step back and opened the door. Mona was still wearing the uncomfortable-looking clothes she'd worn to the parade. Beads of sweat clung to her hairline. Two loose strands of hair hung over her face, and there were dark circles under her eyes. She carried two bulging canvas bags in her arms.

They appraised each other in silence.

"Can I come in?" Mona finally asked, lifting the bags for Ransom to see. "They're heavy."

Ransom stood to the side. Mona entered, kicked off her shoes, and headed straight for the kitchen. Ransom followed her, closing the door to the boys' room as he passed.

Mona set the bags on the table and began unloading their contents. There were a dozen jars of fruit, two loaves of bread, a block of white cheese, several pounds of dried meat, a container of dried milk, a five-pound bag of flour, one of potatoes, carrots, corn, peaches, some peppers, and four onions.

Ransom salivated at the sight of the food. It was enough to last the two weeks until he picked up their next conservation card. As she set the food on the table, he could feel a burden lifting from his shoulders.

Mona opened the refrigerator, stooped down, and began placing the cheese, fruit, and vegetables inside.

"Where did all this come from?"

"Some of it's from my own personal storage. Some of it I bought from a store near my house. It doesn't matter, really. What's important is that you and the kids have enough to eat until your card is replaced."

"How did you know about that?"

"I had a long talk with Teya. She said you lost your card and that you were low on food. I thought I'd help."

The mention of Teya brought back the heated feelings he'd been harboring since her arrest, followed by feelings of confusion. He didn't understand why Mona was doing this. She was fine arresting her sister but cared about their comfort?

"How are the kids?" Mona asked as she straightened and shut the door to the refrigerator.

Ransom looked toward their bedroom door before answering. "They're fine." He softened his tone, not wanting her to rescind the gift. "A little confused, perhaps, but they're doing okay." He looked at the food spread out on the table. "At least they'll have something to eat when they wake up."

Mona held a bottle in each hand. "Where do you keep the canned fruit?"

Ransom shook his head. "Why are you doing this, Mona?"

"Doing what?"

"Showing up at my house with all this," Ransom said, motioning to the food.

"I told you. I talked to Teya. I thought I'd help."

"Is that why you're here? Is it really? Are you sure you're not trying to relieve a guilty conscience?"

Mona set the bottles on the table. She brushed the hair out of her eyes with the back of her hand. "Look, I know this is a hard time for your family right now . . ."

Her sympathy was too much. *Screw the food*, he decided. "You bet it is. Thanks to you."

Mona's eyes narrowed. She opened her mouth, then closed it again, looking down at the bottles of peaches spread out across the table. Her hands were clutching the jars so tightly that her knuckles were white.

"If you didn't have two wonderful kids who needed something to eat, I'd take all this back and let you fend for yourself." Ransom opened his mouth to speak, but Mona held up her hand. "Please, Ransom, just hear me out, okay?"

Ransom paused, then crossed his arms over his chest and leaned against the wall.

"You're frustrated and angry. I would be too, if I were in your shoes. But you can't blame me for what happened today. I had no idea Teya was pregnant until she told me. I can't even begin to tell you how surprised I was. I was shocked, really. I'm out celebrating the most important day of the year, and the person I trust over everyone else just drops a bomb on me out of nowhere. Teya's never been one for drama, but that one took the cake."

Ransom shifted his weight. "You weren't the only one surprised by it."

"Yeah, she told me you've only known for a few days, right?"

Ransom nodded.

"That means you're not going to be charged with concealing her pregnancy."

"Great news. What magnanimous gift are you planning to bestow next? That I have an extra day to find a credit?"

Mona pushed the two jars toward Ransom. "I'll let you put the rest of this away." She picked up the canvas bags from the table, folded them, and placed them under her arm, starting for the door.

Ransom put his arm across the kitchen doorframe. "Hold on. I'm not done."

Mona ducked under his arm and continued down the hall. "I don't care. I've got to go. It's been a long day, and we're both tired. Why don't you give me a call tomorrow night, and we can chat then."

"You said you talked to Teya. I want to know how she's doing."

Mona kept walking.

"Please, Mona. I'll control my temper."

Mona stopped and let out an audible sigh. After a minute, she moved back to the table and pulled out one of the chairs. She sat down and leaned back. "Fine. What do you want to know?"

"How is she?"

"Tired, but she's doing well. She has a private room. I'm doing what I can to make sure she's comfortable."

"Can I see her?"

"Visitors aren't allowed. You know that. And, no, I'm not going to make an exception."

Ransom pulled out a chair and sat across from Teya, the dozen jars of fruit like a wall on the table between them. "Did she say why she told you?"

"Guilt. She felt bad about what happened to Eloise. Blamed herself for it. I don't know why, really. Eloise's pregnancy would have been discovered sooner or later. She did try to convince me to free Eloise. She wanted to trade places with her."

Ransom thought back to Friday night and how Teya had cried as they waited for the sentinels to clear out. At the time, he'd thought it was just fear. "Did you let Eloise go?"

"Of course not. I'd never see her again."

"You lied to Teya?"

"Oh, please. I never promised her anything. I just said I'd look into it."

"So now what?" he asked.

"You have until Friday at noon to present a valid credit or to find someone with a credit who's willing to adopt the child."

"And if I can't come up with one?"

"She'll undergo a surgical procedure that will terminate the pregnancy," she said flatly.

Ransom felt a sad, helpless chasm opening inside him. To escape Mona's gaze, he rose and pushed the button over the kitchen sink, then cupped his hands and let them fill with cold water until the faucet shut off. He splashed the cold water on his face before drying his eyes with a towel.

"I'm sorry," Mona said. "I wish there was something I could do."

Ransom turned so he was facing her. "That sounds really ridiculous, coming from the Population Director."

Mona put her hands over her face. For a moment Ransom thought she was going to cry, but then she pulled her hands away. Ransom wasn't sure if her already puffy eyes were from tears or exhaustion. "Do you think I like seeing my sister in one of those rooms?"

"It sure seems that way."

Mona stood angrily and moved to the far side of the kitchen, leaning against the stove, placing her hands on the edges. She finally turned and looked at Ransom. "I know there's a perception out there that the Population Director is all-powerful, but I'm not. Aside from internal matters, I don't have that much authority."

"Teya's not an internal matter? She's inside your facility."

"I can't pardon her. Only the governor can do that. All I can do is see that she's made comfortable during her stay."

"If you don't like the thought of her being in there, why don't you give her your credit? That way, we'd both get what we want."

His words hung in the air. Mona stared at him for a long minute.

"No. I can't. I'm sorry."

She turned and headed for the balcony. Ransom followed.

"Why not? She's your sister. Your flesh and blood."

"Giving Teya my credit would violate all my beliefs."

"What do you believe in that's more important than your sister's happiness, Mona?"

Mona shook her head and looked over the plaza. "The only way your kids are going to have any future is if we get this world back to a livable condition. The only way we're going to do that is with fewer people. People are the problem, not the solution. You know that. I give Teya my credit, and I'm not only jeopardizing your kids' future, I'm risking the future of every other child in the world too."

"What if this child's special? What if he or she is destined to make this world a better place? What if this baby will grow up and invent something or be the kind of leader needed to clean up the planet once and for all?"

"The world tried that for thousands of years, Ransom. It didn't work. At one point, we had over eight billion people on this planet. What did we have to show for it? Overcrowded cities. Poverty. Starvation. Greed. Wars over finite resources. One more person takes us one step back, not forward. Every living person moves us that much closer to the brink of destruction."

Ransom just stood there, not knowing what to say. Mona was repeating everything he had heard growing up. He had no rebuttal. He'd never heard any arguments to the contrary. But something about what she said didn't feel right. Deep down, he didn't see the threat his unborn child posed to the city—let alone the world.

He decided on another approach. "You didn't have to report her. You could have ignored her and given us time to find a credit."

Mona shook her head. "We're a society of rules and laws. I couldn't just pretend she didn't say anything. Just like the guilt of faking the test ate her up, the guilt of ignoring her announcement would have eaten me up."

Ransom let out a short laugh.

Mona stared at him. "Look me in the eye, Ransom, and tell me that if she'd come home with blood on her hands and told you she'd just killed someone, you'd sweep her confession to the side and hope she could find a way to fix it."

"Those are two very different situations," he said. "Apples and oranges."

"No, they're not. You have a choice to make between your wife and the law. You have to decide what's more important— your relationship with her or our whole society. I had to make the same choice."

"No. It's different. You have to think about your future. It would be the end of your cushy job if word got out that your only sister was going to have a third—especially if you were the one who gave her the credit."

Mona's eyes became slits. "You think I turned her in because of my career?" Her voice rose with each word so that she almost shouted the last.

Ransom was a little taken aback. In all the years he'd known Mona, he'd never seen her lose her temper like this.

"You don't have a clue how things work! If I was worried about my job, the last thing I would have done was show up here with food."

"I didn't realize bringing food to relatives was illegal."

"It's not. And you're missing the point."

"What's the point, Mona?"

"Once word gets out that my sister is pregnant with a third

and concealed it for three months, there's going to be an investigation. Individuals who would like to see someone other than myself heading this division will happily spearhead the proceedings. They'll do everything they can to prove that I knew something about it. Next, since we have a confession by your wife explaining how she concealed everything, they'll try another tactic. If word gets out that I helped your family after the fact, they'll say I'm having an affair with you, or they'll use it as evidence that I give special treatment to those in custody—anything that might raise the eyes of the governor and make him ask for my resignation. So don't think that reporting Teya was about saving my career. If anything, it's put my future in jeopardy. I reported my sister because it's the law, and I brought you food because I love my two nephews and can't stand to see them starve!"

Ransom relented on that point. "Fine, but you could have waited to say something, given us a week or two to find a credit and work something out."

"Here we go again. You want your wife to be an exception to the rule."

"I don't like the rules, Mona—they put good, kind people in horrible places!"

Mona leaned forward. "Do you remember what it was like for women in the Infirmary when the population laws were first passed?"

Ransom didn't say anything. Growing up, he'd heard rumors about women being dragged from their homes in the middle of the night and subjected to horrible trauma. He'd never known anyone with firsthand experience. Those were just stories.

Mona continued, "There wasn't a five-day waiting period. Women were spit out of the place in less than forty-eight hours. Usually their families weren't even notified. You had women still recovering from the procedure walking down the street, blood running down their legs, trying to find their way home." Mona stopped and looked around. "Let's go inside where we can talk in private."

Ransom followed her to the kitchen. They took their seats on opposite ends of the table.

"When I got my first job at the Bureau, they gave me a tour of the place to show me how everything worked. It was all great until the end when they took me to a big, open room in the basement, full of women strapped to beds. Some were talking to each other, but most were screaming or crying or both, and they all looked horrible. At some point, a doctor would come in and just take them away. Then they were put in another room for twenty-four hours to make sure there weren't any medical complications. After that, they were on their own. It was like watching animals in a lab. I went home and cried, tempted to quit and never go back. Then I realized that if I wanted to make things better, I had to stay.

"I worked hard and learned how to play politics. I brown-nosed and did what I had to in order to get the nod of the governor once this position opened. Then after I was appointed, I used my influence to change things—not only here, but throughout the state. Now each woman has her own room. They have some privacy and five days for a solution to be reached. Counselors come around regularly to check on them and talk to them, both before and after the surgery. In addition, there's a fully trained medical staff there twenty-four hours a day to help them."

"That still doesn't make what you're doing right."

"Then you work to change it. Protest in front of the capitol. Write a letter. Tie yourself to the doors of the Census Bureau. Run for office. But don't sit here and tell me that things are unfair, when the only thing you've done is complain. I've done everything in my power."

Ransom could feel frustration building inside him. "Teya's not the first one to conceal a pregnancy. Some women have had thirds no one knows about. The family keeps quiet, and the kids stay hidden in their apartments—sometimes for years before anyone finds out about them. And somehow the world seems to go on just fine."

"Don't tell me you think keeping a child locked in an apartment building their entire life is living. That's child abuse. And, yes, I think it's better for a child never to be born than to face a life of concealment."

"If the planet could feed over eight billion people before these laws were passed, why can't it do so now?"

"It couldn't feed us! Millions of people starved every year, and most people weren't even eating real food. Besides, have you been to the farms recently? We've been fighting an unknown potato disease right now that could wipe out most of the crop. Half of the apricot crop was destroyed by a late frost. Considering how much food is lost to theft, we can barely afford to feed the people we do have. You may stand against the population laws now, but what's your solution for feeding a few extra hundred people a year? Every new mouth means someone gets less to eat tonight."

Ransom leaned forward across the table so his face was just a foot away from Mona's. "I've seen the homes, Mona. I've torn down hundreds of them. They're bigger and nicer than the places we have now. Refrigerators three times as big as what we have. Pantries that were once full of food. Don't tell me it's not possible to feed everyone and then some."

"And look at what it cost the planet! Forests ploughed under to make room for farms. Factories, cars, and cows spewing carbon into the air and turning our planet into a furnace. The polar ice caps were melting, the sea level was rising. There was no sense of stewardship over the earth or ourselves. Back then, most people in this country were overweight slobs, Ransom. You don't know what it was like, but I've seen films of people sitting around in front of televisions all day, eating. Life expectancy was stagnating because we weren't taking care of our health. We were dying from overeating while countless others starved. We were on a path that would have resulted in the death of hundreds of millions, if not billions of people. We had to take drastic action to save ourselves and to force people to care about each other and our earth. I'm not going to defend the system and say it's perfect. It's not. But it's better than what we had. Much better. At least now we have a fighting chance to stop the wars and destruction and leave something better behind for our children. Maybe in a generation or two, they'll have another chance to make changes. I just hope they won't make the same mistakes."

She stood up and walked out of the kitchen.

"If you're not going to give us your credit, can you at least tell me where I might go to get one?" Ransom called after her.

"Try the baby board," she said, putting her shoes on.

"I've tried that already."

"Then I can't help you."

"How can you not know?"

Mona put her hand on the doorknob and turned so she was facing him. "I don't, Ransom. I really don't. You have to believe me."

Ransom stared at her. His gut told him she was telling the truth. "You can still give up your credit," he said.

Mona opened the door. "I need to go. I have a long walk home."

"Wait. Will you give Teya a message for me?"

"Of course."

"Tell her I'll find one. I'm not giving up."

"I'll tell her," Mona said.

She closed the door. Ransom hurried to look through the peephole. Mona stopped at the top of the stairs and looked back at the door. She stood like that for a long moment before finally heading down.

Ransom opened the door a crack and held it there until he could no longer hear her shoes echoing in the stairwell. He shut and locked the door, then turned to the balcony.

Shielding his eyes from the setting sun, he watched Mona walk across the plaza. He still couldn't believe she wouldn't help her sister. He had often heard people bragging about how strong the bonds of family were, and he honestly thought Mona and Teya were those kinds of sisters. Maybe the bond wasn't as strong as he thought. Maybe there was a point where any relationship could break. But being an only child with no living relatives, he had no experience in the matter.

A phone rang.

At first Ransom thought it came from a nearby apartment.

Then it rang again.

Ransom ran to the living room. He picked up the phone on the third ring.

"Hello?"

"Hi," a male voice said. "I'm looking for a Ransom Lawe."

"This is he."

"Great. You're home. I wasn't sure I'd catch you today. I just got back from a trip, and there was a note shoved in my door with a message to call you."

Ransom paused for a moment. "I'm sorry," he said. "It's been a long day. Could you please tell me what the note said?"

"Well, considering it was written on half of a pink note card, I think it has something to do with the replacement credit I have for sale."

Suddenly the day before came rushing back. A feeling of hope surged through Ransom's body. "Yes, that's right. I left the message yesterday. Have you sold it yet?"

"No. Are you still in the market?"

Ransom breathed a sigh of relief.

twenty

Ransom had to walk all the way to 20th
Street to meet Richard Keller, the man who had phoned
him. It took him nearly an hour to reach the building. Thankfully, Eve had been willing to watch the kids for as long as it took.
At least he wouldn't have to worry about them.

He hurried up the stairs to the fourth floor and knocked on
the door of apartment 401. There was silence and then the sound
of feet moving down the hall. The peephole went dark.

"Who is it?"

Ransom identified himself.

A short man with shoulder-length red hair opened the door.
He was wearing a dark suit and a maroon tie. Both looked new.

"Richard Keller?" Ransom asked.

The man stepped back from the door and motioned for
Ransom to enter. "Please, come in."

Ransom stepped past the man into a large entry hall. A spacious living room and kitchen branched off to either side. There
were four closed doors—probably for three bedrooms and a bathroom, if the layout was like other apartments from that era. The
apartment even had twelve-foot ceilings. The gracious floor plan
seemed rather barren though. Upon further inspection, Ransom
realized there was no furniture and no pictures on the wall. In the
middle of the room was a black briefcase with a brass handle—
nothing else. He glanced in the kitchen as Richard started talking.
There were no appliances.

"You'll have to pardon the fact that I can't offer you a seat,"
Richard was saying. "Actually, it was fortunate that I got your

message at all. You see—oh, where are my manners? Come into the living room, at least. Don't bother taking your shoes off—there's not much here to mess up."

He gestured to the living room. Ransom went in, his feet creaking on the wooden floorboards as he walked. The room was twice as big as his apartment. There were dust lines of squares and rectangles on the wall where artwork had been. Ransom commented on the large bay window that looked out over the street below. But even more impressive was the opposite wall, graced by a fireplace—complete with three logs resting on each other.

"The fireplace works," Richard said, noting Ransom's raised eyebrows. He walked over to the fireplace and pushed a button on the wall. There was a hissing sound, then a click. Orange and yellow flames sprang to life. He pushed the button again, and the flames turned blue, shrinking to an inch high before going out.

"The fireplace is run on natural gas, so, as you can imagine, it costs a fortune to actually use. And the logs are fake to make it look more real, I guess. That's how they did it back then."

"I didn't know apartments came with them," Ransom said.

"The first apartments built after the relocation laws had them. And this apartment building was the second one constructed under those guidelines. It was completed just a few months after the first New Earth Day. Of course, it made sense back then. Natural gas wasn't nearly as expensive in those days. But you didn't come here for a history lesson, did you?"

"No, I came here for this," Ransom said as he took the other half of the replacement card out of his pocket.

"You know, I almost forgot I put it up there. I'm so busy with so many other things. Have an unexpected pregnancy, do you? Well, not you—your wife, of course. I'm assuming this is your third child?"

Ransom nodded.

"Well, I'd like to help you if I could. As I was saying earlier, it's a miracle really that I even got your note. As you can see, the apartment's empty. Tomorrow I sign the paperwork and sell it to a family of six. *Six*. Can you believe that? They're the only ones in the city who have four children living at home. Of course, this place will be a big improvement over what they currently have. Imagine—four kids under ten sharing one bedroom. It's an awful situation, if you ask me. I can only imagine what it's like. I'm an only child myself, so space was never really a concern. In fact, I grew up in this apartment. My bedroom was the last door on the left. It's nearly as big as this living room. I'm going to miss this place."

"Why are you selling it?"

"Change of heart. I'm not going to lie to you—I haven't always been conscious of others' needs. My parents ran a chain of grocery stores and made a good deal of money on it, so I didn't grow up thinking of others. But I inherited the stores and continue to run the business—which is no easy task in today's climate, with food rationing and all—but it's given me a perspective of how badly off others are. I finally realized how selfish I was being by keeping a place this size all to myself. I realized that there were other families who were in greater need of this space. So I put it on the market and sold it—for a very affordable price, all things considered. I came back to do one last walk-through and make sure I hadn't left anything behind. That's when I saw your note sticking in the door. It's a miracle you found me."

Ransom eyed the man warily. "What do you want for your credit?"

The man stroked his chin. "Tell me a little about your situation."

Ransom paused. He didn't feel comfortable getting into too much detail with a stranger. "I just need a credit," he said.

"I understand. I don't mean to pry. It's just that I want my credit to go to a family who will really make a difference in the world. I can't have kids, you see. My guys don't swim, or so the doctors say. It took me years to accept that fact. I tried surgery. Potions from the Station too. Nothing worked. It was just recently that I came to grips with the fact I'll never be a father. Ironic, isn't it? About a third of the population chooses not to have children. Half of those refuse to sell their credit. Yet all I want is just one child. But because of the population laws, if I ever find someone to spend the rest of my life with, I can't even get her artificially inseminated. It's the natural way or no way."

Ransom didn't know what to say. This guy was a little too open for him. He mumbled some condolences.

"I don't mean to tell you my life story," he smiled apologetically, "but it's why I eventually put my credit up for sale. If I find a buyer, I want to be sure the right person gets it. Someone who will raise their new child to be someone who will contribute to this world. That person will never have my genes, but I want to die knowing that the couple I sold my credit to raised a child I'd be happy to call my own son or daughter."

Ransom paused for a beat. He still didn't want to share the details of his life, but if a little talking got him the credit, he could do it.

Ransom explained his and Teya's jobs, what they wanted their boys to be like, and a little of the stress he'd been under trying to find a credit and provide food for his family after his conservation card was stolen. Despite his penchant for privacy, talking about it released some stress, and he found himself a little choked up.

"It's obvious that you love your wife and family very much," Richard jumped in, alleviating the awkward moment. "You've gone above and beyond the call of duty. I was going to take some time to think about it, but I believe fate has brought us together, Ransom. Fate. God. Call it what you will, but I'd be happy to sell you my credit."

Ransom cleared his throat. "We don't have much money. All we have is a thousand dollars in savings. But that's nowhere near enough to pay its market value. All we have that's worth anything is our apartment."

"I don't want your apartment. Look around at what I'm giving up. And I'm already a rich man." Richard paused. He locked his lips and looked up at the ceiling. He stood like that for a minute before lowering his eyes. "I'll tell you what," he said. "I want you to value this credit. I've been in business long enough to know that people take care of what they value. If you give them something for free, they don't care about it as much as if they had to pay something for it. So, if you're willing, I'll sell you the credit for the thousand dollars in your savings account."

Ransom couldn't believe what he was hearing. He had never heard of a credit going for so little. He felt as though he had just won the state lottery. He was excited and relieved at the same time. It would wipe out their savings account, but they'd be free of the Census Bureau. Teya would be happy. He'd be happy. He didn't know how they'd work things out, but he felt confident they could handle it. Other people had raised three kids on less. If they could do it, he could too.

"Agreed," Ransom said.

Richard held out his hand. Ransom shook it.

"Great," Richard said. "I'm assuming you want to get your wife out of the Infirmary as soon as possible."

"That's the plan."

"Well, nothing's open until tomorrow morning. Would it be inconvenient to meet in front of the Census Bureau at, say, eight thirty? That should give you plenty of time to go to the bank and get the money. Tonight I'll unpack some crates and get my replacement credit paperwork. We'll go inside together and sign everything over. How does that sound?"

"It sounds perfect," Ransom said.

Ransom arrived at the Census Bureau at eight twenty. He carried the thousand dollars in a small burlap bag tucked under his arm. He looked around nervously at everyone who walked past. He had never carried that much cash in his entire life. He could only image what someone would do if they knew what was in the bag.

He paced around in front of the building. Everything sounded too good to be true—so much so that in the back of his mind, Ransom worried that Richard would get cold feet or still show but demand more money. This was his one last chance to get a credit—and for a steal. If this didn't go through, there wasn't enough time to find another one before Teya's pregnancy was terminated.

His fears were relieved when he saw Richard getting off a southbound tram right at eight thirty-five. He was dressed down from when Ransom had seen him last night. Instead of a suit, he wore jeans and a green shirt—both of which looked new. He carried the same shiny briefcase in his hand.

"Sorry to keep you waiting," Richard said as they shook

hands. "As you know, trams are completely unreliable. One day it takes ten minutes to go a couple of stops, thirty minutes the next day. But I'm here, and I have the paperwork." He held up the briefcase. "I assume you have the money?"

Ransom patted the bag under his arm.

"May I see it?"

Ransom looked around nervously. He didn't like the idea of opening the bag in public.

"I just want a peek," Richard said. "I don't need to count it."

Ransom walked to the side of the Census Bureau and stood so his back was to the crowd. He opened the bag, and Richard looked in.

"Perfect. Why don't we go in and take care of this."

They walked into the Census Bureau together. This early in the day, there was only a handful of people waiting. They took a number and sat on the last row. They didn't have to wait long. In less than a minute, a blonde girl behind window seven called out their number.

At the booth, Richard slid his replacement credit documentation across the window. She examined it, then had both men fill out a form that they were declaring consent to the transfer of the replacement credit. She checked their IDs, then had a supervisor check them too. Then she stamped the document and asked for the twenty dollar processing fee.

Ransom felt his heart drop. All he had was the thousand in cash.

Richard smiled. "Don't worry about it, Ransom. I'll take care of it." He opened his wallet and slid a new twenty-dollar bill to the teller. The woman wrote out a receipt and gave it to Richard.

"Okay," she said to Ransom. "Here's your new credit."

Ransom held the document in his hands. It was made of thick, expensive paper and had the stamp of the Census Bureau on it. He couldn't believe that he had it. He slid it back to the teller.

"I'd like to use this right away, if that's okay. My wife. You guys have her. I'd like to use this to get her out."

The clerk sighed deeply, then grabbed another form and tapped her fingernails on the counter while Ransom filled it out. When he was done, she asked for ID again and had the same supervisor come over and verify the information. Then she slid another paper to Ransom to sign.

"When will my wife get out?" Ransom asked.

The girl shrugged. "They release people most afternoons about three. If this gets processed before noon, she'll be out today. If not, you may have to wait until tomorrow."

"How will I know whether or not it will be processed?"

The girl shrugged. "I'll pass the paperwork on in a minute, but there are no guarantees it will be done today."

"But I need her out today. I have two young kids at home that miss their mommy."

"I'm sorry. I'll do what I can." She looked past them and called out the next number.

Ransom was about to say something when Richard gently took his arm and led him away from the window.

"Hey, you got her out. You should be grateful for that, right?"

Ransom nodded and smiled. "You're right. She'll be out. I don't know how to thank you."

Richard looked at the burlap bag in Ransom's hand. "Well, there is one way you can do that." He smiled, sheepishly.

Ransom handed the bag to Richard with a similar smile. "Here you go. Thank you so much."

Richard just smiled again. He opened the briefcase and put the sack inside, then held out his hand. "It was a pleasure doing business with you. Please make me proud of this child, okay?"

"I will," Ransom said.

Richard slapped Ransom on the back, smiled, then strolled out the doors.

Ransom stood there for a minute enjoying the feeling of success. He just wished there was some way to be sure Teya could get out of the Infirmary today.

He started for the exit and stopped. What was he thinking? There was a way. He turned and headed for the elevators.

twenty-
one

Mona looked through the file of papers one at a time. Occasionally she'd stop and glance up at Ransom. "It bothers me that you're staring at me like that."

"I'm not staring," Ransom said. "I'm looking around the office. This is the first time I've been here."

Mona shook her head. But five minutes later she was done with all the documents.

"So what's the verdict?" Ransom asked.

Mona closed the folder. "It looks like everything's in order."

"So you can get Teya out today?"

"Yes. She'll be released this afternoon."

Ransom stood to leave. "Thanks for pushing this through."

Mona gave him a terse smile. "Anything for my sister."

Ransom headed for the door, glad to be leaving the Census Bureau.

"Wait," Mona called after him.

Ransom turned around. Mona was standing with her hands on her hips.

"Last night you were desperate. You tried to talk me into giving up my credit. Less than twenty-four hours later, you have one. How did you get one so fast? That speed is unheard of."

"I guess you could say it was a miracle."

Mona rolled her eyes. "Just because you're married to my sister doesn't mean you can be smart with me. I've brought you food and will push all this paperwork through for you today—the least you can do is tell me how you got the credit."

Ransom briefly told her about Richard and the string of

coincidences that brought them together.

"And he only charged you a thousand dollars?"

Ransom nodded. "Like I said, it was a miracle."

She looked down at the paperwork and put her hand on the top page. "Yeah, I guess you could say that. Maybe I'll see you this afternoon."

Ransom started down the hall. He wanted to dance down it and click his heels together like in really old movies. But he settled for smiling all the way to the elevator.

* * *

Ransom stood in the alley behind the Census Bureau. He leaned against another building, his hands thrust in his pockets, keeping his eye on the two other men who were also waiting. None of them spoke. They all avoided direct eye contact and occasionally shifted their weight from one leg to another. They were all there for the same reason—to pick up wives, girlfriends, or other family members. Considering the grim circumstances under which they had gathered, there wasn't much reason to talk.

Ransom glanced at the door in the back of the Census Bureau where Teya would soon exit. It was painted black like the building. The door opened to a hundred-square-foot area that was surrounded by a chain-link fence topped by shiny razor wire.

Nice and cozy for expectant mothers, Ransom thought bitterly.

A few minutes later, there was a click from the back door that brought all three men to attention. The door opened, and a short sentinel walked out into the caged area. She took a key from her pocket and unlocked the padlock on the back door.

Two of the men took a step toward the gate.

"Stay back," she said, looking them over. "Everyone will be out in a minute."

The men returned to their places. A moment later, another sentinel opened the door and held it open. Two women walked out into the gated area. Ransom stiffened. Teya wasn't among them.

The first snatcher opened the gate that led to the alley. The two women looked down at the ground as they left the fenced area. They each moved to the men who had come for them. The first couple embraced awkwardly. They exchanged a few words, then started down the alley for the street. The other woman started to cry. Her companion held her in his arms.

Ransom looked back at the gate. Where was Teya?

The short sentinel was relocking the gate.

"Wait," Ransom said, hurrying to the sentinel. "I was told my wife was leaving today. She didn't come out with the others."

The sentinel looked up at Ransom. "We're only releasing two women this afternoon. Maybe you got the wrong date. It happens."

"No. That can't be. I just turned in the replacement credit paperwork this morning. I was told she was going to be released this afternoon."

The sentinel shrugged. "Sometimes they don't process it as fast as they need to," she said. "Try again tomorrow."

"Look," Ransom said. "My wife's name is Teya Lawe. Her sister is Mona Harrington. She's the director. Your boss. She gave me her word that my wife was going to be cut loose this afternoon."

The sentinel looked back at her clipboard. "Sorry, but her name's not on our list," she said. "Why don't you go around front and talk to someone at the desks. Better yet, call your sister-in-law. If there's an error, I'm sure she'll correct it."

"There has to be some mistake," he pressed. "I have a valid credit. My wife should have been released. It's the law."

"Go in the front doors and see what they can do," the sentinel said, clearly annoyed.

She went to fasten the lock. Ransom pulled on the chain-link gate, making it impossible for the guard to lock it.

The tall sentinel pulled out his nightstick and took a step toward Ransom.

"Let go of the gate right now. You're not going to get another warning," he said. His voice was cool and flat.

Ransom pulled harder on the gate.

The sentinel raised the nightstick and was about to bring it down on Ransom's fingers when Mona's voice rang out.

"Stand down!"

Ransom looked over the shoulder of the tall sentinel and saw Mona walking toward them. The sentinel lowered his nightstick and took a step back from the door.

"This guy claims his wife's supposed to be released today," the sentinel growled.

"I know why he's here," Mona said. She came up to the fence. "Let go of the gate, Ransom."

Ransom grabbed the chain link tight enough that he could feel the metal digging into the back of his knuckles. "You said everything was in order. You said she was going to be released. Where's Teya?"

"Let go of the fence, and I'll explain everything to you."

"I had a valid credit. You know that. Where's my wife?"

"Let go, Ransom, or I'll tell Alex to smash your fingers," she said, tossing her voice back to the tall guard who still had his nightstick at the ready.

Ransom gave Mona a hard look, then let go of the fence. With several quick motions, Mona locked the fence, then turned to the two sentinels. "Give us a moment," she instructed.

The sentinels looked at each other, then back at Ransom.

"He's not a threat," Mona said. "I need to speak with him privately."

The sentinels moved over to the door in the back of the building. Ransom noted that the tall one still hadn't put his nightstick away.

Mona lowered her voice. "Teya's not going to be released today,"

"What? Why not?"

"Your paperwork wasn't in order."

Ransom gave Mona a hard look. "Don't tell me you're pulling a bureaucratic stunt. What happened? Did I forget to check a box, or did the clerk forget to put the right stamp on it?"

Mona shook her head. "You were sold a fake credit."

"What are you talking about?"

"The man who sold you his replacement credit—Richard, right? He didn't have a credit to sell. In fact, I bet his name wasn't even Richard. The credit he turned in was a forgery. It was a good forgery—good enough that it fooled the clerk, and me, the first time I saw it. But it was fake. As a result, we can't release Teya."

"You're lying!" Ransom yelled. "You just can't stand the thought of us having more than two kids!"

"I'm sorry, Ransom. I really am. I know you emptied your entire savings to pay for it. I wish there was something I could do for you, but right now my hands are tied until you can produce a real credit."

Ransom swore, then hit the fence with his fist. Mona didn't flinch.

The taller of the two sentinels stepped forward.

"We're fine," Mona said without taking her eyes from Ransom.

The guard paused for a moment and took a step back.

"You're not the first one to get scammed, Ransom. We get two or three of these a month."

"Great. I feel better already."

"I want to help you. Come tomorrow, and we'll file a formal report. You can help us catch this guy before he cons someone else."

"I don't have time to file reports. I need to get my wife out of here!"

"I'm sorry. I can't help you."

Ransom swore again. "Mona, you can solve this entire problem right now if you want."

"Look, Ransom, if I hear about a credit, or if there is some way to get Teya out of here legally, I'll do it. I can promise you that. But that's all I can do. Go home and be with your kids. They need their dad right now."

Ransom tried to keep his voice calm. "I can't do that. I don't have time to sit at home and fill out all your paperwork."

"Then there really is nothing I can do," Mona said as she turned to leave.

"I'll get her out of there one way or another!" he shouted after her.

Mona didn't respond. The tall snatcher held the door open for her and then for the shorter sentinel. He gave Ransom one last look, then stepped inside the building.

The door clicked shut.

Furious, Ransom hurried down the alley and out into the street.

* * *

Ransom arrived at apartment 401 breathless and sweaty. He banged on the door.

"Open up, Richard. Give me back my money, you cheat."

He knew the odds of finding Richard were zero, but he had to at least try. What else was he going to do? He took a step back and kicked the door. The thin plywood cracked. He took another step back and kicked the door again. A second crack ran through the door.

"What are you doing?"

Ransom turned. A gray-haired man stood at the door of apartment 402. He held a glass of water in one hand and was wearing nothing but a pair of cutoffs.

"Do you know where Richard is?" Ransom growled.

"Who?"

Ransom took a step toward the man. The man took an equal step back and started to close the door. Ransom stopped and put his hands in the air.

"I'm looking for Richard. The man who grew up in that apartment. Do you know where he moved?"

The old man raised his eyebrows. "Hate to tell you this, but no one has lived in that apartment for over a decade."

"What do you mean? I was in the apartment just yesterday with Richard."

The old man took a drink of water. "Maybe you were. But I've lived across the hall for twenty-five years, and I can tell you there hasn't been a soul living in that place for the last ten. Before that, a nice family lived there. Our kids used to play together. As far as I remember, they didn't have a kid named Richard."

Ransom looked at the door, then back at the old man. "I don't believe you. I told you that I was here last night. How would Richard get access to the place if he didn't live here?"

"Easy. The door's not locked. When the family left, they didn't lock it or leave any keys behind. Apartment's been open for years. Kind of surprised no one has ever squatted in it, to be honest with you. Guess it's because the entrance to our building isn't that easy to find."

"So you didn't see anyone come or go last night?"

The old man shook his head. "I wasn't here. After the parade, I went over to my daughter's house. Didn't get back until late."

Ransom walked over to the door and turned the knob.

The door opened.

Ransom entered the apartment. It was just as it had been yesterday. He walked into the living room, looking for any clue that Richard might have left behind. Everything was the same.

He headed down the hall and opened the rest of the rooms. The first three were bedrooms. All were dusty and empty. Then Ransom came to the last door on the left—the room Richard had claimed was the bedroom he grew up in. He turned the knob and slowly opened the door. It was a bathroom. An old one too—it had a tub.

The anger Ransom had felt turned to despair. Mona was right. He had been tricked. Whoever this Richard was must have known about the apartment. All he had to do was concoct some kind of story. The rest was easy. Ransom wanted to scream. He wanted to beat up the old man who stood in his doorway. But the pressing matter at hand was to find a way to get Teya out of the Infirmary.

And there was only one way to do that.

He hurried out of the apartment and past the old man, whose water glass was now empty.

* * *

The door to the repair shop was held open by a six-foot metal floor fan. Ransom strode in and noticed Jorge standing behind the counter, talking with a customer.

"I need to talk to Esperanza," Ransom said, interrupting him.

Jorge didn't even look at Ransom. "I'll be with you in a minute," he said flatly, returning his attention to the customer.

Ransom walked behind the counter and headed for the back door.

"Hey!" Jorge said. "You can't go back there."

He stood, blocking Ransom's way. Ransom pushed Jorge to

the side and headed for the back room.

A beam of light shone under the crack to the back room. Just as Ransom reached it, the door swung open, and he was greeted by Nauleo.

Ransom tried to push past the beefy Polynesian, but Nauleo didn't budge.

"Get out of here," Nauleo said.

Before Ransom could answer, someone grabbed him around the neck. Ransom was pulled off his feet. He couldn't breathe. He grabbed the man's arm and tried to loosen his grip, but to no avail. Next, he threw his weight against the man, and they slammed into the wall. His assailant's arm loosened just enough that Ransom was able to escape his grasp. He turned and saw Jorge put his hand to his head, a dazed look on his face.

Ransom jumped to his feet. Nauleo was right in front of him. He swung his arm back and punched Ransom in the stomach.

Ransom felt the air go out of him. He fell to his knees. Nauleo raised his fist again when Esperanza's voice echoed through the dark hallway.

"Enough!" she said.

The light from the back room poured over Ransom's face. The next thing he knew, Esperanza was kneeling next to him.

"Are you okay?" she asked.

"I'm fine," Ransom said. He was slowly getting his breath back. The only thing hurt was his pride. He wanted a shot at Nauleo without Jorge's arm around his neck. He decided not to tell Esperanza that.

Esperanza looked at Jorge and pointed to the door leading to the front of the store.

"Get back and mind the shop," she said. "We have a customer who's probably wondering what on earth is going on back here."

Jorge started to speak, but Esperanza interrupted him.

"Go!"

He finally headed to the front of the repair shop, but not before giving Ransom a hard look.

"Go out there and help Jorge," Esperanza said to Nauleo.

"Someone needs to watch the monitors."

"Everything the monitors show, you can see from behind the counter. Now go out there and help Jorge." When he was gone, Esperanza offered to help Ransom up.

"I'm fine," he said, sucking in a breath. He used the wall as a brace as he moved to stand.

Esperanza looked him over, then headed to the back room. Ransom followed her. The room was just how he remembered it, except this time there was no food on the table. Her baby was sleeping in a crib against the far wall.

"Have a seat," Esperanza said, motioning to the chair in which Ransom had refused to sit the last time. This time he sat, letting his body sink into the cool leather.

Esperanza walked to the refrigerator and returned with a cold bottle of water. She held it out to Ransom.

"I'm fine."

"With all that sweat running down your face, I'd say you need to cool off. What did you do? Run here?"

"Something like that."

She held out the bottle again. This time Ransom accepted it and took a long drink. The cold rushed straight to his head. He set the bottle on the table and grabbed his head in pain.

"Put your tongue on the roof of your mouth," Esperanza said.

"What?"

"Press your tongue against the roof of your mouth. The headache will go away in a few seconds."

Ransom obeyed, surprised to find the headache dissolving. "How'd you learn that?" he asked.

"Most people don't have experience drinking ice-cold liquids nowadays. It's something I learned when I was a kid. My brother and I used to see how many ice cubes we could shove in our mouths. That helped me get past it."

"Where'd you live that you ate ice as a kid? Alaska?"

"Why don't you tell me what brought you here in such a hurry?"

Ransom noticed that she had sidestepped the question, but he decided against trying to follow up. There were more pressing matters. "Teya's in the Infirmary."

"I've heard," Esperanza said.

"How'd you know?"

"I told you, we have sources." She paused and laced her fingers together. "So what does her imprisonment have to do with us?"

"I've tried to buy credits, but nothing's panned out. I have three days to resolve this before I'm out of options."

"And you thought we might be able to help."

Ransom wiped the sweat from his brow with his arm and nodded.

Esperanza leaned forward. "I'm a little confused. Last time we spoke, you said you wanted nothing to do with me or my group. 'Terrorists,' I believe you called us."

Ransom shifted uncomfortably in his seat. "I want you to get her out," he said quietly.

Now it was Esperanza's turn to pause. She seemed genuinely surprised by the request. "What makes you think we can get your wife out of the Infirmary?"

"Because I think you've done it before."

Esperanza smiled. "And what makes you think that?"

"You said you have sources in there. I'm sure you pay them well enough to help with other things."

"We use our sources for information. Nothing more."

"I know that women escape from the Infirmary occasionally. The general public may not know about it, but being married to the sister of the director, I hear things from time to time. Besides, everyone knows there are people who leave the city for a day hike or something and never come back. These folks go somewhere. Maybe to your hideout in the Green States. Maybe somewhere else. But the only reason I can see you staying around is to help people get out when they're ready to go."

"That's an interesting theory."

"I don't have time to play games. I want you to help get my wife out of the Infirmary. Can you do that or not?"

"Sorry, but I'm afraid we can't do anything for you."

Ransom sat in stunned silence for a moment. "Why not? The other day, you were gung-ho about helping me."

"That was before your wife decided to turn herself in. That

made your situation much more complicated."

"Complicated, or impossible?"

Esperanza pursed her lips. She closed her eyes for a minute, then opened them. "I need to talk with some friends before I can give you any promises."

"Fine. When will I know?"

Esperanza let out a short laugh. "We're not some kind of service. You can't just snap your fingers and expect us to jump to attention. Even if we agreed to do it, these sorts of things take planning and time."

"Time is the one thing we don't have."

"Well, if we do decide to help you, you need to have a plan too. For example, where are you going to go once we've freed your wife?"

Ransom stopped. He hadn't thought past the first step. He now realized going home would be impossible. Women didn't just walk away from the Infirmary unnoticed. Once the government knew she was missing, the apartment would be the first place they'd look.

"I—I don't know. I guess our apartment is out of the question."

"That's right. They know where you live," Esperanza said. "They know where your family and friends live. You can't just walk past the city walls without a permit. But let's say you had one and got out before the city guards were told about your wife's escape. Where would you go? What would you do? You can't go far or survive for long—especially with a three-month-pregnant wife and two young children. You don't have the supplies or the know-how to stay alive out there. And, if by some stroke of luck you happened to make it to a nearby town, odds are that alerts would be sent out and photos of your family would be in the hands of every law enforcement agency. You'd be arrested the minute you showed up."

Ransom sighed. "You know what? You're right. I don't have a plan. I'd probably be caught within an hour. That's why I'm here. I think you know how to get Teya out of the Infirmary and my family out of the city."

"You realize our help comes with a price."

"And what price is that?"

"As soon as we get Teya out, we take you and your family with us—you remain silent about our help the rest of your life. You become acquainted with the way we live, and you can raise your family in safety and security."

Ransom thought about the proposal. He felt that saying "yes" was making a deal with the devil, but there was no other option. If he waited, and they lost this baby, he knew his relationship with Teya would never be the same—their family would never be the same. Going with Esperanza was a risk too, but at the very least it would mean they'd have a third child and be together. And if things didn't work out, he could always find a new place for his family to live.

"I need to think about it," Ransom finally said.

"There's no point in even asking my people to risk a break-out unless you're on board one hundred percent. Even then, I can't guarantee they'll agree to it."

"Don't try to pressure me into this."

"You came to me, Ransom. The only thing I'm doing is explaining your options. Take all the time you want to think about it, but I'm not even going to broach the subject with anyone until I hear back from you."

"She undergoes the procedure in three days."

"Then you'd better make up your mind sooner rather than later."

Ransom knew that every minute he waited lessened the chance of getting Teya out. "Okay," he growled in frustration. "I'm in."

Esperanza smiled. "Great. First thing we need to do is run to your house and get some supplies."

"I thought you said you had to consult with your team."

"We've already agreed to take you, Ransom. We just had to make sure you were committed. I think we can get Teya out of the Infirmary tonight, but we need to start now. You want to know how we're going to do it?"

Ransom nodded. He might as well know what the devil had signed him up to do.

twenty-two

Ransom walked briskly down the street toward his apartment, Esperanza trailing fifty feet behind— or at least, she had been a block ago, when he last looked over his shoulder. Esperanza had warned him that a sentinel or someone else from the Census Bureau might be watching them, and that, for the time being, they couldn't be seen together. But he couldn't seem to resist. It somehow reassured him that he'd get Teya out of the Infirmary and wasn't dreaming up a solution.

He headed down the alley and across the plaza, stealing another glance at Esperanza as he entered the building. She was on the far side of the plaza. As Ransom took the stairs to the apartment, he realized how eerily quiet the building was during the day. The sounds of people's lives that leaked through the doors and echoed down the hallways was gone. The stillness of the building unnerved him, and he hurried up the last flight of stairs to his apartment, his footfalls the only sound.

Inside the apartment, he was greeted by a blast of hot air. He was glad the boys were with Eve. Her apartment faced north and always seemed cooler in the summer. Leaving the door slightly ajar, he started opening windows and then the balcony door. He was downing warm water when he heard the front door click open.

Esperanza entered and shut the door behind her. The sound of the door shutting echoed through the apartment. She brushed black strands of hair out of her eyes and took off her shoes.

"Thirsty?" Ransom asked.

"I'm fine," she said. She looked around the apartment. "Where's your bedroom? We need to hurry."

Ransom set the cup on the counter and showed Esperanza to the bedroom. He took a large, dark green canvas bag from the top shelf of the wardrobe, momentarily noting the faded logo of the Recycling Center. Then he got on his hands and knees and pulled out a large drawer at the foot of the bed, retrieving a blue backpack.

"This is all you have to carry everything?" Esperanza said, looking at it as he tried to dust them off.

"I can't say that going camping is at the top of my family's priority list."

Esperanza grabbed the backpack. "These will do, but you'll need to stuff that bag as full as you can. You won't be able to take everything, you realize. Just clothes, medicine, and some hygiene items like toothbrushes, soap, and a comb."

"What about food?" Ransom asked. He couldn't imagine leaving everything Mona had brought over the previous night.

"We'll have enough for our needs."

"There's a lot of food in the kitchen. Should I give it to someone?"

"Leave it. It would look odd if you just gave the food away—even to a trusted neighbor or family member. Nobody does that. If you want this plan to work, the last thing you should do is draw attention to yourself. Besides, there's no guarantee that we're going to get Teya. You realize that, right? If it doesn't work and we have to abort the mission, you might be coming back here with the boys tomorrow. If that's the case, it's best that you have food and other supplies until we can regroup and figure out something else. Now, where does your wife keep her clothes?"

Ransom pointed to the chest of drawers. "Bottom three are hers," he said. "And she hangs some dresses and other things in the wardrobe."

Esperanza knelt down and opened the bottom drawer. "I'll pack for Teya. You take care of yourself and the boys."

Ransom reached into the wardrobe. He pulled out some shirts and his other pair of jeans and shoved them in the canvas bag.

"Those are all short-sleeve shirts," Esperanza noted. "Make sure you pack something warm."

"What are you talking about? It's August."

"It gets cool where we're going—even in the summer. Trust me, the last thing you want is for you or your boys to get sick. We need you to be healthy. It makes the trip easier and faster."

Ransom pulled a threadbare sweatshirt from the chest of drawers and a worn jacket from the wardrobe and put them in the bag. Then he headed to the boys' room and crammed as much of their summer and winter clothing into the bag as possible. He was about to zip it when he noticed the wooden elephant and lion sitting on the window shelf. Even though they weren't essentials, he decided to pack them anyway. Holding a familiar toy might be something that would help comfort the boys during their long journey.

When he was done packing, Ransom set the bag in the hall and headed to the kitchen. Hunger was gnawing at his stomach. He opened the refrigerator and grabbed a peach, eating it over the sink. Esperanza was cinching up the backpack as he walked back into the bedroom.

"Ready?" he asked.

Esperanza hoisted the bag over her shoulder. "All set."

They walked to the door. Esperanza put her hand on the doorknob and turned around.

"Okay, this time I'll leave first. Wait a minute, then head over to your neighbor's and get the kids. I'll be sitting in the alley on the bench closest to the street. When I see you come out, I'll start walking to the shop. You'll have two kids with you, so staying a good distance from me shouldn't be a problem. Remember, we don't want to stand out or be seen together. And two people with two kids, each carrying bulging sacks, will stand out."

"Understood," Ransom said.

"If the police stop me on the way to the shop for some reason, turn around and head back here. If it's you that gets stopped, I'll head to the shop. Whatever happens, don't try to find me. When things settle down, I'll find a way to communicate with you again."

"I got it," Ransom replied, though her comment simply reinforced the growing feeling in his gut that anything could go wrong.

"Good. I'll see you at the end of the alley then."

Esperanza opened the door and headed down the hall. Ransom

shut the door and watched her through the peephole until she disappeared down the steps. He started counting to sixty in his head. As he did, he turned and looked over the apartment. As small and impractical as it was, it was the only home his children had ever known. He looked down the hallway into the living room and remembered countless wrestling matches with the boys on that floor. He walked through the kitchen onto the balcony and into the hot summer air.

His eyes rested on the bench where he and Teya had often talked late into the summer nights when they'd first moved in. It was also on that bench that she'd announced the news of their second child. Ransom smiled. Those times seemed so simple and so long ago. A new home was waiting for them somewhere. He only hoped his choice would allow him and Teya to raise all their children in peace.

Esperanza came into view on the plaza below. Ransom finished counting to sixty when she was halfway across. He didn't move right away. Instead, he watched until she reached the end of the alley. This was it. Ransom took a breath, then heaved the bulging duffle bag over his shoulder and headed to the door.

He stopped in the middle of the kitchen and grabbed a burlap bag from under the sink. Despite Esperanza's warning, he filled it with most of the food Mona had given him the night before to give to Eve. When the bag was full, he hurried to her apartment.

He didn't bother locking the door behind him.

✳ ✳ ✳

Ransom emerged a few minutes later with the two boys in tow. He made a beeline for the alley. Esperanza picked up the bag and turned the corner before Ransom and the boys were halfway across the plaza.

Ransom felt seized by a sense of urgency once Esperanza was out of sight. He grabbed the boys' hands tighter and picked up the pace, going as fast as he dared.

"Why aren't we going home?" James asked.

"We need to go see someone who can help us get Mom."

"Are we going to see Mom today?" James got excited.

"Maybe."

"I miss Mom."

"I do too."

"Me too," Warren said.

Esperanza already had a half-block lead on him by the time they reached the 'Vard. It wasn't that Esperanza was walking fast as much as it was that Ransom was slowed due to the boys. He picked up the pace, and his sons jogged alongside to keep up.

Halfway to the repair shop, Warren stopped. "My shoe's untied," he said.

"You'll be fine. We'll be there soon. I'll tie it then."

Warren wrangled free of Ransom's grip, then sat on the sidewalk and reached for his shoes. Suddenly he jumped to his feet. He looked at his hands and started to cry. "Hot," he said, panicked.

Ransom took Warren's hands and rubbed them together.

"Your hands will be fine," he said.

"Tie my shoe please, Daddy," Warren asked between sniffles.

"Wait until we get to where we're going. It's cool there, and it will just take a minute." He started to move down the sidewalk.

"No! Tie my shoe!" Warren was crying now, his tantrum fueled by his recent injury.

Ransom tried to carry him with one arm, but Warren writhed in the air, making it impossible. Ransom glanced down the sidewalk at Esperanza. She was over a block away and walking fast.

Ransom continued walking. Warren continued to wiggle.

It was too much.

Ransom set Warren on his feet, then knelt down and started tying his son's shoe. The heat radiated from the sidewalk like an oven. He tied the shoe in a double knot and stood.

"Everything okay?"

Ransom spun around. A police officer stood behind him, his arms folded across his chest.

"Yeah," Ransom said. "Everything's fine. My son's shoe came untied."

The officer looked at the kids, then back at Ransom. "Can I see some identification, please?"

Ransom's heart skipped a beat. He reached into his back

pocket and pulled out his wallet. He fished out his identity card and handed it to the officer.

The officer looked it over, then handed it back to Ransom. "What's in the bag?"

"Clothes."

"Where you going with it?"

"Thrift store," Ransom said, relieved the thought had come to him in time. "Going to give them a second life."

The cop paused. "Open the bag."

Ransom shrugged. "Sure." He set the bag on the ground.

"Unzip it," the cop ordered, although he was still being relatively friendly.

Ransom knelt down and opened the bag. Two of Warren's shirts spilled to the ground.

"That's a lot of clothes."

Ransom said nothing, smiling as if he agreed.

The cop lifted up one of the shirts with his shoe. It certainly looked like something worthy of a thrift store. "Everything seems to be in order," he said. "Have a nice day." He nodded to Ransom and headed down the street.

Ransom stuffed the clothes back in the bag while James and Warren watched the cop. When the bag was again slung over his shoulder, he made his way to the repair shop as fast as they could manage.

When they arrived, the shop was empty except for Jorge. He was putting an old tube television back on a top shelf.

His face darkened when he saw Ransom, but he motioned with his head toward the back door.

"What's all this stuff?" James asked as they walked by the glass counter filled with tools.

"Junk," Ransom said, though it was more to Jorge than to James.

He took the kids to the back room. Esperanza was attempting to calm Gabby, who was crying. A look of relief crossed her face when she saw Ransom.

"What happened? I thought you were right behind me."

Ransom explained about the shoe and the police officer.

"Did anyone follow you here?" Esperanza said.

"I don't think so," Ransom said, though he really hadn't paid much attention.

Esperanza looked over at Nauleo.

"For the next hour, keep an eye open for people who walk past the shop more than once. Ransom may have been followed."

The baby continued crying. Esperanza grabbed a blanket from the crib and moved to the couch. She rested the baby's head on her shoulder, then covered it with a blanket. Esperanza looked at Warren and James. "You boys look tired. Would you like something cold to drink?"

Ransom looked down at his sons. Their faces were red and sweating, their eyes darting back and forth between Esperanza and Nauleo. Ransom coaxed them toward the two chairs. They both climbed into the same chair, still looking around suspiciously.

Ransom went to the refrigerator and took down two bottles of cold water. He twisted off the caps and handed the bottles to the boys. James quickly set his bottle on the table. "It's cold," he said.

Warren, on the other hand, seemed happy to have something to drink and sipped it quietly.

Ransom sat on the chair next to the boys. "When do we move?"

"Tonight," Esperanza said. "Late."

"Until then?"

"Relax. Eat. Take a nap if you want. It could be a long night."

The boys were looking confused by the conversation, so Ransom opened the bag at his feet and took out the wooden elephant and lion. The boys' faces brightened, and within a minute, they were on the floor playing with the toys.

Ransom leaned back in his chair and watched them play. He wondered what Teya was doing—or what was being done to her—at that very moment. He hoped she knew he was coming.

twenty-three

At exactly 10:00 p.m., Esperanza, Jorge, and Ransom left the repair shop and headed south down the 'Vard. It was a warm, moonless night. A breeze blew in from the west. Ransom, tired of the heat, hoped this meant a storm would arrive in the next day or two.

At the nearest stop they waited five minutes for the next tram. The tram took them to the 25th Street stop and, without saying a word, the three of them headed toward the Census Bureau. Without looking behind them, they cut across the alley where Ransom had waited for Teya the previous afternoon.

The only light in the alley was a spotlight over the back door. It bathed the alley in a cold, white glow. It was the brightest artificial light Ransom had seen. He wondered how much it cost to keep on and how the Census Bureau had received a waiver for the light-pollution laws.

They walked down the alley at a brisk pace. Ransom glanced over at the chain-linked area where he'd spoken with Mona earlier that day. The light glistened off the razor wire.

At the end of the alley, they turned left and walked another block until they reached Gore Park. They followed the meandering sidewalk inside the park until they came to a metal picnic bench.

Jorge pulled a cloth out of his bag and wiped the dirt and dried bird droppings off the seats and the table. Esperanza sat down.

"The padlock on the gate isn't the same one that was there last week," Esperanza said to Jorge. "Can you pick it?"

"Shouldn't be a problem. Didn't look like anything fancy.

They'll probably have something better next time."

Esperanza leaned back and looked over at Ransom. "Have a seat. Relax," she said.

"How long do we have to wait?" Ransom asked.

"Depends on when our people can get in place. Could be ten minutes. Could be a couple of hours. Don't worry. They'll let us know a few minutes before it happens."

Ransom shuffled his feet impatiently, then sat on the far end of the table. He rested his feet on the seats, thinking about James and Warren. The hardest part of the plan was leaving his children asleep in the back room of the repair shop. They both went to bed reluctantly, clutching their wooden animals and staring around the room with big eyes. It had taken over an hour for both of them to fall asleep. Nauleo's wife had come with their own child to watch the boys and Gabby, but all Ransom could think about was his sons sleeping on the couch, bathed by the icy glow of the security monitors. Esperanza had given Ransom the option of staying behind, but he had refused. Without him, he knew that Teya was unlikely to walk away with two strangers.

He heard the crunching of shoes on gravel. A group of teenagers were cutting across the park. They stopped at a picnic bench two down from where Ransom sat. One of the teens said something, and the rest of them laughed. He kept his eyes on them.

"Ignore them," Esperanza said. "They aren't going to bother us."

"I just want things to go smoothly."

"Everything's going to be just fine. We've done this successfully a dozen times over the last two years. We know when to abort and when to go forward. You do what we say, and everything will work out. What you need to do is relax the best you can. Being uptight will simply waste energy and make you tired. You'd be better off closing your eyes and resting until we're ready to roll."

Ransom knew Esperanza was right but said nothing. He turned around on the bench so he was facing the apartment building across the street. Half the windows glowed with dull yellow-orange light. There were silhouettes of a dozen people standing on various balconies. He counted up five stories to the last window on the left, where Mona's apartment should be. Her light was on, the blinds open. From where he was sitting, he couldn't see anything through her windows except the ceiling. He wondered if she was thinking about her sister or if she even cared anymore.

Thinking about Mona made Ransom angry—not exactly a low-energy emotion—so he focused his attention elsewhere. He looked across the park to 24th Street. In five minutes' time, he counted thirteen people hurrying down the street. Some of them entered and exited the nearby apartment buildings. Others walked down the block. He swatted a mosquito that landed on his arm. He looked over at Jorge and Esperanza. They spoke in low voices in Spanish. They talked for a few minutes, then became quiet. Esperanza leaned against the table and closed her eyes. He looked back up at Mona's window. It was dark. He wondered how she could sleep when her sister was locked up.

After a while, he did some stretches, watched the teenagers, and walked around. When his anxiety was nearly out of control, Esperanza stood and pulled something out of her pocket. Ransom couldn't tell what it was, but when she pushed a button, a small screen lit up, bathing her face in a dull, blue light. She pushed another button, and the screen went dark. She slid the object back in her pocket.

"Lights will be going off in a few minutes," she said.

"What was that?" Ransom asked.

"A messenger," Esperanza said.

"A what?"

"It's a computer that sends and receives short messages." She took it out of her pocket and held it up for Ransom to see, pushing the button. Ransom read the message on the screen.

In place. Lights off in 3.

As if reading his mind, Esperanza said, "No. You can't find these anywhere in the city. Not even at the Station. This is something we've made." She pushed some buttons and put the device back in her pocket, then climbed on the table and slowly turned in a circle.

"I don't see anyone, Jorge," she said. "I think we're good to get the equipment out now."

Jorge stood and unzipped the backpack. Esperanza jumped off the table and pulled three objects out of the backpack. She handed one to Jorge, tucked another under her arm, and held the last one out for Ransom.

It was some sort of mask, with something that felt like binoculars attached to the front. It weighed about ten pounds.

"What is this?"

"Night vision goggles."

"What do they do?"

Esperanza let out a short laugh. "You can't be serious. You've never heard of these before?"

"I've never recycled anything like this before."

"They'll help you see in the dark. They'll magnify even the slightest amount of light and let you see as if it were day. It gives everything a green tint, but you'll be able to navigate your way around without a problem. Here, let me help you put them on."

She took the goggles from Ransom's hand and reached up, putting them over his face and then adjusting the head strap.

"I don't see anything," Ransom said.

"You won't until I turn them on. Trust me—you don't want to do that until the power goes out."

Ransom pulled them away from his eyes so he could look at Esperanza.

"Once it's dark," Esperanza said, "we're going to run at full speed toward the gate. It will be dark, so no one should see us. However, if we run into someone with a candle or another light source in the alley, we need to abort the mission. It's bad enough to be caught with this equipment. It will be even worse if we're caught with it inside. Got it?"

Ransom nodded.

Esperanza continued, "Keep in mind, these goggles are close to sixty years old. They may not work that great. If you can't get yours to work, don't worry about it. Just let me or Jorge know, and we'll guide you in the dark. Finally, if the lights come on and you're wearing them, you'll be temporarily blinded. When we say take them off, you'll need to do it. Got it?"

Ransom was about to ask another question when everything went dark. Someone walking on the sidewalk near the park cursed. Ransom couldn't blame him. A power failure in the middle of the night was rotten luck for anyone trying to enjoy the evening.

He quickly put the goggles back on and felt Esperanza push something on the side. For a moment, all he could see was a wall of green. Then the world came into focus.

Esperanza was looking at him through her goggles. She waved. "Can you see me?" she asked.

Ransom waved back. "You're green."

"Can you see your way out of the park?"

Ransom looked down the sidewalk. He could see it snaking its way through the park, past the cactus garden. "I'm good," he said.

"Excellent. Now keep quiet and follow us. We're hoping they can keep the power off for twenty minutes or so, but they may have to turn it on again sooner, so we have to be quick. Our goal is to get in and out in less than fifteen minutes."

Ransom nodded. "I'm ready."

He saw Esperanza hold the cross around her neck to her lips, then she and Jorge took off down the sidewalk. Ransom followed, staying close behind them. They ran past a man shuffling his feet, his hand out in front of him, as he slowly made his way along the sidewalk.

Ransom followed Esperanza and Jorge into the service alley. The night vision technology didn't work as well here, but Ransom was still able to see well enough to keep up. They stopped when they reached the fenced area.

Ransom wiped a bead of sweat from his forehead and heard Jorge say something to Esperanza in Spanish. He looked up as she reached into the backpack and handed him a small kit. Jorge took out some wires, then inserted them into the padlock. There was the faint sound of metal scraping metal, then the lock popped open. Jorge removed the lock and pushed the gate wide.

Ransom and Esperanza stepped inside the fenced area. He watched Jorge shut the gate and put the lock back in place without locking it, and then they moved to the door.

"How are you going to open it?" Ransom whispered. "There's no lock on the outside."

"The door is sealed electronically. If the power's out, the door doesn't work," Esperanza said.

Ransom watched Jorge stick something under the door. He pulled back, and the door silently swung open.

"Once we go inside, Ransom, there's no backing out," Esperanza warned. "Are you sure you want to do this?"

Ransom nodded even as apprehension bubbled up inside of him. Nothing was going to stop him from freeing Teya.

Jorge stepped inside.

"After you," Esperanza said to Ransom.

He took one last look around the alley, then stepped inside the building.

twenty-four

Ransom followed Esperanza and Jorge down the hall. On either side were office doors with frosted glass windows, the names of staff stenciled on each. Though he hadn't known what to expect when he'd entered, he was strangely disappointed that these halls were just like those of the Recycling Center's office building.

Esperanza and Jorge turned right, and Ransom followed them down an identical corridor. Just as they reached the end of the hall, Ransom saw a flickering green light playing off the walls.

Jorge stopped in his tracks and turned around. "Snatcher. Hide!"

Esperanza reached for the first door on her right. Locked. She raced back to another door while Jorge checked the doors on the left.

"Over here," she hissed. She motioned for Jorge and Ransom to follow. When they were all inside, Esperanza shut the door quietly, then took a step back, pulling the blowgun out of her pocket. She flicked her wrist, and the blowgun extended. Jorge did the same with his.

Ransom looked around for something he could use for a weapon. There wasn't much. A pile of papers was stacked neatly on one corner of the desk. A ceramic coffee mug with three dull pencils was placed on the stack of papers. A typewriter sat in front of the chair. Aside from the desk, the only other furniture was a coat rack in one corner and a framed photograph of a smiling couple on the wall closest to the desk.

Suddenly Ransom became aware that the room was getting

brighter. He turned just in time to see flickering light, followed by a dark shape moving past the door.

They waited until the light disappeared. Then Jorge slowly opened the door and peeked into the hall. He paused for a moment, then, clutching the blowgun in his right hand, he stepped through the door. Ransom moved to follow him, but Esperanza grabbed him by the arm.

She held her finger to her lips and shook her head.

Ransom took a step back and waited. Thirty seconds later, Jorge popped his head in the office.

"It's clear. Let's go," he said in a low voice.

Ransom followed them out to the hall and down the corridor. At the intersection where they had seen the flickering light, they turned left. Twenty feet later, they came to a flight of stairs.

They descended in silence. There must have been less light for the goggles to pick up, as Ransom was having a difficult time seeing the stairs. He took them one at a time, gripping the rail.

As he reached the final landing, Ransom could just make out Jorge as he put the blowgun to his lips and blew. It was followed by a sharp cry, then, a moment later, the sound of something heavy falling to the floor.

Ransom looked down the stairs. The body of a sentinel was crumpled against a large metal door on the far wall. Jorge approached the body. He bent over and took a nightstick from the holster, then searched the man's pockets and pulled out a ring of keys. He flipped through the keys and found the one he was looking for.

He motioned for Esperanza and Ransom to join him.

Esperanza took the keys, and Ransom and Jorge picked up the body and sat it in the far corner. By the time they finished, Esperanza had unlocked the door.

"Take your goggles off before I open the door," she said. "This place is always well-lit—even when the power's out."

Ransom removed his goggles. It was pitch black. He felt Jorge take the goggles from his hand and unzip the backpack to shove the goggles inside.

Then Jorge said something to Esperanza in Spanish. There

was a click as the door opened.

Flickering yellow-orange light flooded the stairwell. Ransom looked past Esperanza down the hallway. The walls were cement and painted white. Every few feet was a door painted the same white color as the walls—ten doors on each side. Each door had a small glass window with a number above it, and between each door, white candles of various shapes and sizes lit the corridor. Ransom could hear voices and laughter from a room down the hall.

Esperanza turned to Ransom and whispered, "Jorge and I will take care of the guards. There's a chalkboard in the room to your left. Your wife's name and room number will be written on it."

Ransom nodded. He took a step toward the hallway, but Esperanza grabbed his arm.

"There's one thing I need to make absolutely clear," she hissed. "There have been times in the past when the women we've tried to rescue don't want to come. I don't know why. Maybe some of them really don't want the third child. Others may not like the thought of leaving their world for the unknown. It doesn't happen often, but it does happen."

"Why are you telling me this?" A feeling of dread was slowly rising in Ransom's body.

"Because if Teya doesn't want to come, Jorge and I won't wait around for her to make up her mind. Hopefully when she sees you, she'll come quietly. If not, you have about a minute to convince her. Otherwise, we're going to leave, with or without you. We can't afford to get caught, and we will put ourselves above the two of you. Got it?"

Ransom looked at Esperanza. "Understood," he said.

Jorge and Esperanza stepped into the hallway, blowguns at the ready. Jorge peeked around the corner to the room on his left. He looked back to Esperanza, pointed to his eyes, and held up three fingers.

Esperanza nodded.

They paused for a moment, then simultaneously ran into the room. Before Ransom could enter, he heard the sound of blowguns and two sharp cries. He entered the room just in time to see a nurse slump forward on a table covered with wooden chips and playing cards. A snatcher crumpled to the floor at the same moment.

The only person still standing wore a white lab coat and was holding his hands in the air. "Don't shoot," he said.

Ransom stopped. The man was Dr. Redgrave.

He surged past Esperanza and Jorge and grabbed Dr. Redgrave by the collar. "You work here? How does it feel to treat one of your employees like an animal?"

"I—all the clinic doctors take shifts here. Tonight was just my night. I haven't even seen Teya."

Esperanza ran up to Ransom and pushed him back. "We don't have time for this. Let's work on getting Teya out of here. Better yet, let's have the doctor unlock her door." She reached into the doctor's white lab pockets and brought out another ring of keys. She held them up to the doctor's face. "Why don't you unlock the door for us, doctor?"

Dr. Redgrave shook his head. "I'm not going to be any part of this. You open the door yourself."

Suddenly the doctor's body jerked, and he grabbed his neck where a silver dart protruded from the spot. His eyes rolled back in his head and he collapsed on the floor just as Jorge said, "No time for this."

Esperanza threw the ring of keys at Ransom. "The board says she's in room thirteen. You and Jorge go get her. I'll clean up here."

Ransom took the keys and hurried down the hall. He stopped at the door with the number thirteen over it and began inserting keys into the lock. It took him a minute to run through the keys. None of them worked.

Ransom swore and started over. One of the keys had to work—he must have gone through the keys too fast.

"We're running out of time," Jorge said, pushing Ransom to the side and pulling his pick lock tools from his back pocket. He furiously started working the lock.

Ransom looked past Jorge into the cell. It was dark inside. He pounded on the door with his fist. "Teya! Are you there? We're going to get you out."

Esperanza hurried down the hall.

"What's the holdup? We've been in the building almost ten minutes. We need to get out of here!"

"The keys didn't work," Ransom said.

Jorge swore as he fumbled with the lock.

Esperanza rested her free hand on his shoulders. "It's okay. Keep trying. Feel the tumblers. You've done this before, and you can do it again."

"It's dark inside," Ransom said. "I can't see her. What if this is the wrong room?"

"Then we run as fast as we can," Esperanza said.

Suddenly there was a loud click. Jorge wiped a bead of sweat from his forehead and swung the door open. Ransom could just make out what seemed like a toilet against the far wall. To the right of that, he could just make out the top third of a bed, and a pillow.

Esperanza gave Ransom a push toward the cell. "You've got sixty seconds" she said.

Ransom took a few steps into the dark room, then stopped. From the area of the bed, he could hear what sounded like faint, rapid breathing.

"Teya?"

Silence.

"Teya?" he repeated. "It's me. Are you in here?"

"Ransom?"

There was the padding sound of bare feet on the cement floor, then Teya emerged. She was wearing a threadbare white night-gown that came halfway down her thighs. There were bags under her eyes, and her hair was unkempt.

"Ransom!" she said, then threw her arms around him. "I thought it was the doctor or one of the guards."

Ransom held her close, then kissed the top of her head. Loose strands of her hair brushed against his cheek. He could smell her warm, familiar scent. For a moment, all his cares were forgotten. He was just glad to be with her again.

"Hey," Esperanza whispered loudly. "We need to go. Now!"

Teya looked over Ransom's shoulder and took a step back.

"What is she doing here?"

"I'll explain later. We need to get you out of here." He didn't want to scare Teya with a complicated discussion just yet.

Teya studied them suspiciously. "Where are the kids?" she said.

"They're fine. They're safe," Ransom answered. He reached down, grabbed Teya's hand, and pulled her toward the hall. "If you want to see them, you need to come with me."

Teya pulled the nightgown around her as she stepped into the hall. Jorge closed the door behind them, and without a word, he and Esperanza headed toward the exit.

Ransom started after them, holding Teya's hand as he followed them. He'd taken about a dozen steps when Teya stopped dead in her tracks. He was walking at such a brisk clip that he almost fell flat on his back.

He spun around. Teya was staring at a door with the number seven painted over the window.

"What are you doing?" Ransom hissed. He looked back over his shoulder. Esperanza and Jorge were almost to the door.

"It's Eloise. She's in this room," Teya said. She took a step toward the door.

Ransom pulled her toward him. "Eloise? How do you know?"

"I saw her staring out the window when I first came here. Her eyes grew wide when she saw me. She yelled something, but I couldn't hear it through the door."

Ransom stared down the hall, pulling Teya behind him again. "You can talk to her later. Right now we need to go."

Teya shook her arm free of his grasp. "I'm not going unless Eloise comes with us."

By her tone of voice and the look in her eyes, Ransom knew she was serious. He had seen that look before. Deep down, he knew he wasn't going to be able to change her mind. But he had to try. "We don't have time for this."

"It's my fault she's here," Teya hissed. "You found a way to open my door, so I'm sure you can open hers."

Ransom looked back at Esperanza and Jorge. They were impatiently waiting at the entrance of the hall, looking back at the two of them. Esperanza motioned for them to hurry. Ransom shook his head and pointed to Teya.

He turned back and faced her. "What are you thinking? Do you know what's going to happen if we get caught? Not only will both of us end up in a cell, but we stand a good chance of losing our kids."

This made Teya pause. For a second Ransom thought he had convinced her to come. Then the determined look came back to her eyes, and he knew he had lost.

"Then go without me. I'll be out in a few days. Come get me then."

Ransom grabbed her by the shoulders and pulled her close. "What is wrong with you?" he asked. "Our whole future is at stake!"

"No, Ransom, I can't live with myself if I walk out of here without Eloise. Either she comes, or I stay."

Esperanza came running down the hall toward them. "If you don't come with us now, we're leaving."

Ransom motioned to Teya. "She says she's not coming unless we take someone else with us."

Esperanza looked at Teya. "If you love your husband and children, you'll walk out with us."

"Open this door. I know you can do it. You opened mine."

Esperanza turned and looked at Ransom. "Jorge and I are leaving. We can't afford to stay here any longer. Stay with her if you wish, but keep in mind that you're on your own. I'm not taking any responsibility for you two from this point on."

"I'm not going anywhere unless Eloise is with us," Teya pressed, anger and fear warring in her voice.

Esperanza's eyes went from Ransom to Teya, then she turned and hurried down the hall. Jorge followed her up the stairs, and the door slammed shut after them.

Ransom grabbed Teya around the waist and started dragging her down the hall.

"Leave me!" Teya yelled.

At the same moment, the florescent lights on the ceiling cut into the candlelight, flooding the hallway with bright, white light.

Ransom swore. "Now we really need to hurry."

He was almost to the exit when the door burst open and Dragomir entered the hallway. His eyes registered surprise for a brief moment, then narrowed once he recognized Ransom.

"You!" he said, then whipped out his nightstick and ran toward them.

twenty-five

T here was more than simple malice in Dragomir's dark eyes. Ransom realized that the man wasn't going to be content with beating him up and hauling him off to jail—he was out for the kill.

Ransom looked over his shoulder at Teya. "Run!" he yelled even though he didn't know where she could go aside from her own cell. They were on the wrong end of a dead-end hallway.

He turned to face Dragomir just as the sentinel raised his nightstick. In a hand-to-hand fight, Ransom was confident that he could at least hold his own, but he knew he didn't stand a chance against a man with a weapon. A raised arm would be shattered. One well-placed blow to the head, and Ransom would be knocked unconscious or killed. Dragomir was thirty feet away. Then twenty. Ransom took a step back. He thought about their previous encounters. Dragomir was faster, stronger, and an overall better fighter. But he also had a short temper. The man would be less likely to think and more prone to make mistakes if Ransom could entice him to anger and to fight on emotion.

But there wasn't any time for taunting. Dragomir closed the last ten feet and swung at Ransom's head. Ransom threw himself backward at the last possible second. He could feel the air from the nightstick rush by his face. Suddenly off-balance, Dragomir was unable to stop the momentum of the nightstick as it hit the cement floor with a loud crack. Ransom could see the pain in the snatcher's face as the force of the impact traveled up his arm.

Before his assailant could react, Ransom took a step forward and kicked Dragomir in the chin. The sentinel looked momentarily stunned. He rubbed his jaw, then smiled. His teeth were covered with blood. "Is that all you got?" he snarled.

He raised the nightstick and swung again, leaning into his swing. Instead of jumping back, Ransom threw himself against one of the doors. The nightstick connected with air.

Quickly Ransom jumped to his feet and looked around for Teya. She was several paces behind him. She had a terrified look on her face. Ransom knew he couldn't dodge forever. He was quickly running out of hallway. And, sooner or later, Dragomir would connect. He had to take the offensive.

As Dragomir raised the nightstick and started forward, Ransom charged. His right fist connected with the sentinel's jaw while his other hand landed squarely in the man's stomach.

Dragomir gasped and took a step back.

"Run!" Ransom yelled to Teya. "Get out of here!"

She started running forward.

He turned just in time to see Dragomir swing his weapon. The nightstick connected with his left shoulder, and a searing pain shot through his arm. He fell to his knees.

Out of the corner of his eye he saw Teya run past.

"Where are you going?" Dragomir said.

Ransom looked up and saw the sentinel's beefy hand grab Teya by the arm and pull her close.

"Don't run out on me. You still owe me some one-on-one time," Dragomir said.

"Let me go!" Teya screamed.

His heart pounding, Ransom struggled to his feet. He moved his shoulder and grimaced as pain shot through his arm. He could still rotate it—slowly. He hoped that meant nothing was broken.

Dragomir turned his head, locked eyes with Ransom, and grinned. A trickle of blood ran from the corner of his mouth, down his chin, and to the floor.

"I'm going to beat you within an inch of your life, right in front of your pretty little wife," Dragomir snarled. "And when all your arms and legs are broken, you'll watch me do the same thing to her."

With one swing of his arm, he threw Teya against the wall.

Her body hit the cement with a sickening thud, then slid to the ground. A soft whimpering noise escaped her lips.

Rage flowed through Ransom's body. There was no way he was going to let Dragomir lay another hand on his wife. Ignoring the pain in his shoulder, he ran at Dragomir as fast as he could.

Dragomir raised his weapon, his knuckles snow-white from gripping the handle so hard. He swung, hard and fast. Ransom ducked again, but this time Dragomir took a step forward, and the nightstick came down. It caught Ransom on the temple. It wasn't a direct blow, but it was enough for stars to appear before Ransom's eyes and his legs to feel suddenly wobbly. Ransom took a step to the side, then stumbled against a door before slumping to the floor.

Everything seemed like it was in a fog. He saw Dragomir's boots stop inches from his body. His mind told him to move, but his body didn't respond. Then one of the boots shot forward and connected with Ransom's stomach. The air rushed out of him. He curled up in a fetal position, gasping for breath. A kick connected with his face. Ransom's head snapped back, his world momentarily filled with darkness and pain.

The coppery taste of blood filled Ransom's mouth when he finally opened his eyes. His head throbbed, and there was a ringing sound in his ears. Then he felt something heavy on his chest. He looked down and saw Dragomir's black boot firmly planted on his breastbone. The pressure on his chest increased until he started panicking, the air slowly being squeezed from his lungs.

His chest felt as though it was going to explode, and Ransom clawed at the boot with his hands. He tried to cry out, but there was no air in his lungs, and only a soft gurgle escaped his lips. Kicking his legs wildly, Ransom struggled to get some leverage so he could take a breath.

Dragomir jabbed Ransom's face with the stick. "Cat got your tongue?" he said. He smiled a wicked pink grin.

He jabbed again. "Keep those eyes open. I don't want you to miss a second of me and your wife together. It will be the last thing you ever see."

Blackness crept around the edge of Ransom's vision. He made

one last attempt to push the weight from his lungs. Then the darkness closed in.

Suddenly air filled his chest. He took in a deep breath and coughed, sending blood and spit onto the floor.

His vision returned, and he looked up at Dragomir. The man was wheeling around in the hall like a drunk. When he turned away, Ransom saw Teya on Dragomir's back, her long fingernails dug into the sentinel's eyes and nose. Blood ran from Dragomir's face. The sentinel took four blind swings with the nightstick, the last one hitting Teya on the top of her head. Teya screamed and dug her fingers deeper into his face until Dragomir howled and dropped the weapon. It clattered to the floor and rolled toward Ransom. Dragomir reached his arms over his head, trying to grab Teya.

Ransom grabbed the nightstick and got to his feet. The world spun. He reached out and balanced himself just as Dragomir threw himself against the wall. Teya's body made a dull thump as it connected once again with the cement. She lost her grip and fell to the floor.

The sentinel spun around and grabbed Teya by the shoulders. He picked her up and threw her down the hall.

Dragomir turned and looked at Ransom. He had three deep scratch marks on each cheek. Blood was still flowing from his right nostril, and one eye was shut over a line of blood. Drops of it fell from his face to the floor.

The sentinel swore, lowered his shoulder, and charged. Ransom swung the nightstick, but he was in too much pain to swing it fast. He missed Dragomir's head, but hit his right shoulder. It didn't slow Dragomir down. He slammed into Ransom, knocking him back into the wall. Then he grabbed Ransom by the shoulder.

Ransom screamed at the pain as he was tossed to the floor. He struggled to his feet, but Dragomir pushed him back down. He looked on helpless as the sentinel knelt next to him and delivered blow after blow to Ransom's kidneys. Ransom writhed in pain. He raised the nightstick and brought it down on the guard's back. It had no effect. More punches landed. The pain became unbearable, and the nightstick fell from Ransom's hand.

The punches stopped, and Dragomir leaned forward.

Ransom looked at Dragomir. He opened his mouth to speak, but no words came out. He coughed up blood.

"That's it?" Dragomir said. "No final words?"

A gurgling sound escaped Ransom's lips.

"What was that?" Dragomir said. He turned his head and leaned closer so his ear was just inches from Ransom's face.

Mustering every ounce of his strength, Ransom grabbed Dragomir's head and pulled it toward his mouth. He bit into Dragomir's ear as hard as he could.

Blood squirted into his mouth. Dragomir screamed. He punched Ransom in the face and jumped back, grabbing his ear. Blood flowed between the cracks in his fingers and down the back of his hand.

Ransom looked over at Teya's still body. He picked himself up on his hands and knees and crawled toward her.

Halfway there, Dragomir's strong arms grabbed his feet. "Where do you think you're going?"

Dragomir flipped Ransom on his back and started dragging him down the hall.

Out of the corner of his eye, Ransom saw the nightstick. He reached out and grabbed it as he went sliding past. Ransom sat up and hit Dragomir's wrist as hard as he could. Dragomir screamed, letting go of Ransom and clutching his wrist with his free hand.

Ransom staggered to his feet. Pain exploded through his body. He felt as though his legs were about to collapse. He looked up just as Dragomir lunged toward him. Ransom flipped the night-stick so it was pointing straight at Dragomir's stomach. He felt the stick sink deep in his combatant's flesh. Dragomir's eyes grew big as the breath rushed out of him. He grabbed his stomach, dropped to his knees, and rolled to the floor, gasping.

Breathing hard, Ransom stood over him and raised the night-stick and brought it down as hard as he could above the guard's bloodied ear. The guard's eyes rolled up in his head and closed.

Ransom heard the door at the end of the hall close. He started to his feet, ready to take on another sentinel. Instead, he saw

Esperanza and Jorge running down the hall.

"Looks like you took him out before we could come and help," Esperanza said, nodding to Dragomir's limp body.

Esperanza held out her hand. Ransom took it and stood on his feet. "You came back," he said between breaths.

"Don't flatter yourself," Esperanza said. "We're stuck in the building. The lights came back on and engaged the electronic lock. We need a passkey to get out of here. Since I forgot to take one from the guards, we had no choice but to find one."

Esperanza moved to Dragomir's motionless body. She knelt down at his side and checked his pulse, then determined whether he was breathing. Quickly, she searched his pockets at the same time, pulling out a white ID card and a set of keys. She threw the keys into her backpack, then slid the card into her pocket. She glanced up at Ransom. "You going to leave him like that?" she asked.

"Like what?"

"Alive. Now's your chance to take him out for good. End his threat to your family forever."

"I can't do that. I'm not a killer."

"He would have killed you. Teya too."

"But he didn't. Besides, if I hadn't stopped him, you would have got him when you came back."

Teya shook her head. "From the way you look, you're lucky to be alive."

Ransom looked at the snatcher. "Forget about him. It's over. We're leaving with you, and I'm never going to see him again."

Esperanza let out a short laugh. "Unless you're willing to take care of the problem now, you run the risk of him coming back one day. The only way you can ensure he'll never bother you or your family is to eliminate him. Now's your chance. It may be the only one you get."

Ransom took a long look at Dragomir. A small pool of blood had formed next to his face. There was a part of him that wanted to finish the snatcher off. But inside, he couldn't kill someone—at least when they no longer posed a threat to his family. Soon they'd all be on their way out of the city, and he would never have to worry about Dragomir again.

"He's not worth it," Ransom finally said. He turned and staggered down the hall toward Teya.

"Well, I still owe him one," Esperanza said.

Ransom turned just in time to see her kick Dragomir in the face. The sentinel's head snapped back, his neck limp.

"That's for threatening my baby," she said.

Esperanza moved past Ransom, suddenly aware of this further complication. "Are you going to be able to get out of here?"

Ransom nodded. "I'll be fine."

Esperanza pulled the messenger from her pocket and typed a quick note, then waited a moment before closing the device. "I'm letting someone know we'll need help once we leave the building. Let's go."

Ransom held out his hand and pulled Teya to her feet. Her hands were sticky with blood.

"Do you have the strength to make it out of here?" he asked.

Teya nodded. They started down the hall after Jorge and Esperanza.

Teya stopped as they passed door seven. "What about Eloise?"

There was a metallic jingle as Esperanza impatiently grabbed the keys from her backpack. She sorted through the ring, pulling out a big, silver one. Before she unlocked the door, she turned and looked straight into Teya's eyes. "I'm opening this up on one condition. You have thirty seconds from the time the door opens to convince your friend to come with us. If she doesn't, you leave and follow us out of this place. Agreed?"

Teya nodded.

Esperanza shoved the key into the lock and turned. It opened with a click. Teya stepped into the darkness.

Ransom mentally counted the seconds off in his head.

Seven . . . eight . . . nine . . . ten.

He could hear Teya's hushed voice coming from the cell.

Fifteen . . . sixteen . . . seventeen.

He looked down the hallway at the door. Jorge had his eye on the door too. He looked nervous and antsy. Ransom hoped he was able to hide his nerves better.

Twenty-six . . . twenty-seven . . . twenty-eight . . .

Ransom was about to call out to Teya as Eloise emerged from the room. She leaned her head against Teya's shoulder and pulled her own nightgown tight around her body.

Ransom let out a breath. He didn't realize it until then, but he had been holding his breath the whole time Teya was in there.

Esperanza didn't bother with introductions. "Let's go," she said. "We need to get out of here *now.*"

Ransom took Teya by the arm and led her and Eloise down the hallway, following Esperanza and Jorge. He helped them step over the body of the guard who lay outside the entrance. He moaned and started moving as they headed up the stairs.

"We've only got a few minutes," Esperanza said. "Hurry!"

Ransom ignored the pain and followed Esperanza as fast as he could. Jorge stopped them when they reached the main floor. He took a quick look down the hall, then walked forward to another door before motioning everyone else to follow.

They made it to the back door without encountering anyone. Esperanza took the ID card and swiped it against a small black box with a pinpoint of red light near the top. The light turned green, and Ransom heard a clicking sound as the door unlocked.

Esperanza held it open, and they stepped out into the warm summer air.

twenty-six

Ransom ran through the blinding white spotlight, pulling Teya and Eloise behind him. Then they were in the dark alley. He ignored the pain that shot though his body and pounded against the side of his head. He could make out the orange glow of the streetlight at the end of the alley and picked up the pace. The footsteps of people running behind him filled his ears.

When he reached the end of the alley, he turned right, heading for the 'Vard—just as Esperanza had told him to do.

"Ransom, this way!"

He stopped and turned. Esperanza started across the street, motioning for him to follow. "Where are you going?" he said, each word a ragged gasp in his throat. He was breathing hard, and his sides ached where Dragomir had punched him. He thought he might vomit.

"There's a safe house in the building across the street. We'll stay there tonight."

"I thought we were heading back to the shop."

"We were, until everything went downhill."

Ransom grabbed Teya by the arm and followed Esperanza through the door of the apartment building and up the stairs.

"I don't understand," Ransom said, wincing from the pain. "The plan was to go back to the shop."

"The plan was to get out of the Infirmary undetected. The area's going to be swarming with cops in a few minutes, and I don't plan on being here when they show up. So hurry back to the shop if you want. But just so you know, as soon as they realize

245

who's missing, they're going to be searching every corner of this city for you and your wife. I doubt you'll make it two blocks before you're picked up."

"What about my boys?"

"They'll be fine until we can get there. You'll be able to see them in the morning. I promise."

Suddenly there was a shout from the alley behind the Census Bureau. In the spotlight, Ransom could see sentinels emerging from the back door. They held flashlights and nightsticks, ready to go.

They all hurried inside the door to the apartment building. On the fourth floor, there were four apartments that branched off from the landing, two in the middle and one each to the left and right. Jorge stood in the entrance to the door on the right. Light from the hall flooded the landing as he held a finger to his lips. Everyone hurried inside before he shut the door and locked it.

Esperanza pushed past them and led the way down a short hall to a large living room. "Get comfortable, everyone," she said. "We'll be right back." She and Jorge exited through a door down another hallway to the kitchen.

Ransom stopped just inside the room and turned to Teya. "How are you doing?" he asked as he looked her over. She was pale, but otherwise looked okay. "Did the sentinels or anyone else mistreat you?"

Teya shook her head. "Aside from being locked up, I was fine. Mona came and talked to me every night, just to make sure."

Ransom felt some of the night's tension leave his body.

"I'm more worried about you," Teya said. "You took a big beating in there. You have blood on your chin." She raised her hand to wipe his face but stopped halfway there. Her fingers were covered in blood.

Dragomir's blood.

She shuddered, and Ransom guided her to a bathroom he had seen in the hall as they entered. As Teya washed her hands, Ransom looked himself over in the mirror. Blood from his mouth had run down his chin and neck. He waited for Teya to finish, then took a washcloth from next to the sink and washed his face.

When he was done, he looked at Teya. She appeared ready to burst into tears. He held her tight as she cried.

"I thought you were going to die," she said between sobs. "I thought we both were."

"It's okay," Ransom said. "He's won't be able to hurt us again."

There was a knock on the bathroom door, causing them both to jump. Esperanza was standing in the hall with a basket full of small jars and white cardboard boxes.

"I brought some medicine," she said as she entered the bathroom and set the box on the toilet. She turned to face Ransom. "Lift up your shirt."

Ransom grimaced as he pulled it up. His shoulder and sides were throbbing. He heard Teya gasp, and he looked down at his waist. His sides were covered with large red welts where Dragomir had kicked him. His previous bruises were so dark, they looked black instead of purple.

Esperanza unscrewed a bottle cap and shook two white pills into her hand. "Take these. If the pain doesn't subside in the next hour, let me know."

Ransom swallowed the pills as Esperanza took the cap off another bottle. "I'm going to need to put some of this lotion on your bruises," she said.

"*I* can do it," Teya said stiffly.

Esperanza paused, then handed her the bottle. "I'll be on the balcony if you need me," she said.

Teya took the bottle and rubbed the cold lotion over Ransom's injuries. He grimaced each time her hands touched him.

"Is that who I think it is?" she asked in an icy tone.

"Yeah," Ransom said, hoping she'd drop the subject for now. He was worried that sentinels would come bursting through the door any minute.

When she was done, they headed back to the living room. Eloise was sitting on a worn eight-foot leather couch against the far wall. It was old, and the leather was cracked and peeling. A handful of times Ransom had seen similar couches left behind in the larger homes he recycled, but this was the first time he'd seen one in an apartment. Directly across from the couch, next to the wall, was a small table with a television on it.

A large square device that looked like a complex radio was bolted to the wall, and in the far corner sat a queen-sized bed with a yellow, lumpy mattress.

Teya took a seat by Eloise.

Ransom watched the two women for a moment before he went to look for Esperanza.

The lights in the kitchen were off, but Ransom could make out Esperanza and Jorge standing on the adjacent balcony. Behind them, he could see beams of white light playing off the back of the Census Bureau.

He moved to the balcony for a better look. From four stories up, they had a perfect view of the alley. A dozen flashlight beams weaved along it. The door they had exited only minutes earlier was propped open. Sentinels and cops walked in and out.

"Told you we needed to hurry," Jorge said peevishly.

Ransom didn't bother with a reply. Instead, he watched the action below. A few minutes later, four officers came out of the door carrying a stretcher. From their awkward pace, Ransom could tell they were carrying a heavy load. As they passed under the light, Ransom caught a glimpse of Dragomir's bloodied face.

He felt relieved to see the guard carried off, partly because the man wasn't dead, and partly from knowing he was being taken away—somewhere he couldn't harm Ransom or his family. It felt good.

Two sentinels emerged from the alley and ran across the street in the direction of the apartment. Ransom felt his body tense. He took a step closer to the edge of the balcony and looked over. Out of the corner of his eye, he saw Jorge doing the same. The sentinels turned right and stopped a couple walking in front of the building.

"Are we safe here?" Ransom asked quietly.

"Should be. They don't know about this apartment," Esperanza answered.

"And if they do?" he pressed.

Jorge shrugged. "Then God help all of us."

Below, the sentinels were showing their badges and shining flashlights in the faces of the couple. The man and woman fumbled around for their identification and finally gave it to the sentinels. The sentinels spoke to each other briefly, then hurried up the street toward the 'Vard.

Ransom was about to head inside when he spotted Mona running down the middle of the street. She was dressed in one of her business suits, but even in the dim light from four stories up, Ransom could tell that her hair was unkempt and her blouse wasn't tucked in. As she approached the area, a sentinel shone a flashlight on her face, then escorted her down the dark alley. Within moments, she was ushered inside.

Ransom wondered if there would be any fallout for Mona once it became clear Teya had escaped. Would it cost Mona her job, or would they just cover up the breakout to avoid the embarrassment? Ransom stopped in his thoughts, decided he didn't care, and moved back into the apartment.

Esperanza followed him inside. She opened the refrigerator and grabbed three bottles of water, giving one to Ransom.

"How are you feeling?"

"Aside from the pain, I feel great."

"Drink the water—it will help. I have something that will help you sleep if the pain gets too bad."

"Thanks, but I'll be fine."

Esperanza handed him two bottles. "Take these to Teya and the other woman. Tell them to drink and rest. There's a lot of activity across the street. We're not going anywhere until morning."

Ransom returned to the living room with the water. He handed Eloise her bottle, then sat on the couch next to Teya. "Drink up," he said, holding the bottle in front of her.

Teya just looked at the bottle, then gave Ransom a look that he knew meant she was deeply worried.

Ransom opened the bottle for her. She took a quick sip. "It's cold."

"You'll get used to it." Ransom took the bottle from her and drank deeply.

"Where are our kids?" Teya whispered.

"Back at the repair shop," Ransom answered in the same quiet voice.

"I can't believe you entrusted our kids to these people. Are you crazy?"

"I didn't really have a choice. I was pretty sure you wouldn't come out of your cell unless I was there."

Ransom set the bottle on the floor between his feet. They sat in silence for a minute.

"Thanks for taking me with you," Eloise said quietly, breaking the silence. "You didn't have to do that."

"It was the only thing I could do," Teya said. The anger and worry that filled her voice moments before was gone. "I'm sorry about switching the tests."

Eloise looked at the ground, then back at Teya. She surprised everyone by giving Teya a hug. "I probably would have done the same thing, but your rescuing me is where we differ. I have to forgive you based on that alone."

Esperanza came into the living room with a stack of pillows and blankets. Eloise rose to help.

"Sit," Esperanza said. "You need to rest. I'm just going to make up some beds real quick."

She set the pillows and blankets on the lumpy mattress.

"You two can sleep here. We'll put Eloise in the other room. Jorge and I will take cat naps on the balcony."

"What about our kids?" Teya asked.

"They're fine," Esperanza said. "They're probably sleeping. You'll see them first thing tomorrow."

Teya stood. "I want to see them now. I don't want them being watched over by strangers. I want them with us."

"We can't leave the apartment until things quiet down outside," Esperanza said. "You leave tonight, and you'll be arrested. I promise you that both your boys are being treated well. As is my baby."

"I don't believe you. I'd rather be arrested than leave them with your people."

Ransom took Teya by the arm in an attempt to calm her down.

"It's okay, Ransom," Esperanza said. "Teya can see her kids right now if she wants."

Esperanza turned on the television on the far wall, then fiddled with some buttons on the radio-looking device. A moment later, a black-and-white image of the repair shop's back room appeared on the screen. They could see the couch with James and Warren, their heads on opposite ends, covered with a blanket. In the background, Nauleo walked back and forth with Gabby in his arms. His wife sat in the far corner, looking at the monitors.

Teya moved toward the screen and touched it where the boys appeared.

"You can watch them all night if you want," Esperanza said. "Just keep in mind, we have a long journey tomorrow, and you'll need your strength."

Teya shot Ransom a look, and he knew he'd have to bring her on board with leaving the city before the night was over.

Esperanza made up the bed, then took Eloise to the other room.

As soon as they were out of sight, Teya said, "What were you thinking, joining up with terrorists?"

His wife's rebuke surprised him. He had to struggle to keep his voice under control. "I was trying to save you and our baby. Don't tell me you'd rather be in your cell right now."

"In some ways, that's a better alternative. Besides, if we're caught with them, we'll go to prison and never see our kids again."

"If they catch us, I don't think it's going to matter if we're with them or not. We're both looking at serious jail time if we stay."

"I can't believe you did this."

"Don't get upset at me, Teya. You started this. I was looking for a solution when you decided to open up to your sister."

"These people killed my father!"

"I doubt it was Esperanza or Jorge. They would have been kids when your father died."

"I'm not going with them."

"They just saved our lives—our baby's life," Ransom said. "Right now, the only way we can keep this family together is to leave the city and start over somewhere. It doesn't have to be permanent, but we need their help to get out of here."

Teya turned away, staring at the monitor. From the way her body trembled, Ransom could tell she was crying.

He put his hands on her shoulders and gave them a squeeze. "I know this isn't an ideal situation, Teya, but I need you to cooperate. This is the only way to keep our family together. Staying here isn't an option."

Teya turned and wiped her eyes. "I really don't have a choice, do I?"

"There's always a choice, Teya. I just don't want to see our family broken up. Right now, going with them keeps us together."

"There's a part of me that would rather take my chances here than spend any time with those people."

"I know this is hard for you, sweetie. But I promise you that if we get to their city and things aren't perfect, I will take you and the kids and find somewhere else to live. I won't let them hurt you or the boys."

"I guess we're going with them then," Teya said in a less than convincing tone.

Esperanza walked into the room with some clothes and a pair of shoes under her arms. "These are for you, Teya," she said as she placed them on the couch. "There's something to sleep in and clothes for tomorrow."

Teya got out of bed and picked up a pair of dark blue shorts and a white T-shirt. She went into the bathroom and returned a moment later with them on. Then she turned and got into bed. She lay on her side, keeping her eyes on the monitor.

Ransom sat on the bed next to her. It wasn't until then that he realized how tired he was. The last few days he'd had very little sleep. The adrenaline that had been keeping him awake all night was definitely gone now, and the pain was beginning to subside.

Ransom took a final drink from his water, then flipped off the light. He wrapped his arms around his wife and felt their bodies rise and fall simultaneously as they breathed.

He wanted to talk to her more—make sure they were on the same page—but decided to wait a moment before broaching the subject. He closed his eyes.

Then he was asleep.

twenty-seven

Ransom awoke to an empty bed. He sat up and looked around at the unfamiliar surroundings, momentarily unsure of where he was. Then he noticed Jorge asleep on the couch, snoring softly. The events of the previous night rushed back to him. He sat up and winced from pain in his midsection. His head hurt, and his entire body felt stiff.

He looked over at the monitor. His boys were sitting at the table with a bowl of fruit and some kind of bread in front of them. They seemed happy.

The sound of female voices wafted in from the kitchen. He sat on the edge of the bed for a moment, collecting his strength, then stood up and slowly made his way in that direction.

Esperanza and Eloise were sitting at the small kitchen table. In front of them lay a bowl full of apple slices and a half-eaten loaf of sweet bread. Teya stood against the far wall, her arms folded across her chest. She was wearing the jeans and faded orange blouse Eloise had put on the couch the night before. The shirt looked two sizes too big. From the balcony came sunlight and the noises of people going about their day. The clock on the wall said it was five after seven.

Esperanza stood and offered Ransom her seat. Ransom shook his head and stood by Teya.

His wife looked up at him. "How are you feeling?" she asked.

"Sore."

"Eat something," Esperanza said, motioning to the food on the table. "You'll need all the strength you can get."

Ransom tore off a piece of bread and took a bite. The yellow bread was thick and moist. It tasted like honey. He offered a piece to Teya. She shook her head.

"She needs to eat something," Esperanza said. "We've got a long journey ahead of us today."

Teya shot him a look and walked out of the kitchen. Ransom followed her to the bathroom. Once inside, she shut the door and leaned against it.

"I didn't sleep much last night," she said. Ransom opened his mouth to speak, but Teya held up her hand. "Hear me out, okay?" she said.

"Fine," Ransom said, folding his arms.

"I spent most of the night watching the boys sleep. I—" Her voice cracked, and she wiped away a tear.

Ransom felt his frustration with her melt away. He pulled her close and kissed the top of her head.

Teya took several deep breaths, then stepped back so she could look Ransom in the eye. "I'm sorry about turning myself in. Even though it was the hardest decision I ever made—even if it meant losing our baby—I did it because I couldn't live with the pain I caused Eloise and her family. But as I watched our boys last night, I realized I endangered our entire family too."

Teya took a piece of the gray-colored toilet paper and blew her nose.

"While I was sitting in my cell, I realized I had made a mistake. I had a strong feeling this baby needed to be born and thought there was no way that was going to happen. I cried myself to sleep, wishing I could take it all back, or, at least, find another way to save Eloise. Then the next thing I knew, I heard my cell door open and your voice calling my name. At first I thought it was a dream, but I sat up in bed, and there you were."

The tears welled up again, and Teya rested her head on Ransom's chest as she continued.

"You risked so much to save me and our baby. And everything happened so fast last night that I never thanked you for what you did. I'm so sorry for everything, and I want you to know that even though I don't fully trust those people, I know you wouldn't have gone to them unless you trusted them. So I'm willing to follow them, as long as you're by my side."

Ransom breathed a sigh of relief that she was willing to go. Life was so much easier when they were in agreement. "It's okay, love," he said. "Don't feel bad about it. Everything worked out. I'm just happy you and the baby are all right and that I can hold you in my arms. And I promise you that if I get any hint that these people are dangerous, I'll do everything I can to make sure you and the kids are kept safe."

Teya looked up and smiled at him. "I know you will," she said. Then she leaned forward and gave Ransom a long kiss.

They walked back to the kitchen, holding hands. When they entered, Esperanza motioned to the counter, where two white pills were laying on the counter next to a bottle of water.

"You looked like you were in some pain this morning," she said.

Ransom popped the pills in his mouth and chased them down with the water. "When are we leaving?" Ransom asked, wiping his mouth.

"In about an hour," Esperanza said as she glanced at the clock on the wall.

"How are we getting out of here?"

Esperanza smiled. "You'll see."

* * *

Ransom watched as the recycling truck moved silently up the alley behind the apartment building, stopping at the back entrance. Esperanza waited a moment before heading out to the alley and banging the truck three times. A moment later, there was a click as the back of the truck opened on hydraulic hinges. Esperanza scanned the interior, then motioned for everyone to climb in.

"You're kidding," Ransom said.

"It's the quickest and safest way out of here."

"How'd you get one of these things?"

Esperanza just smiled. "I told you. I have contacts."

Ransom looked inside the container. Warm, musty air suffocated him as if someone had recently sprayed the inside with water.

255

"How long are we going to be in the back?" he asked.

"Depends on how long it takes to get through the checkpoint. My best guess? Thirty minutes."

Ransom felt the sun's heat searing on the back of his neck. "If we're in there too long, we'll die from the heat."

"If it makes you feel any better, we'll run out of air long before we cook to death," Esperanza said. "These things are airtight. But you probably already know that."

Ransom shook his head doubtfully but climbed into the truck anyway. He turned and helped Teya inside.

"We're going to the shop to pick up supplies and your kids," Esperanza continued. "If you don't want to come, you can always go home. Or you can ask Eloise if she has room to hide your entire family."

Ransom turned to Eloise. "You're not coming?"

She shook her head. "I'm staying in the city. I know people who will hide me until the baby comes."

"Are you really going to spend the rest of your life holed up in some room? They know you've escaped. You're going to be on their search-and-find list for a long time."

"I'll take my chances," she said. She glanced at Esperanza and Jorge, who were now loading a few belongings into the truck. Then she lowered her voice so only Ransom could hear. "Besides, I don't trust them. Don't get me wrong—I'm grateful. But I'm sticking with friends and family."

"How are you going to get back to your husband and kids?"

"There's a network of people who are more than willing to help. They'd help you too. I'm sure we can find a place to hide your family."

Ransom looked back at Esperanza as she tossed the last of the bags in the truck. He knew that following them was taking a big chance. Their upcoming journey was going to be hard and dangerous. Even so, there was no longer a place in this city for his family. Getting Teya out of the Infirmary had meant an end to their lives as they knew them. If they were found now, it would be a long jail sentence for him. For Teya, it meant a trip back to the Infirmary, in addition to jail time. They might never see their boys again. As far as he was concerned, hiding in a room or moving from apartment to apartment to avoid the authorities was just like living in prison. At least with Esperanza and Jorge, he'd have a chance to start over.

He realized Eloise was waiting for a response. "Thanks, but leaving with them is the best option for us," he answered, helping Eloise into the truck as he said it.

"Have a seat, everyone," Esperanza instructed as she and Jorge climbed into the truck. "It might be a bumpy ride."

Ransom moved to the front of the container and sat next to Teya. He took her hand in his.

Again, Esperanza pounded on the side of their hideout three times, and the door to the container silently began closing. As Esperanza took a seat by Jorge, the door snapped shut, and they were in complete darkness.

* * *

The truck made its way quickly through the streets. The muffled sounds of the driver leaning on the horn and yelling at people in his path made their way through the metal walls of the truck. During the ten-minute ride to the repair shop, the air became hot and sticky. Even this early, the sun's heat was pounding through the truck, turning it into an oven.

Suddenly the truck came to a stop, and Ransom's head smacked into the wall with a loud thump that made a dull echo through the container. It was quiet momentarily, then someone inside pounded on the side of the truck three times. There was a click, and the back door hissed open.

Sunlight and cool air streamed into the container. Being in the dark only a short time required that Ransom's eyes adjust to the light for several moments. When Ransom could finally see, he focused on Nauleo handing four backpacks they had packed earlier to Esperanza and Jorge before hurrying back inside the shop.

Ransom stepped down from the truck, then helped Eloise down.

"I want you to know that I do appreciate you for getting me out of there. And if things don't work out for your family wherever you're going, you'll always have a friend here who will be happy to help you out," she said.

"If you're going to be hiding, how will I find you?"

"You know where we live, right?"

Ransom nodded. "In the apartment right above ours."

"I won't live there anymore, but if you go there in the future, I promise there'll be someone who can help you. I'll tell them about you. When you do come back, just be sure to tell your name to whomever opens the door."

Ransom nodded. "When you get a hold of your husband, tell him I left the door to our apartment unlocked. If sentinels haven't already ransacked the place, your family is welcome to whatever you can take."

"Thank you," Eloise said.

The back door of the shop opened, and Nauleo emerged, holding Gabby. James and Warren poked their heads out of the door and looked around the alley. Their faces lit up when they saw Ransom.

"Dad!" they exclaimed at the same time. Ransom kneeled to the ground and embraced his sons.

"I had peaches for breakfast! Fresh ones!" James said.

"Me too!" Warren chirped.

"That's great, guys," Ransom said and smiled as he looked at their excited faces. "Guess what? I have a surprise for you."

Ransom picked up the boys and set them on the edge of the container. "Look who's inside," he said.

The boys looked curiously into the container. Teya took a step forward so the boys could see her. They let out an exultant cry and ran to their mom. Ransom felt his eyes water as he watched them happily hug Teya and pepper her with information on what they'd been doing. It was nice to see his family together again.

Esperanza threw the last of the packs in the back. She took the sleeping baby from Nauleo, then turned and looked at Eloise.

"Follow Nauleo inside. He'll make sure you can contact your husband. After that, you're on your own."

Eloise nodded. Then she turned and looked at Ransom and

Teya. "Best of luck on your journey. I hope to see you and your family again one day."

"Me too," Ransom said.

"Everyone inside," Esperanza commanded. "We need to get moving. Ransom, how are your boys going to handle the dark?"

Ransom paused, remembering how frightened he'd been of the dark when he was much older than the boys. "I don't know."

"These walls may be made out of metal, but they're not that thick. If anyone starts crying, they'll know we're inside." Esperanza rummaged in the bag nearest to her, then walked over and handed him a long, black flashlight. "You know how to use one of these?"

Ransom clicked the flashlight on and off.

"Use this as a last resort if the boys have a hard time with the dark," Esperanza said. "It's the only one we have, and it has to last our entire trip. Trust me—you don't want the batteries going out in the middle of nowhere." She rummaged through her bag and pulled the yellow sling from it. Then she picked up her baby and placed her inside.

Ransom turned to the boys. "You guys want to go for a ride in the truck?"

"Yeah," James said. Excitement filled his voice.

"Okay, that's what we're going to do. But they have to shut the back door for us to go. It's going to be dark. You have to promise not to get scared, okay?"

James looked up at Ransom. His eyes looked worried. "Are you going to be with us?"

"Yep. I'll be sitting next to you the entire time."

"Then I'll be okay," James said.

"Me too," Warren replied.

Ransom led the boys to the front of the container. He stacked two packs on their side so they'd have something to lean against. The boys sat down, full of excitement and anticipation. Ransom and Teya sat on either side of them.

Esperanza banged the wall of the truck three times and sat next to Jorge. When the door clicked shut, the truck started down the alley.

It took ten minutes to arrive at the city gates, but they had to sit for what Ransom figured was another fifteen minutes before the guards got around to inspecting their truck. Either the guards were taking their sweet time, or there was simply a long line of vehicles ahead of them. He hoped it was the latter. The temperature inside the truck has risen dramatically. The air was hot and humid and smelled like the trams. Ransom's shirt stuck to his body, and an occasional bead of sweat ran down his face.

James and Warren, who had been fairly quiet on the drive over, had grown restless. More than once, they had complained about the heat and the smell. Ransom had quieted them, hoping their voices couldn't penetrate the container. He gave them each a bottle of water to drink in an attempt to cool and distract them.

Then, without warning, the truck jostled forward. Ransom could hear the muffled words of the guard and driver talking in familiar, friendly tones when they stopped again.

Then there was the crunch of gravel underfoot as the guard walked around the truck. Ransom assumed the guards were inspecting the truck with mirrors, looking for something hidden underneath. He heard the guard and the driver chatting again, though he couldn't understand what they were saying.

Suddenly his heart pounded in his chest as he remembered that the guards always opened up the back of the truck to inspect it. No doubt the guards had been informed of Teya's escape and were probably passing out copies of the photos to everyone leaving the city. Once the back hatch was opened, they'd all be caught, and there was nothing he could do about it.

The heat in the back of the truck became unbearable, and Ransom tried to think of what he could do once the hatch opened. Maybe he could rush the guard and give Teya and the boys time to run away. Maybe—

There was a gentle bump as the truck moved forward. It sped up, going straight for several minutes. Then the truck slowed, shifting to a lower gear. The road became bumpier. Ransom figured they must be heading east toward Idaho since roads leading to the Green States were never maintained.

The truck stopped a few minutes later. Without any prompting, the back door clicked open, and fresh, sweet-smelling air blew inside, displacing the humidity. Ransom looked at his boys. Their hair was wet and stuck to their foreheads.

Out the back, Ransom saw the verdant banks of the Spokane River. It had been at least a decade since he'd been this far east of the city. It looked pretty much as he remembered it, green and beautiful. But today, there was something exciting about being back. It wasn't just another pretty walk. It was the first step toward a new life.

The boys ran to the end of the truck and looked out excitedly at the river.

"Is this our new home?" Warren asked.

Ransom moved so he was standing behind the boys. "No. Our home's a long way from here."

"But where we're going has a river too, and it's just as pretty," Esperanza said.

While the boys looked on, Ransom helped Jorge unload the packs, then helped the boys down onto the ground. They ran to the side of the road and looked down at the sparkling water. Then they picked up some rocks and took turns tossing them down the bank and into the river.

Esperanza slapped the side of the truck three times, and the back hatch slowly shut. The truck pulled forward to a wide spot ten yards farther up the road and turned around.

Ransom helped Teya put on her pack, then pulled his own over his shoulders, wincing from the pain. The pack was surprisingly heavy, and Esperanza walked over to help him loosen the straps.

"What have you got in here? It weighs a ton!" Ransom exclaimed.

"It will be a lot lighter by the time we reach our destination."

"And where's that?"

"The Green States."

"There are a lot of Green States. Can I get a little hint before we start?"

"We're going to Wyoming—the western part of the state. It's about a two-week journey from here. A city called Star Valley."

Ransom tried to remember his geography. "You really think we can get there in two weeks?"

"I know we can. I've walked it more than a dozen times." She looked Ransom over. "How's the pain?"

"Bearable."

"If it gets worse, let me know. I have plenty of pain medication in my bag to get you to your new home."

Suddenly Ransom was aware of the sound of gravel popping under tires. The truck was slowly making its way toward them and down the road.

Esperanza reached into her pocket and pulled out a piece of paper. "Why don't you give the driver this," she said, smiling.

"What is it?"

"His reward for a job well done."

Ransom raised his eyebrows, took the paper from her hand, and walked over to the driver's-side window. "Dempsey!" he exclaimed.

"You keep your wife and those kids of yours safe," Dempsey replied, laughing. "You've got a long walk ahead of you."

"You've worked for them this whole time?"

Dempsey shook his head. "I'm not officially part of the group. I prefer to think of myself as an independent contractor."

"But you've been helping them."

"I do what I can to earn a little extra income."

"How did you get us through the checkpoint? They always open the back."

Dempsey smiled. "Let's just say I get a weekly update of the guard rotations. Some of them are our friends. Others can be bribed. Lucky for you, the east gate was the best option today. It meant I could shave some miles off your trip."

"Why don't you come with us?" Ransom said, thinking how great it would be to have his friend along for the journey.

Dempsey shook his head. "I'm too old. Doubt me and the wife would last a day outside the city. Besides, staying around and helping out has its benefits. Speaking of which, I believe you have something for me."

Ransom handed Dempsey the paper through the window.

Dempsey opened it and scanned its contents. "Looks like every-thing's in order," he said.

"What is it?" Ransom asked.

Dempsey smiled. "Just a note telling me where to pick up some extra supplies. It looks like they were able to get me ten pounds of roast beef. Guess I'm going to have to eat more of it myself, now that you won't be around to share those sandwiches." He folded the paper and put it in his pocket. "I need to go. I'm already ninety minutes behind on my recycling duties."

"Will you be able to handle a house by yourself?"

"Oh, I'm sure I'll get some help as soon as the center gets notice you're a wanted man. I just hope they don't stick me with the new guy."

Ransom smiled, thinking of how uptight Jesse had been when Ransom left the water on. "Thanks," Ransom said. "Thanks for everything."

"Good luck."

"I'm sure Esperanza will let you know how it goes."

"I know she will."

Ransom stood on the stair below the driver's door, and he and Dempsey embraced. Then Dempsey nodded and put the truck in drive. Ransom watched the truck until it disappeared behind a bend in the river.

Esperanza and Jorge walked past, backpacks in place. "Let's get going," she said. "We've got to make it to our campsite tonight. Tomorrow we'll cross into Idaho."

Ransom called to the boys, who were still throwing rocks into the river. They each tossed one last stone down the embank-ment, then hurried to their dad.

Ransom took Teya's hand in his. "You ready for this?" he asked.

Teya squeezed his hand. "I hope we've made the right deci-sion," she said.

They looked at each other for a long moment before starting down the road.

The boys ran on ahead of them, following Esperanza and Jorge, heading east.

book club questions

1. The author chose to tell the story through Ransom's and Teya's eyes. How does this storytelling technique add to the mystery and tension in the novel?

2. Did Teya's decision to keep her pregnancy a secret for three months strengthen or hurt her relationship with Ransom? Does keeping secrets from a spouse hurt or strengthen a marriage?

3. What was Ransom willing to do to save his family? What would you be willing to do to save your family?

4. Is the city where Ransom and Teya live more environmentally friendly than the city you live in now? Is it a city you'd want to live in?

5. How would you describe Teya and Mona's relationship? In what ways are they close? In what ways are they far apart?

6. Is family size something that should be mandated by the government, or is it best left to families to decide?

7. If you were Ransom or Teya, would you have followed Esperanza and Jorge to Wyoming or stayed with Eloise in the city?

acknowledgments

I t's not easy to write a novel while working full time and being husband and father. If it wasn't for my wife, Julianna, giving me the time I needed to write, *The Third* would still be nothing more than a jumble of thoughts in my head. Thank you, my love, for letting these characters and this story come to life. Your sweet influence and love mean more to me than words can express.

Thanks to Marcus Varner whose feedback on my initial drafts was invaluable to steering the story and the characters in the right direction.

Finally, special thanks to Dr. Michael Wutz of Weber State University whose riveting Technology and the Novel class planted the seeds of this novel and many more to come.

about abel

Abel is the author of the memoir *Room for Two* and numerous short stories and poems. For nearly a decade he has worked as a professional copywriter and composed hundreds of print and online pieces of marketing collateral for technology, real estate, health care, and education organizations—including several Fortune 500 companies. *The Third* is his first novel.

Abel and his wife, Julianna, are the parents of three boys and a girl. Learn more at www.abelkeogh.com.